HEYDRICH WAS THE DEVIL – AND STAHMER HIS DISCIPLE!

The Devil's disciple shrugged. He knew that the grenades in his suitcase would provide the first explosions of the Second World War, and that its first battle would take place inside the radio station at Gleiwitz. And that he could be setting up the first death here . . .

The dance-bar's windows were open, but the air inside was almost unbearably close. Somewhere out there, columns of troops were tramping under a heavy sky, to the East. Hermann Göring, the Luftwaffe chief, had already informed the people that 'No enemy aircraft will ever fly over the borders of the German Reich', and civil defence units were rehearsing the blackout.

Hitler was drivelling about peace. His tailor was measuring him for a uniform that was intended, not for the front, but for his Reichstag speech. The farmers were cutting their corn; soon the scythe of war would bring home a bloody harvest. The August days of 1939 were like a dazed calm before the storm . . .

Prinz-Albrecht-Strasse

WILL BERTHOLD

Translated by Fred Taylor

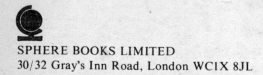

SPHERE BOOKS LIMITED
30/32 Gray's Inn Road, London WC1X 8JL

First published in Great Britain by
Sphere Books Ltd 1981
Translation Copyright © Sphere Books 1981
Reprinted 1984

Publishers Note

This novel is a work of fiction, in which no reference is
intended to any person living or dead, except that many
historical characters are mentioned, and some occasionally
appear on the scene.

TRADE
MARK

Set in Plantin

Printed and bound in Great Britain by
Cox & Wyman Ltd, Reading

1

It was one of those fine, cold winter days when frost wields its razor with a smile. From the Urals to the Atlantic, a high-pressure zone lay across Europe; and at the centre of that zone was Germany, a nation that was in the process of transforming itself into one huge prison.

A dark Mercedes limousine glided steadily along the icy-smooth surface of the country road. The car's heating system was fighting a losing battle against the cold, and its two passengers, a man and a woman, both young, had wrapped their legs in thick travelling-blankets. Two pairs of skis were strapped to the roof.

The young woman in the passenger seat brushed her hair out of her eyes. She was in her mid-twenties, pretty and athletic-looking; with her blonde hair and blue eyes, she represented the statuesque embodiment of ideal German womanhood in Hitler's new Reich. Ira Puch, gymnastics teacher from Berlin, leaned back, letting the winter sun stroke her face, stretched like a cat and yawned lazily.

'We'll be at the Czech border in ten minutes,' the man said.

She nodded.

'There's no need to worry,' he added. 'It will be all right.'

Ira stole a sideways glance at him. She didn't know his real name, or who he was. She didn't even know what he intended to do, still less how she was supposed to fit in. All she was sure of was that he held the wheel of the car tight with both hands, hands that were strong, skilled, and confident. Those hands could run through a woman's hair,

1

or over her body; and with the same sureness they could wield a machine pistol . . .

The hands went with his face, she thought; with his firm chin, strongly-chiselled nose, high forehead, thin lips and grey eyes, the man's appearance was virile but somehow emotionless. The close-set eyes, with their thick, dark eyebrows, gave his features an unnerving coldness. Here was a man who combined courage with complete ruthlessness – a typical product of the German Secret Service that was coming into being under the sign of the swastika.

'When we see the customs barrier, we start to call each other by the familiar "Du". Is that clear?'

The young woman nodded again.

'What's your name?' he asked suddenly, like an interrogator.

'Ira Stahmer,' she answered with a playful pout. 'Née Puch.'

'Married?' he cut in.

'To you.'

'Good,' he said. 'And what's my profession?'

'Technical manager.'

'Where were we married?'

'In Breslau ... Registry Office 111 ... The witnesses were ... ' Ira recited mockingly.

'How long have we been married?'

'Since December 2nd.'

'Good.'

The driver lit a cigarette. He was called Werner Stahmer – at least on this trip, because he changed his names like other men changed shirts. The names were false, but the passports that bore them were genuine; the forger was none other than the Nazi state. Stahmer's work-place was hell, and his employer was the Devil. The Devil's name – his real

2

one – was Reinhard Heydrich, boss of the organisation that was to become internationally notorious as the R.S.H.A. – the security branch of the S.S.

'Just keep cool,' Stahmer said to the woman. 'All you have to do is to play the part of my wife ... ' He grinned humourlessly. 'I hope that doesn't come too hard.'

Ira's face expressed nothing, but inside she was both frightened and curious. These people had come to her with a proposal, and she had accepted. She had known the man in the driver's seat for exactly two hours, and already she felt like a piece of military equipment. She had been thrown to him as if he were a recruit collecting his rations at the platoon stores.

'We'll have to look like a couple,' murmured Stahmer. 'Completely intimate.'

He flashed her a look of appraisal. Then he added: 'I can understand that you might not find that bit easy, but the people on the border have to believe that we're still on honeymoon. All right?'

'Yes,' she replied, unable to summon up much conviction.

'You're not exactly talkative,' he said, then, as if to himself: 'Which is all to the good.' He looked at her searchingly again. 'But you took this job on of your own free will?'

'Certainly,' she answered with a wry smile. 'It's just that I have no idea what the job really is.'

'Be glad that you don't!' he hissed. Then he stared fixedly ahead again in the direction of the border. The closer it came, the more his face tensed, though his eyes darted from side to side, checking the terrain. He was a relative newcomer to this business, but he intended to make sure he did everything right . . .

Ira had no idea of what lay ahead of them, nor did she care much. Someone had told her that it was for the good of

Germany, but even that hadn't impressed her, despite the fact that her father had been a Nazi party member for donkey's years and always had his ear glued to the propaganda on the radio.

Ira understood nothing about politics, and didn't want to. Her dislike of the brownshirts had more to do with her femininity than with high ideals; she would rather wear high heels than 'sensible shoes', and preferred making a splash in a low-cut cocktail dress to marching through the streets in some shapeless Hitler Youth uniform.

'Have you got any money with you?' Stahmer asked.

'Yes,' she answered, 'but not much.'

'Give it to me.'

'Why?'

'You'll have to get used to the fact that your "husband" pays the bills from now on.'

The car had passed the little village of Boderbach. Stahmer saw the customs post ahead and changed down into first gear.

The German border officials behaved correctly but coldly, like typical robot products of the new Germany.

Stahmer put up with the lengthy exit procedures with a look of affable boredom. His special pass, which would have had these men grovelling at his feet, lay in a safe in Berlin. On this trip, he had to go through the business of showing the meagre fifty Reichsmarks he was allowed to take out of the country.

The barrier was raised, and the black limousine continued on its way.

The border officials on the other side were more human, but also more suspicious. They checked every piece of baggage, even searching their toiletry bags, riffling through their suitcase and unfolding Stahmer's pyjamas.

'What is your business in the Republic of Czechoslovakia?' one of the uniformed guards asked.

4

'Skiing,' Stahmer said laconically.

'Why here?' the Czech border official persisted.

'Why not?' Stahmer answered cheekily.

The man shook his head in irritation. He knew that no one could get far on fifty marks, particularly as visitors also had to pay a toll for use of the roads. He also knew that every other person who came out of Germany was either a refugee or a spy, and he didn't have much time for either.

'I have relatives in Prague,' Stahmer explained, as if he had read the man's thoughts.

The border official became a little friendlier.

'Nevertheless, I could do with some extra cash . . . ' Stahmer said with a wink, pointing to his wristwatch. 'It's gold,' he said, 'eighteen-carat . . . Could we do business together?'

'Not possible.' But the guard indicated in the direction of a wooden cabin that acted as the officials' rest room.

Stahmer smiled and nodded, then left the car and went over into the building. In full view of a policeman, he exchanged the gold wristwatch for a hefty wad of Czech crowns.

The engine roared into life, and the limousine set off once more in the direction of Prague. Ira, who had had to go through the same indignities at the border in silence, shivered as she snuggled against the back of the seat and drew the blanket more tightly round her.

'A pity about the watch,' she said.

Stahmer shrugged his shoulders, then looked wordlessly back at the road.

'Are we that poor?'

'We're supposed to be normal, and that little transaction was "normal",' he said. 'Good camouflage.'

She felt an irrational surge of fear as she realised what he meant, then she laughed. 'Do you always have to go through this kind of skulduggery?'

'The real meat comes at the end,' he answered brutally.

Driving didn't seem to tire Stahmer. Hours went by, and the car sped on; through Prague without stopping, and beyond. The driver had no need of a map, because he knew exactly where he was going. The roads became narrower, the snow drifts deeper.

The journey went on. In silence. The forests they passed seemed petrified, threatening, like Stahmer's face.

'You're not so talkative, either,' said Ira this time.

'Later,' he answered. 'In half an hour, we shall arrive at a secluded hotel on the Moldau . . . First we'll spend a while in the bar, then we'll try to get a room for the night. Is that clear?'

The woman nodded. Her face, red with the cold, darkened. Suddenly she couldn't look him in the eye. He noticed that she was disturbed, and he smiled coolly.

'Just a formality,' he explained. 'We're on state business, don't forget. Or are you frightened of me?'

'Not especially,' Ira said. 'And what do we do then?'

'Winter sports.'

'No, I mean really . . . '

Stahmer thought for a moment.

'I'm looking for a man,' he said slowly. 'You don't need to bother yourself with that side of it. You just hand me my breakfast toast . . . stroke my hair now and again like a loving wife . . . and do as much skiing as you can. Understand?'

'Yes . . . And when you've found your man?'

'I don't know,' Stahmer said. 'I get my orders from Berlin. And so do you . . . '

There was no sun now. The thermometer had plummeted down to well below zero. From time to time, Stahmer took one hand from the wheel and shook it to restore the circulation. Suddenly his face changed and became friendlier, warmer.

'Not long now,' he murmured, taking Ira's hand as if to

6

comfort her. 'In a moment you'll get a glass of hot rum punch.'

The road veered off along a rocky mountainside that skirted high above the river Moldau. It was only two or three kilometres to the village of Zahorski, but there was an atmosphere of lonely melancholy about the countryside they were passing through. They met not a living soul; there were no other cars on the roads. Once the car got stuck in the snow, and Ira had to get out and push. But at last the Mercedes rounded the last bend and arrived at a parking area that had been cleared of snow.

Stahmer got out of the car, shook his frozen limbs, then crossed to the other side and helped the woman out. 'We'll leave the luggage here for the moment,' he said.

Ira took his arm as they crossed the car park. When they entered the dimly-lit bar of the hotel, the few customers seemed to stop talking, and the temperature in the room seemed to drop. Everyone seemed to be sizing them up. There was no move to serve them.

They sat down in a corner which gave a view of the whole room. Stahmer had to call the waitress four or five times, and the rum punch took twenty minutes to arrive. When it came, it was lukewarm. Guests from Germany were not popular in this place – and soon they would be hated ...

Stahmer moved closer to Ira on the bench, looked into her eyes, and smiled with fond affection. He was really very convincing, she thought. Anything for the service ...

She smiled back. For the moment, the game was fun.

The crackling stove in the bar warmed their frozen limbs. But it couldn't melt the icy hostility of the people all around them.

Werner Stahmer's eyes had picked out one particular man the moment they stepped into the hotel. He had focused on him, then looked away again quickly, but in that second he had photographed him, searched the index of his memory, compared, established: that was the one . . .

Rudolf Formis, exile; forty-five years old, medium height, slim build; a man with the head of a scholar, the expressive hands of an artist and the passion of a martyr. In his eyes there burned hatred and love. Love of his country, and hatred against its oppressors. His features told of knowledge: the knowledge that every hour of every day, wherever he went, he could expect death from the enemy he was fighting. His role in the struggle against Hitler might have seemed trivial, but to those who knew the realities of power, it was a vital one.

Rudolf Formis looked around and sat down in a seat that had obviously been kept free for him. The waitress brought him hot lemon tea and a newspaper, without having to be asked. He read with deep concentration. Once he looked over the edge of the paper, brushed Stahmer's face with his eyes, met Ira's gaze, and then looked away, polite and withdrawn.

'So,' said Stahmer to Ira. 'Now we'll get ourselves fixed up with somewhere to stay.'

He stood up and approached the landlord.

'May we have a room?' he asked.

The man shook his head unsmilingly. *'Nerozumim nemécky,'* he answered. 'I don't speak German.'

'Just for a few days,' Stahmer persisted, harrying the old man.

'Nemame nic volney, bohuzel,' the hotel owner said, firmly and with a hint of anger. 'Sorry, none free . . . ' He turned on his heel and left Stahmer standing there.

For a few seconds the German seemed downcast, then he shrugged his shoulders helplessly and turned to Ira with a sour smile.

Rudolf Formis had been listening to the conversation, though he had kept behind his newspaper. He was a kindly man, and under any other circumstances he would have been glad to help a fellow-countryman in trouble. But to befriend any German who turned up in this place would be much too dangerous. Perhaps even fatal ...

Formis watched Stahmer round the edge of his paper as the German walked back to his table. He glanced at the woman again.

Then Stahmer said, loudly and with feeling: 'We should have stayed at home ... Except that it would have been good to go skiing for once in a place where the dogs don't piss swastikas ... '

Formis raised his head. His heart beat faster. After all, he was alone and isolated here. He wished he could talk to someone who had just come from Germany – but who had stayed human. At that moment, Formis felt something close to shame at the fact that his way of life forced him to see every one of his fellow-countrymen as a potential spy or assassin.

He stood up and went slowly over to them.

'Can I help you?' he asked Stahmer quietly. 'I speak some Czech.'

'Oh, many thanks,' said the agent. 'I wouldn't mind travelling on, but my wife ... Damned cold today.'

'I'll see what I can do,' the emigré said. He went over to the landlord, and the two Germans heard him arguing with the man in the rich, flowing language.

After several minutes, Formis returned. 'You can stay here,' he announced. 'Room nine.'

The agent put out his hand. 'Stahmer,' he introduced himself. He motioned in Ira's direction. 'My wife.'

'Formis,' said the other with a slight bow.

'We're very grateful,' the woman said.

For a moment, Formis looked embarrassed. Then he nodded and went back to his seat. He carried on reading for a few minutes, then he looked up at the clock.

'What's the time?' Stahmer whispered to Ira.

'A quarter to eight.'

It was on him. The tension. The fever. The almost sexual

9

excitement. As it always was when he had the target in his sights. If he was right, the agent thought, Formis would leave the room in ten minutes at the most and go upstairs to one of the rooms in this hotel ...

'I'll be back soon,' he said to Ira.

Stahmer stood up and went out. In the hotel entrance, he lit a cigarette. Then another. When he had almost smoked the second, he heard the door close behind him. Formis, he thought. He already had the emigré's walk taped. A swift, sidelong glance was enough to confirm it.

Stahmer left the building and walked aimlessly about. No one paid any attention as he crouched down and ran the snow through his hands, his eyes fixed on the front façade of the hotel.

Second storey. Corner room. The antenna.

Their sources had been right: here, in this crummy little country inn, was the secret transmitter, the radio station that broadcast to Germany every night at eight o'clock, beaming out the message for the nation to rise up against Hitler.

Stahmer packed the snow together, threw a snowball away towards the car park, then strolled slowly back into the bar. It was a minute or two before eight o'clock. The landlord peered at him suspiciously for a moment, then seemed satisfied.

Ira was absently spooning her soup. So far as those around them were concerned, the man beside her was whispering sweet nothings in her ear. What he was really saying was: 'When Formis shows up here again, I'll take our luggage upstairs. Try to get him into conversation ... All right?'

The woman nodded.

Exactly fifteen minutes later, the man who operated the secret transmitter came back into the bar. He had

10

completed his broadcast. He walked past the Germans' table, smiling politely at Ira.

'Excuse me,' she called after him, bringing him back on his heel. 'Do you know the ski slopes round here?'

'Oh, yes,' Formis said.

With a wave of the hand, Ira motioned him to come and sit by her.

'Are you German?' she said.

'Yes. From Berlin.' His gaze was suddenly distant, as if he were searching within himself for the heart of Germany.

Stahmer stood up. 'Excuse me, darling ... I'll just take our cases upstairs ... '

He was lucky. No chambermaids about. He took all the luggage up the stairs at once and got it as far as the first floor. Then he waited at the door and listened. No movement.

He padded further, silently. To the second floor, corner room. He examined the door and saw that it had a special lock. He smiled. So that was all that stood between him and the transmitter-room. With cool efficiency, he made a wax impression of the lock to send to Berlin, then returned downstairs, joined in the conversation for what seemed a decent interval, yawned, and indicated to Ira that it was time for bed.

They went upstairs together.

When they got into their double room, the embarrassment came – for Ira, at least. She stood hesitantly in front of the long mirror over the wash-basin, then looked at the French bed with the flowery bolster. Now, in this room, Stahmer seemed like a real stranger. Even his silence was unnerving.

She could feel that this odd man, whose 'wife' she was playing, was examining her from the darkness.

She turned when she heard his voice nearby.

11

'I'll fetch a bottle of wine from downstairs,' he said with a laugh.

For a moment longer, Stahmer stood at the window and gazed out into the darkness. The woman didn't interest him; he was concerned only with Formis. So far everything had gone according to plan. Yet again, he had carried out his orders to the letter, and that was what it was all about.

When he got back, he switched on the light. He noticed with amusement that Ira was already in bed.

'A pretty nightdress,' he said, without looking at her. 'Listen carefully,' he went on. 'We have found our man.'

'The old one?' Ira asked. 'The man who got the room for us ... Formis?'

He nodded. 'I have to go away,' he said. 'Meanwhile, you stay here.'

'Me?' she whispered incredulously. 'Alone?'

'Make friends with him,' he said coldly. 'Don't let him out of your sight. But for God's sake don't be too obvious.'

'What's going to happen to him?'

'Don't be sentimental, dear girl,' he said, handing her a glass of wine. 'That decision's up to Headquarters.'

'When will you be back?'

'Provided everything goes all right, in about two days.'

'And ... what's the man done wrong?'

'That depends what you mean by ... Look,' he said slowly, 'he runs a propaganda transmitter attacking the Führer ... here in the hotel.'

'But ... '

'It doesn't concern you,' said Stahmer, and his voice was harsh and a little cruel. Then he forced himself to become more friendly. 'Can I do anything for you in Berlin?'

'No ... Are you going all that way?'

'Go to sleep,' he said. 'Tomorrow you can tell Formis that I had to go to Prague on urgent business. Prague ... not Berlin. Got that?'

12

The light went out, and the man at Ira's side soon seemed sound asleep. He was in control of the situation.

When she awoke the next morning, the space beside her was empty.

2

The aircraft made a smooth landing at Tempelhof airport. The Berlin that greeted Werner Stahmer was overcast and cold, but he didn't have much time to consider it; a car with civilian number plates was waiting by the customs building – and brought him straight to the Prinz-Albrecht-Strasse. Within twenty minutes, he was at the head-quarters of the R.S.H.A., in the old mansion that had been turned into the nerve-centre of a repressive machine without equal in the history of humanity.

One man, hated by his friends and enemies alike, ruled over this empire within the Third Reich: Reinhard Heydrich. His trade was death, his tool was power, and it was acquiring power that was his only concern. To get it, he would have served anyone: communists or catholics, freemasons or atheists, Nazis or Jews. For its sake he blackmailed, tortured, killed, burned and gassed. Six thousand or six million: what did it matter? To his chosen trade he brought the same icy hatred, the same indifference to human life. Heydrich was the Devil in human form, right down to his manicured fingertips.

The overlord of the R.S.H.A. was standing when he received his agent, and he seemed in a good mood. That could be dangerous. Stahmer knew his boss, and he kept on his guard.

'Well,' Heydrich rasped. 'Success?'

'Yes, Gruppenführer.'

'That was quick ... ' Heydrich smiled, but his face remained strangely unmoving. He was tall and whipcord-strong; his eyes reflected nothing but a bottomless contempt for humanity. Above thin and cynical lips, a

14

long, narrow nose jutted out like a piece of artillery directed against the world. But he was a strange mixture: in contrast with the rest of the party leadership, who were included in his contempt, he possessed courage and intelligence. He radiated a personal magnetism that put everyone, even his superiors, in awe of him. With a playful gesture, the Gruppenführer offered his underling a cigarette.

'You have brought a wax impression of the door lock?'

'Yes.'

'And the transmitter is in the hotel?'

'Exactly.'

'Good,' Heydrich murmured. He gave another of his frightening, emotionless smiles. 'Bring the man Formis here.'

'To Berlin, Gruppenführer?'

'Where else?' Heydrich said languidly, savouring the effect of his words on Stahmer. 'I want him alive – here.'

'I have to get him over the border ... '

'You have no choice. Knock him out, put him in a car ... And if the Czechs cause trouble during the border crossing ... ' His hand imitated the flight of a hand grenade. 'You can take someone else with you,' the R.S.H.A. boss said finally. 'Blow up the transmitter.' He paused. 'Is the girl performing well?' he added, with a hint of a leer.

Stahmer nodded absently.

'It will have to be quick,' Heydrich said, his voice commanding now. Then, with a dangerous, hissing softness: 'I have waited a long time for Formis.'

It was idiotic, Stahmer thought. Impossible. How was he supposed to get a prisoner across one of the most heavily-guarded borders in Europe? How could they be expected to blow up the transmitter and then leave the country inconspicuously?

He looked at Heydrich again, but the watery-blue eyes were cold and merciless.

'You will do it?'

'Yes, Gruppenführer,' answered Stahmer. There was nothing else he could say ...

Whenever he was summoned into his boss's presence like this, he came out in a cold sweat. He knew he should refuse. His missions were becoming more desperate, more dangerous all the time. But it was precisely because of that greater fear that he was able to summon up vital reserves of courage. And Heydrich knew it, he always knew it. When he faced Heydrich, Stahmer, the agent who was prepared to risk anything in the field – including his life – was a coward. Because if anything went wrong, Heydrich would deal with him – in his own very unpleasant way.

But now the secret police boss was offering him a slim, cool hand.

'The Devil take the hindmost,' he said.

Stahmer clicked his heels in a reflex action, even though he was in civilian clothes.

'A good motto, eh?' Heydrich grinned.

'Yes, Gruppenführer,' answered the agent helplessly.

He had no choice. Only when he had left Heydrich's office could he start to control his own mind again. This place was full of Stahmers. They came and they went; but, whether they survived a mission or not, the fear was always the same ...

Stahmer left the building in the Prinz-Albrecht-Strasse as swiftly as he had arrived. Meanwhile, the machinery of the R.S.H.A. was already in motion. In the laboratory a key was being cut with the aid of the wax impression he had made. And in the personnel department, they were searching their files to select a trained killer.

At the same time as Stahmer was seeing the Devil in Berlin, Formis was in his room at the hotel, the 'studio' where the secret transmitter was hidden. He was

16

speaking into the microphone, his words echoing like a thin cry of agony through the night, a voice in the wilderness that was Germany. Soon it would be silenced, and he knew it.

At first the Nazi government had made repeated protests about the transmitter. The Czechs had claimed that they could not find it. But Formis knew that he was being tracked down, that each time he made his speeches over the airwaves he was giving himself away. One day they would come for him – and use the same ruthless, brutal methods that were the reason for his fighting this desperate, lone battle.

He stood up. His broadcast was over. Then he cleared away the small transmitter to one side and went downstairs. The bar was almost empty; the sudden spell of extreme cold had persuaded most of the tourists to head for home.

The young woman from Berlin was still there, alone. Formis greeted her politely. Something drew him to her: perhaps his longing to hear his mother-tongue, perhaps loneliness.

'Not much to do here, is there?' he began shyly.

'I suppose not,' Ira said. 'And today my husband had to go to Prague.'

'That's not very gallant of him,' Formis said with an awkward smile. 'Have you been married long?'

'No. We're still in the first flush of love,' she answered with a laugh.

Already she could lie coolly, naturally, she thought. And the man was so genuinely kind and friendly. The lamp flickered as the wind outside battered against the walls of the building.

'I'm not a very good conversationalist,' said Formis slowly. 'I'm not sure how I can help you out.' His eyes darted over to a little chinoiserie table in the corner, on which stood a chess board.

'Do you play chess?'

'Yes,' Ira answered.

'Well?'

'Well ... for a woman.'

The man stood up and went to the corner. He picked up one of the pieces, a rook, and it left behind a small, clear spot on the board. Ira realised that the chess set was unused, covered in dust. Formis turned.

'Long-distance chess,' he explained. 'I have a partner in Australia. We have been playing this particular game for two years.' His smile was tired.

'Have you been here that long?'

'Yes. That long.' Formis's mouth was suddenly fixed in a deep, bitter line.

'Isn't it boring?' Ira continued casually.

'Boring?' he echoed. For a moment, his grey eyes showed suspicion. 'Why?'

'I mean ... two years in this little place.'

'The air is better,' Formis said. 'Better than in Berlin ... much cleaner.' He smiled with his mouth, but his eyes glimmered with a hard brilliance. 'Haven't you noticed?'

'Yes, of course ... ' Ira was suddenly confused. 'I had a bit of a cold when I arrived,' she gushed, 'and now it's gone.' She knew that it didn't ring true. And that it wasn't true.

Formis seemed oblivious. He nodded. 'It was the same with me,' he said. 'The moment I arrived here, I found I could breathe freely again ... ' He surprised her with a wry, staccato laugh.

Ira looked at him carefully. His cheeks were flushed, his gaze seemed distant and somehow lost. She sat down opposite him and went through the motions of setting out the pieces. When they came to play, her moves were all wrong. She couldn't summon up the concentration; instead of watching the positions and the moves, she found

18

her eyes fixed almost obsessively on her partner's face.

He was making allowances for her. He could have checkmated her several times, but he made deliberate mistakes. The one mistake he failed to realise he had made was the most serious of his life: he had showed hospitality to the agents of the Devil.

Once again the girl's eyes were on him.

'Why are you looking at me like that?' he said with a forced smile.

'I'm sorry,' Ira countered quickly. 'I'm really playing badly this evening.'

'I'll take out my queen,' he offered.

His warmth and kindness suddenly washed over her like a wave. She could sense what this man was doing, the sufferings he had to undergo, how lonely he was, what incredible inner strength must exist within him to keep him in this miserable place and to risk his life.

Ira's face paled. She saw that grave head with its noble features covered in blood, waxen, sightless. And at that moment she understood what kind of orders Werner Stahmer would bring with him from Berlin. Loathing coursed through her like acid in her veins. And I am the bait, she thought – the nice German girl. God, I shall be guilty too ...

'What's wrong?' Formis cut gently into her thoughts.

'Nothing,' Ira said, trying desperately to cover her distress.

She got to her feet, took a few unsteady steps, then turned to him again, her face chalk white.

'I ... I don't feel well,' she said. The words echoed through the near-empty room, as if mocking her.

Formis shook his head as she left. Then his thoughts were back with the long-distance games he was playing.

The match with his friend in Australia. And the deadly contest against the barbarians in Berlin.

Stahmer had to stay in the Reich capital for another day. The R.S.H.A. was making its preparations, gathering its forces. He wandered around in the Berlin crowds and felt fear pulsating through him when he thought of the flight back to Prague. Neon signs glowed almost ghostly through the evening mist; the headlights of the endless streams of cars seemed to throw a golden chain on the dark, wet pavements.

Stahmer let himself be taken up and carried by the mass. The din, the car-horns, the shriek of the tramways, the bellowing of the newspaper-sellers surrounded him, but they couldn't touch him. It was always the same when he came back from seeing Heydrich. The world of warmth and life seemed so unreal. And he seemed like a spineless, helpless puppet, with a new trick to perform for his master. Yes, Gruppenführer ... He could almost feel the taste of those words on his tongue: metal, explosives, bile. Perhaps blood, too. Yes, Gruppenführer ...

Some schnapps, he thought. The best thing was to get drunk. And when he had that process under way, he started to look up addresses in his notebook. It would be even better to look up a girl; one of the many, the too many, the disposable ones, the ones who knew too much about life, or too little – the girls he had had by the dozen and then thrown away. They were always there, to help him get through a night like this.

He got to a phone and made a date. Someone. Somewhere. To go to some place. The schnapps was already taking effect as he walked to the taxi rank; he was finding it difficult to control his legs – or his thoughts. Tomorrow. He forced himself to think about it, saw Formis's face. He crossed the border, threw hand grenades, with Ira by his side. Then he saw himself as he would be one day, somewhere; he had the same waxen face as Formis, the man he had destroyed ... One mission had to go wrong. Some day, some year. There were many tortuous paths in this dirty, invisible war, and for the men who travelled them there was no life insurance. And all the ways, no matter how they might seem separate, led to the same place. To evil. To the abyss.

To hell ... which had temporarily taken up its seat of residence in the neon-lit city of Berlin.

The wind hissed its icy breath against the lonely hotel above the Moldau. Inside, it sounded like a far-off moan, sad and sinister. The light flickered constantly, and the bar lay in half-darknesss, warmed faintly by the ancient, log-fed stove.

The tall, hard-faced man entered the deserted hotel. He was back from Berlin, by way of Prague. With his orders.

Werner Stahmer parked the black Mercedes in the little car park by the hotel, listening for a while to the healthy revving of the engine before he cut the motor and got out with a grunt of satisfaction. He didn't lock the door. If tonight he was going to have to drag an unconscious Formis to the car, he couldn't afford to lose a second. A single moment could decide everything.

As he walked across the crisp, new snow to the hotel, Stahmer permitted himself a brief thought of the girl in Berlin the night before, of her warmth, her ingenuity, the writhing of her oiled body. Then the hotel door grated on its hinges, and he was back in a different world. He let himself in and heard his steps cutting through the eerie silence of the place. Soon that stillness would turn into an inferno ...

First Ira, he thought.

Stahmer glanced quickly at the board in the entrance lobby. No key there for room nine, so Ira must be upstairs.

21

The man from Berlin nodded to himself and went on his way, the stairs creaking gently under his feet as he climbed. As he entered the corridor on the first floor, a shape loomed out of the gloom.

'Well, back with us again, Herr Stahmer?' said Rudolf Formis with a friendly smile.

Stahmer felt a strange fear, even though he had been thinking of this man all the way back on the plane from Berlin. He had thought of him in every possible form: unconscious, tied up, a bundle in the car boot. This meeting, so normal and amicable, had been the one thing he hadn't been prepared for. A Formis who walked around, who drank his coffee and got into polite conversation on the stairs, just like any other human being.

'I hope your trip was successful,' said the emigré pleasantly.

'Yes ... ' Stahmer swallowed hard.

'While you've been away, I have had some pleasant conversations with your wife.'

'My thanks,' Stahmer answered stiffly, trying desperately to play his role. For a moment he toyed with the crazy idea of going for Formis here and now, beating him senseless on the stairs. Then he managed to get a grip on himself.

The next moment, Ira Puch appeared on the stairs.

'You?' she said, in a puzzled voice.

'Ira ... darling ... ' Stahmer called out quickly. But a smiling Rudolf Formis was already on his way down to the bar.

When Stahmer and Ira were alone, the woman smiled nervously. Now that Stahmer was back, the fear had returned, too. She watched, tossing her blonde hair and pursing her full lips, as he threw his coat onto the bed and became curt and businesslike.

'Everything all right?' he asked quietly.

She nodded, a little too energetically, as if she were trying to shake off some unclean thing. 'And you?' she said lamely, her face showing the strain.

The agent grinned crookedly. 'It's on ... in seven hours, it'll all be over, or ... '

Very slowly, she lowered herself into a chair.

'What is ... on?'

Stahmer lowered his voice; he spoke in a half-whisper, harshly, quickly: 'Yes,' he said. 'The man's got to go. The transmitter as well. Straight away ... Headquarters has decided. He is to be taken alive ... stupid business, but we can do it. One minute past eight. Tonight.'

The girl's eyes looked past him into an emptiness of her own creation. Her lips parted slightly.

'Who do we have to take alive?' she asked dully, as if she had not understood him.

'Formis,' Stahmer hissed. 'Who the hell else?'

He held out a packet of cigarettes, and she took one, mechanically. It stayed unlit.

'But so that you don't have to get involved,' the agent continued matter-of-factly, 'we'll do it alone.'

'Who do you mean by "we"?' Ira asked, twisting the cigarette nervously between her fingers.

'There will be a second man,' Stahmer explained. 'I'll smuggle him into the hotel at seven.'

'And what's he for?' Ira's cigarette was already coming apart, unnoticed, in her hand.

'Security.'

'Security against whom?'

'Everybody,' he answered.

'And then?'

'Then we'll all sit ourselves nicely in the car and take our treasure home to daddy,' Stahmer said, with a hint of real bitterness.

The woman shook her head. 'And if it doesn't all happen ... nicely?' she said stubbornly. 'At the border, for instance ... '

'Glad you're starting to think my way,' Stahmer said, looking down at her with a cruel smile. 'Then, my dear, we start throwing hand grenades at people.'

Ira sat stiffly in her chair, her fingers tugging at the remains of the cigarette, pulling the tobacco out in long strands.

'And what am I supposed to do while all this is going on?' She leaned forward slightly.

'Nothing.' He moved closer to her and gripped her face between his palms, forcing her to look up at him. 'Frightened?'

She pulled her head away.

'I don't know,' she said softly.

'There's no need, anyway,' he continued, ignoring her. 'All you have to do is to keep Formis sweet. Between half-past seven and eight o'clock, he must not leave the bar. You have to keep him there. That's where your duty ends.' He smiled mockingly. 'And your "marriage" to me. All right?'

Ira nodded.

'We'll do the dirty work on our own,' he said.

The girl got slowly to her feet.

'So ... the dirty work.' There was a distinct catch in her voice. 'I think,' she said with an effort, 'that my part is the dirtiest.'

'How's that?'

Ira turned her back to him, swivelling sharply on her heel.

'Have you thought of what will happen to that man in Germany?'

'Of course,' Stahmer said. He strode over to her and spun her roughly round to face him again. 'And have you thought what will happen to us if this thing goes wrong?'

Ira shook her head, bewildered. 'Have you no compassion?'

'Plenty,' he answered coldly. 'But on these trips I'm careful to leave it at home.'

They stared at each other for a moment, each refusing to break. Then, with swift, brutal motion he took a tight grip on her wrist.

'Don't think of him,' he said, his voice breaking with urgency. 'Better to think of yourself ... and me.'

He let her go and made to turn. At that moment, there was a loud banging on the oak door of the room.

'Come in!' Stahmer called hoarsely.

In the doorway stood two men in leather coats. From their faces, you would have thought they were looking into an empty room. One of them turned out the lapel of his coat, to reveal the dull glimmer of an official badge.

'Police,' he said in heavily-accented German. 'We ... speak with you.'

Ira, ashen with fear, had to support herself against the wall.

Stahmer felt his heart constrict, sensed an aching pressure against his ribs. Forcing himself to look calm, he slid one hand languidly into his trouser pocket. He was relatively new to this business, but he knew that the invisible war, like any other, could be ruled by luck.

'Feel free,' he said evenly to the policemen.

'First your wife,' the man said. 'We will fetch you later.'

Ira felt a shiver of terror.

As she went downstairs between the two policemen, she could feel the handcuffs already tightening round her wrists.

For a moment Stahmer considered open conflict with the Czech policemen. Then he managed to get his nerves under control. He waited until the detectives and Ira had

25

disappeared, then went soundlessly across to the bathroom on the other side of the corridor. From its window he could see their car. A grey sedan with a Prague number plate. A police number.

His brain racing, Stahmer went back to his room. What did they know? Who sent them? Why plain-clothes police and not Intelligence? Maybe the whole thing was perfectly harmless; after all, they had left him unguarded. So long as Ira would keep her mouth shut.

So long as ...

He cursed Heydrich and his boss's idea of bringing a 'wife' with him as bait. Right at this moment, he could have summoned the courage to refuse Heydrich, to scream at him, tell him: 'Do your own dirty work!'

But Headquarters had thought of everything; this was a precise, stopwatch operation. A helper had been arranged. A rendezvous point set. A code word agreed. The bomb was in his suitcase, the hand grenades as well. They had failed to think of just one, incalculable factor: two dumb-ox policemen from Prague.

Stahmer lit a cigarette. Keep calm, he told himself, glancing at the clock. Just five minutes since they had taken Ira away; even a routine interrogation wouldn't be over yet. Should he go downstairs? No. Wait it out. He could taste his own saliva, like sour milk in his mouth, and in that moment he knew he was taking the way into hell. He shook his head wryly, but then his smile became a grimace.

Ira would talk ... If only she knew nothing; if only those bumpkins of cops had turned up ten minutes earlier, before he had had time to let out any details ...

Twelve minutes now, and still silence. If Ira didn't come back soon, then something was going wrong, badly wrong. It would mean a sudden, permanent goodbye to Werner Stahmer's glittering career. Maybe that wasn't such a bad thing, he mused for one fleeting moment. He knew what had brought him to this place: the craving for adventure, the terror of sitting in some office for the rest of his life. He didn't ask himself questions about the people he served. But now, for the first time, he had some inkling of where it was all going to lead.

Downstairs a door creaked open, and then there were footsteps in the corridor, coming closer. Quietly Stahmer shut the door and went to the window, checking out the best firing position. Be prepared: back against the wall. His hand, damp with the sweat of anticipation, went to his pocket and tightened around the butt of his gun. He manoeuvred the weapon so that its barrel pointed through the material and straight at the door. Aiming somewhere close to the heart of whoever came through it first ...

It was the two policemen.

'We would like to see your passport, please,' one of them said, gruffly but politely.

Stahmer took his hand slowly out of his pocket and handed over his passport.

The cop examined it carefully and grunted. 'It seems to be in order,' he said in a slightly bored voice. 'Our apologies for the inconvenience.'

'That's all right,' Stahmer said icily, playing the stiff but correct German.

He noticed how the two of them made way for Ira as she came into the room. They bowed awkwardly and left.

'What did they want?' he asked quickly when they had gone.

'Our names, where we were born, when we were married ... '

'Bastards,' Stahmer muttered. 'All the big scene just for that.'

He wondered how they had come to turn up here. Had the landlord sent for them? Or Formis? Or was it just a routine check on foreigners? Who cared? In a few hours, the whole thing would be over ...

'Listen,' he said to Ira sharply. 'I've got to go away again. Don't leave the room until I get back. Is that clear?'

He didn't wait for her to answer.

3

Stahmer gunned the Mercedes along the icy road, risking his life at every touch on the brakes, every curve in the road. But there was something driving him on ... the thought of Heydrich's cold, nerveless face. The fear of that was greater than any fear of an accident. To have to say 'We failed, Gruppenführer ... I missed contact with our second man' was more dangerous than the sheet-ice. His imagination was enough to keep him in a sweat, despite the cold – and to keep his foot on the accelerator.

Ten minutes late for the rendezvous. At five o'clock Stahmer reached the meeting-place: outside a bookshop with an unpronounceable name in the small town of Zahorski. Stahmer peered through the window and saw no one; either the man had gone, or he hadn't yet arrived. Stahmer carried on gazing vaguely at the book titles, feeling time hanging on him like a rippling dead weight.

Then he saw the man with the over-long arms walking, almost loping across the street. A gorilla. Slowly he came up to Stahmer.

In the distorting reflection of the window he looked even more grotesque. Stahmer recognised the type: a Gestapo heavy, the kind of animal who was most at home in an interrogation chamber, who made a career out of savagery.

The man came close up to him and looked at him penetratingly, without any attempt to conceal his interest. Christ, a real bloody beginner, thought Stahmer, with angry resentment against the men who had sent him.

'Homesickness,' Stahmer said quietly.

'Georg,' the man answered when he heard the code word.

'Are you sure no one followed you?' asked Stahmer, still almost whispering.

'Sure.'

Stahmer nodded imperceptibly and they walked away together. The other man took his hand out of his pocket; the knuckles were red and bruised. Straight from the torture-cellars to picturesque Czechoslovakia, Stahmer thought sourly, feeling a wave of loathing for the creature. The sooner he could get this over, the better ...

'What do you know about the job?' Stahmer asked baldly.

'Nothing detailed,' Georg answered. His voice was like iron filings.

'You have the explosives?'

'Yes.'

They carried on the bizarre conversation in short bursts, stopping whenever they encountered a passer-by.

'You know the hotel?'

'Yes,' the gorilla mumbled. He obviously didn't have a very large vocabulary.

'Be there at seven tonight. On the dot. At the back. Use the post office van, but don't drive right up to the place. I'll stand at the window and signal with a torch. Then I'll lower a rope and pull you up. It's all got to go quickly. Got that?'

'Yes.' Georg really wasn't a great conversationalist: more like a human blunt instrument.

'Have you got a gun?'

'Sure.' His smile was feral.

'You won't use it,' said Stahmer sharply. Georg nodded, obviously disappointed. He was tall and broadly built, with a narrow, apelike forehead. His look was somehow wandering, unsteady. God, thought Stahmer, what went on inside a head like that?

'At seven our target usually goes downstairs,' Stahmer said briskly. 'I've got a pass key, so we can get the bomb in. Detonation will be an hour later. Meanwhile we'll go to my room and wait for Formis to come back. Then we knock him out with chloroform ... all quick and quiet ... All right?'

'Yes,' the gorilla answered, with a gap-toothed grin.

'We'll get out straight away. He can be tied up in the car while we're on the move. Any questions?'

'Yes ... ' the man's narrow brow furrowed. 'I need twenty minutes to set up my bomb. What happens if the bastard comes back while I'm busy?'

'He won't,' Stahmer said coldly. 'The girl will look after him.'

'What girl?' the gorilla asked. There was suddenly an animal glint in his narrow, deepset eyes.

'There's no need for you to worry about her,' Stahmer said brutally. 'She's been sent by Headquarters, too.'

'Girls are O.K.,' said Georg, obviously finding the thought a great strain. 'But mixed up in something like this ... '

'I told you, it's none of your business. We part at the next corner. Until seven.'

Stahmer gave a grimace of relief as he walked quickly away from his backup man. If only he had been able to rid himself of his mission as easily ...

It was six fifty-seven. Stahmer was getting nervous. Their victim was still up in his room; on this night of all nights, he wasn't running according to schedule.

31

Stahmer could feel an ache in his temples; he had put out the light, and his torch was waiting on the sill. Outside the snow had stopped falling. It was a clear night except for some drifting cloud.

He turned abruptly.

'You will go downstairs now,' he said to Ira.

'Yes,' she said.

'Right. From half-past seven until five to eight, he mustn't come upstairs – under any circumstances.'

'Yes.'

'It will soon be over.'

When Ira had gone, he looked back into the night, watching the road where it merged into the dark shadows of the forest. For a moment he tensed; then the silhouette by the roadside turned out to be a tall milestone ... He tore his eyes away and listened for noises in the house. Downstairs there was the clatter of crockery in the kitchen. Then a sound on the stairs ... He held his breath and realised he had been imagining things.

Why the hell wasn't Formis moving out of his room?

Six fifty-nine. Formis slowly put the cap back on his fountain pen and glanced through the final part of his manuscript. He rubbed his eyes and looked round at the transmitter, then to the alarm clock on the shelf. Seven-four. Formis shook his head in irritation. If he didn't hurry, he was going to be late for dinner ...

His chair scraped against the uneven wooden floor as he leaned over and switched on first one knob, then the other. A tiny red light glowed into life; the transmitter was warming up. Formis checked the window frame and the security catches and drew the curtains. For a second, his eyes scanned the field of snow behind the hotel.

How peaceful, he thought; just as he looked, the moon came out from behind the clouds, bathing the white landscape in its pale light. But this peace was not for him. This lonely, cheerless building was his fortress – because wherever he went, wherever he found a place he could call home, he would take the struggle against evil, the war against Hitler.

Suddenly the lonely man in the hotel room felt a deep longing. God, he would like to stop fighting, crying in the wilderness. He would like ... There was a man coming out of the forest road now – he would like to go home like that man to his wife and children, to be able to put his feet up by a warm fire ...

Then Formis's mouth tightened. After all, that was what it was all about, he thought. The fight went on so that men like that could live in peace, work, enjoy life, even reach out for freedom.

How could he know that the man on the road, whom he so much envied, was Georg, or that what he was after was something very different from peace, wife and children, and freedom?

The emigré's shoulders slumped in resignation. He sat there for a few minutes more, then got to his feet and left the room. Sometimes, when he thought of the burdens he carried for others, he felt sure that he couldn't go on.

The hand on the clock was pointing to seven minutes past seven. A torch flickered in the night, flashing with the sign of Cain. Then a window opened wide and a rope snaked out. Stahmer leaned cautiously out: Georg was there. He felt the rope tense when the gorilla grabbed its end.

Suddenly a door opened down below. A shaft of light from the hotel cut across the snow. Stahmer froze, and glimpsed another moving shadow as Georg hurled himself to the ground and pressed himself against the shelter of the wall. The rope, the bloody rope, Stahmer thought; there was no way he could explain it if anyone saw it ...

Georg was no longer visible. There was only the sound of someone clanking a bucket behind the house; then a woman's voice shouting something in Czech, and the sounds of footsteps, coming closer.

Despite the biting night air, Stahmer was hot, almost feverishly hot. Any moment and the woman would see the rope ... Then, just as he had given up hope, the steps turned and retraced themselves. A few seconds and silence again, followed by the faint sound of a door shutting on the other side of the building.

Stahmer's nerves were as taut as the rope that Georg was now shinning up again. Christ, he thought, why couldn't the fool climb more quickly? The door could open again any minute – it could be that the woman had just gone for reinforcements ...

But all he could hear was the gasping breath of the man on the rope. Then a head appeared over the window ledge, and an arm gripped Stahmer's wrist.

It was eleven minutes past seven. Ira sat in the bar like a spectre, ordering one coffee after another. She sent the menu back; she felt too miserable to eat. Formis was later than he had ever been before. Suddenly she had an overwhelming, irrational hope that he wasn't going to come, that he was going to stay upstairs, that she wouldn't have to talk to him and keep him down here – that she wouldn't have to be responsible ...

She started when someone slammed the kitchen door – with the state her nerves were in, it sounded just like a pistol shot. At that moment, Formis walked into the room, stooping slightly to get through the low doorway. A frozen smile clung to the woman's lips. No, it hadn't been a shot ...

The emigré nodded to her absently, and for a moment he stood undecided in the middle of the room. One table was occupied by an elderly couple, while at another a taciturn peasant sat with his ham-like hand curled round his beer glass.

'Herr Formis,' Ira called out, painfully aware how loud her voice sounded, how unnatural.

The man looked round and then walked slowly over to her.

'I don't want to intrude … ' he murmured.

'But please … '

Ira felt a shudder of self-loathing. The whole dirty game was under way, and she knew that she wanted it to fail. She was carrying out Stahmer's instructions, but she was hoping against hope that Formis would see through the deception, run, escape …

'My husband isn't feeling well,' she said dully. 'He's upstairs, having a lie down.'

'Oh,' was Formis's only comment. He gave an embarrassed wave of the hand. He came closer, then sat down awkwardly at the table.

She was supposed to keep him here, Ira thought desperately. She had to … But why? Suddenly she felt that she was buying time for herself, and not for the man upstairs.

'How is the Australian chess game?' she asked.

Formis shook his head and looked at the young woman in wry amusement. Perhaps the honeymooners had had a row …

'It looks as if we shall end up with a stalemate, sooner or later,' he said, still smiling.

'A draw,' she murmured lamely, taking a long sip from her coffee cup. If only her hands would stop trembling.

'In the game as in life, it's usually the best we can hope for,' he said with a grim smile.

'Yes.' Ira looked at her watch: seven twenty-seven. God, another half hour to go …

35

Shortly afterwards, the clock on the wall whirred into life and struck once. Seven thirty. The beginning of Stahmer's upstairs curfew.

Formis called the waitress and ordered himself something to eat. Suddenly he put his hand to his forehead, as if something had just occurred to him. He stood up – maybe he wanted to change some phrase in tonight's broadcast.

Ira was swaying slightly.

'Herr Formis ... ' she said softly.

He looked at her in surprise. She smiled back at him, with pain in her eyes, and his kindly face clouded with concern.

'Is there something wrong?' he asked gently. Without thinking, he stretched out his hand and laid it on her arm.

Ira felt the hand's warmth, its life, the slight pressure. Her eyes were becoming heavy and moist. The pressure increased.

'Can I ... help in some way?' Formis asked calmly.

He glanced quickly at the clock. Still only twenty-seven minutes to eight. He gave up the idea of going upstairs and sat down again. The woman shut her eyes for a moment. He was the one who needed help, she was thinking, not her ... The warmth of his voice, his friendly concern, cut into her like a slashing knife.

It was shortly before a quarter to eight when Werner Stahmer shut the door of the transmitter room silently behind him and beckoned the gorilla to follow. Then he eased the key out of the lock. Georg was leaning casually against the bannister. Stahmer took his arm and led him downstairs.

Neither of them said a word until they were back on the first floor, in Stahmer's room.

'The thing's in position,' Georg said. 'Timed to go sky high at exactly nine o'clock ... bloody tight,' he added with a throaty growl.

'I believe you,' said Stahmer. 'Any chance that Formis will spot the bomb before it goes off?'

The gorilla smiled contemptuously.

'I've been well trained.'

The room still smelled of Ira's perfume.

'She seems to be my sort of girl,' Georg leered. His yellowed teeth showed in a wolfish grin.

'Quiet!' hissed Stahmer. Yes, Georg would be the type who liked women. Particularly when he managed to get them down into one of the interrogation cellars ...

The two men's cigarettes were points of light in the gloom, like glow-worms.

Stahmer stood at the door and listened. Everything had gone smoothly until now. And it would have to carry on just as smoothly when it came to stealing a man out of this place.

A quarter to eight. Rudolf Formis checked the face of the wall-clock in the bar against his own wristwatch. Fifteen minutes to go. It was his routine ...

He was still talking to the young woman at his table. And he still couldn't work out what was wrong with her – only that she seemed to be disturbed about something to do with her husband. Maybe only he could tell Formis ... but then the emigré had no desire to become involved with anyone who came from Germany.

Nevertheless, it had been the landlord, not Rudolf Formis, who had summoned the police. Formis had been told the results of the detectives' check: that the two young Germans were 'clean'. He believed them, with the true naïvety of the civilian.

37

Still five minutes to go. When Ira looked away, he took the chance to observe her. She was carrying a burden with her, he thought; she wanted to tell him something, but he would have to wait for her to do it in her own good time. He stroked his newspaper and lit a final cigarette, blowing out the smoke through his nostrils. He was a sensitive man, with an instinct for atmosphere, and he could feel the unease in the hotel. But then maybe the constant danger he had always lived with had hardened him.

He would stand up in a moment, Ira was thinking, and then ...

Formis stubbed out his half-smoked cigarette in the ash tray.

'I have something to sort out,' he said. 'I shall have to leave you alone for a short while ... ' To his astonishment, he saw that her eyes were imploring him now.

'Please,' she said throatily. 'Stay, please ... please ... '

'That is not possible,' he answered, more harshly than he would have wished.

He got to his feet, then hesitated for a moment.

Ira leaned over the table, almost reaching out to grasp his arm.

'I have to tell you something ... ' she whispered hastily. 'I'm ... not married to Herr Stahmer.'

Formis shook his head in wonderment. Then his eyes sparkled. Ah, so that was the problem, he thought. He gave her a discreet, understanding smile.

'Listen,' she said. 'He is ... listen ... ' she repeated more loudly when she saw that Formis was about to go on his way ' ... he is an agent ... from Germany ... '

Formis stood there as if turned to stone. Now he understood. At first he felt fear. Then exhaustion. Then disappointment. And last of all, he realised what it meant for her to tell him this.

'Stay here,' he said. For a moment, their eyes met. 'Thank you,' he added quietly.

Then he acted. He strode over to the landlord, drew him to one side, and launched into a few swift sentences in fluid Czech.

'How long will it be before the police can get here?' he asked.

'Normally about ten minutes ... What's wrong?'

'Get hold of the nearest station ... I think that this evening someone's out to kill me.'

'Who?' said the astonished hotel owner.

'Just get on the telephone,' said Formis firmly.

The landlord rushed over to the phone on the wall and rang Zahorski. Then he turned and said to Formis: 'Stay here!'

'No,' the man answered quietly.

Ten minutes, he thought. He was no coward, and his life had been one long fight. The fact that the fight had been pitched onto this level was not his fault. But he wasn't going to kneel before the God of violence now ...

Formis reached into his pocket. His gun was loaded, the safety catch was off. He straightened, and his eyes took on a hard gleam. Good, he thought. If your name is Werner Stahmer, I'm ready to meet you.

Ira watched him with fear in her eyes. Why didn't he just stay down here? He didn't know that there were two men upstairs waiting for him. But she didn't dare go after him, not now ...

Before the landlord could call him back a second time, Rudolf Formis was already on his way up into the transmitter room. To face the Devil's disciples.

Two minutes to eight. A shadow slipped along the wall, bent but whipcord-tense. The man it belonged to had been hunted, deceived – and warned. And he moved forward, his hands in his pockets, his finger on the trigger of his revolver. His name was Rudolf Formis, and he came from Germany – a Germany that had cast him out. Step by step, he went with his eyes open into the trap ...

First floor. He stood still for a moment, peering at the thin band of light under the door of room nine. He nodded to himself, then he inched forward again and up the stairs.

Second floor. The hotel was as quiet as death. Formis stopped again and listened hard, fancying he could already hear the roar of the police-car engine. But it would be another eight or nine minutes, the emigré calculated – and by that time he would have killed, or been killed.

Formis entered his room. His hands were calm and his head was clear now as he stared at the red light on the transmitter. But he failed to see the clock attached to the bomb ... Formis reached for the microphone; it was a few seconds before eight. He took a deep breath and pressed the transmitter key.

'Here is the Voice of Freedom,' he said firmly. 'Calling our friends in Germany ... '

Formis held the mike in his left hand, the revolver in his right. He would not hesitate. He would shoot, and he would kill ...

As he spoke, his eyes kept watch, probing the half-light. From his fortress, his words were carried to the country that had been his homeland, and behind those glinting eyes he was picturing a scene that was something close to hope.

'Calling our friends in Germany ... ' he said a second time.

A floor below him, Werner Stahmer stubbed out his cigarette. The backup man nodded to him, and a grin spread over his bruiser's face. Stahmer went to the door and listened, catching the sound of Formis's steps on the stairs, the rustle of the key as he opened the door to the transmitter room.

'He's started transmitting,' Stahmer said tersely.

He felt the tension in the air, and suddenly it made him feel almost nauseous. He had no idea why: the laws he obeyed didn't concern themselves with decency, humanity, or reasons. For the R.S.H.A.'s men, those things didn't exist – all that existed was Heydrich's face, blank, threatening, bloodless and corpse-pale ...

'While he's broadcasting,' Stahmer continued in a low monotone, 'he'll be distracted. If we do it properly, he won't notice the door opening. I'll get him round the neck, and you give him the chloroform ... and no shooting, understood?'

'Sure,' Georg said indifferently.

'You carry him downstairs ... I'll keep watch in the corridor and fetch the woman out of the bar. Christ, I hope the car starts straight away.'

Stahmer opened the door hesitantly, then Georg followed him out into the hallway. They were wearing rubber-soled shoes to deaden the noise, and carrying revolvers and small grenades. Georg held the chloroform bottle in his hand. They managed to reach the second floor unnoticed, then stood for a few seconds to get their breath back.

Stahmer could hear scraps of conversation from the bar below. A man was speaking quickly, excitedly – the landlord, he thought, and it sounded as if he was talking on the phone. He shrugged. So long as Ira hadn't done anything stupid ...

The girl was sitting as though she had been glued to her seat. She understood that the landlord was on the phone to the police for a second time, urging them to hurry, even though she didn't speak a word of Czech. She was paralysed with terror. It was only now that she was beginning to realise that her feelings of pity had pitted her against 'Secret Reich Business' and all that that implied. It was a woman's feelings against the long arm of evil. God, she thought – so long as Formis got out of this alive, she would be able to save herself as well ...

Ira stared at the face of the clock. A minute past eight, but still not a sound from upstairs. The landlord was standing at the counter, hopping anxiously from foot to foot, glancing suspiciously at Ira occasionally, then looking at the clock again. He knew that time was the decisive factor, and half of him wanted to go upstairs and help.

But he stood and waited. Standing and waiting: like so many millions who hated Nazism.

At that moment, Werner Stahmer poked his backup man in the ribs. The two of them moved slowly to the left, moving towards the door. Behind that door, their victim was making his broadcast – and waiting ...

The heavy police car went into a skid on the second curve of the pitch-black, icy-smooth road. The four detectives said nothing, just stared into the night, at their watches, at the speedometer. The car was eating up the miles – but maybe not fast enough.

The landlord's emergency call had reached them four minutes before, and they had rushed out of the station straight away. They knew Formis, and they liked him. They respected what he was doing, and they had been expecting an attack.

The car shuddered to a halt by the side of the road. For thirty seconds or so, the battery whirred and roared. A cold start, and in this weather ... Finally the engine spluttered into life. Twice the driver killed it, then the car started up, slowly and in first gear, with the choke full out. The engine screamed, but they were moving.

Much too slowly. The man beside the driver switched on the radio; he knew the Freedom wavelength.

At first the airwaves crackled, making the speaker sound as if he had a sore throat. Then the Inspector sitting by the driver leaned forward and put his ear close to the radio. He could hear the transmission now, calm, clear and firm. The words had an eerie, final solemnity – a final call to the oppressed people of a nation of poets and philosophers that had found itself ground under Hitler's jackboot: 'Hold on ...' came the clarion-call. 'Rise up against Hitler! Keep waiting for the hour of liberation that will come, must come, one day ... Bring your children up to be human beings! Tell them over and over again: Hitler means war, and war means death ...'

'Step on it!' said the Inspector to the driver.

Formis's saviours still had three kilometres to go – through the night, the ice and the cold.

Two minutes past eight. The attack was a minute late. Werner Stahmer carefully slipped the key into the lock, with Georg standing a short distance behind him. The gorilla took out his revolver, released the safety-catch and pointed it towards the stairs. From inside the room they could hear the steady drone of the lone man. Georg grinned contemptuously. We'll make short shrift of this bastard, he thought. In the old days, we could smash his kind with a chair leg, but now ... His hand tightened on the gun with a tenderness that was the only love he knew.

The door below opened, and again they could hear conversation drifting up from the bar. Stahmer hesitated. The gorilla peered down the stairs. They didn't know it, but Ira was leaving the bar.

The girl couldn't stand it any longer; she was escaping from the unbearable torment of the passing minutes. Only she and the landlord knew what was happening: the taciturn peasant was ordering his third glass of Pilsener; the elderly couple were discussing their grandchildren; the waitress was putting her feet up for a moment and reading the newspaper; the cook was washing up ... There was a crash as she dropped a cup.

They had come.

Rudolf Formis could feel them, with an instinct that was surer than his hearing. He stared at the door, holding his finger curled round the trigger. But he stayed calm. He may have been used to a different kind of fight, but he was astonished to realise how comfortable he felt with the weapon, how it seemed to fit his hand; how his pulse stayed normal; how strong hate made him; the way he put his script to one side, speaking extempore, leaving his hand free ...

Rudolf Formis knew that people in Germany, somewhere, were listening, knowing that this was someone from the underground who was speaking out, despite the persecution and the terror.

'If my voice ceases,' the emigré said, loud and clear, 'then it is because I have been murdered. It is possible that the man who will kill me is already on his way – perhaps in the corridor outside, perhaps opening the door ... Men can be killed, but not the conscience of a nation. I will only be silent when I am dead ...'

Just as Formis was speaking his final, grave words into the microphone, the door opened, silently, with an almost uncanny smoothness. First a small opening, then the gap grew, inch by inch. A shadow loomed out of the doorframe. A human shape. A man: Werner Stahmer.

Stahmer was preparing to launch himself at his victim.

Suddenly, Formis switched off the transmitter. The shot reverberated off the thick walls of the room.

44

Twice. Three times. Four ...

Three minutes past eight. The police driver had managed
to work up some speed. The tyres ground crazily over the
packed ice, following the faint trail of the headlights. The
four men in the car were almost choking on their own
freezing breath, but they were all listening to the
passionate speech from the radio, oblivious of the cold,
with a chill running down their spines that had nothing to
do with the weather.

At the crossroads they met a truck, and the police car
had to swerve sharply to the right. It ended up rotating
insanely like a merry-go-round. The driver managed to
right them. Then they heard the bark of a gunshot over the
radio. Then another. And another ...

Suddenly, there was an unnerving quiet. Nothing
coming over the airwaves. The Inspector cursed.

'Move!' he hissed to the driver. 'Faster!'

Another kilometre to go. And they might be too late. As
to who had fired, and who had been hit, they would know
that in a few minutes' time ...

At first, Werner Stahmer felt as if his hand had been
struck with a whip. He had understood, with some weird
instinct, that Formis was prepared, that their victim had
been warned, and he had hurled himself to one side. He
heard the sound of shots from behind him. Three in all.
Georg hadn't hesitated – he liked shooting ... it was the
kind of thing he'd learned in the Night of the Long
Knives ...

Formis slumped to the floor, and Stahmer got slowly
out of cover.

'Fucking idiot!' he oathed.

Then he acted. Quickly. He gave the killer an almighty shove, sending him flying out into the corridor, then took the steps, two at a time. Georg stumbled after him, still clutching his smoking revolver.

They made it to the ground floor. A man was standing in the hallway: the landlord, staring at them with terrified eyes. By his side, a pale, trembling figure was leaning against the wall: Ira.

'Come on!' Stahmer shouted.

The girl hesitated.

Georg battered the landlord to his knees with the butt of his pistol, then turned as the waitress came through the door, screaming. The killer straightened, as if from habit, then lashed out with one foot, straight in her stomach. Again and again, even when she was writhing on the ground. Just like the old days ...

Stahmer took hold of the helpless Ira and wrenched her out through the door. Georg delivered one more loving kick at the body of the waitress and followed.

For a few seconds it looked as if they had had it. The battery whined ... But finally the engine started up, and slowly the car rolled over the cleared space in front of the hotel and towards the road. By rights, Stahmer should have turned left. Instinctively, he wheeled to the right. After a few hundred metres, he felt secure enough to switch the headlights on. No oncoming cars. He pushed the car up to ninety.

Stahmer bit his lips together. There was blood on the steering wheel, and it was his own. Formis had hit his hand, and now the pain was coming. No time for bandaging the wound – he had to get away, move. The police would to be arriving at any minute.

Christ, it had all gone wrong, Stahmer mused bitterly. The Gruppenführer would love this. If they were taken prisoner, and if they were put on trial ... The world would know how Heydrich dealt with his enemies ... And Ira would talk – she was so innocent, so inexperienced ...

The engine was howling like a hungry wolf. Move! The Czechs would have their guts for this one ...

'Slow down!' the gorilla snarled.

'Belt up!' hissed Stahmer.

His left hand felt as if it was being boiled in oil, but his mind was still functioning at full efficiency. Formis had been warned. But by whom? Had he been careless? No. Georg? No one had seen him. Stahmer's eyes moved towards Ira, who was crouched by his side.

She returned his searching gaze. He knew, she thought. It was all over ...

'What ... What went wrong?' she asked.

'Nothing,' he said harshly.

'Who ... Who fired?'

'Don't worry, Fräulein,' the man in the back growled. 'He's not telling anyone.'

For a moment, Stahmer felt like hitting the woman with his good hand, feeling the satisfaction of bruising, hurting. It was your idea, Heydrich, he thought. Your marvellous idea – to saddle me with an amateur, a weakling, a traitor, a ...

They hurtled through the first town. Stahmer didn't need to look at a map. Turn right now; he could still use the car for two or three hours longer, then he would have to dump it and go on by foot. If they captured Georg? The gorilla would keep his mouth shut. So would he. But they had to get rid of Ira. Straight away. If they got her, the other two of them would be in real trouble. He bit his lip. He would get even with the girl, he thought. But not here – over in Germany. They would show her the penalty for stabbing a mission in the back!

Ira was beside herself with terror. Suddenly she began to talk, compulsively.

47

'I ... ' she began hesitantly. 'I ... with him ...'

'Shut up!' Stahmer bellowed at her.

'I mean ... Formis ... '

'I said for you to shut your trap!' Stahmer hissed brutally. Then he forced himself to calm down.

'Listen,' he said. 'Nothing happened ... You didn't talk to anybody, no one ... ' His cold eyes seemed to prick at the skin of her face. Then he reached into his briefcase and took out a ticket wallet.

'I'll drop you off in a minute,' he said, turning to face her. 'Take the train to Prague, and you should make it to the airport by eight o'clock tomorrow morning. There's a Lufthansa flight at a quarter past. Your name is Ira Puch again ... This wallet contains your passport, money, and a plane ticket ... Understand?'

Suddenly she began to cry. She was shuddering with relief.

'That's all we need!' Georg muttered with a grin.

Stahmer stared ahead through the windscreen. Still nothing. He drove through the next village, and the next. The villagers were soundly in their beds. This was no night to be out and about.

He reached over and gripped Ira's arm. 'You'll be out of this very soon,' he said. 'What are you going to do?'

'Fly from Prague to Berlin,' she said dully.

'And when you get there, you speak to nobody. Otherwise ... '

They had reached the local market town. There were still lights on in the railway station. In any case, Stahmer had the timetable in his head: eight thirty-three, so there were still four minutes before the last train left for Prague.

'Go on! Quickly!' he yelled at the girl.

Ira clambered out and stumbled towards the ticket

48

office. She can't have noticed that he knew she had betrayed him, he thought.

But when she got to Berlin ...

The police car had long since reached the remote hotel above the Moldau. The cops had leapt out of the car and stormed the building. As soon as they saw the terrified, bloody victims of the attack, they knew they had arrived too late. They only stopped cursing when they saw the dying man's face.

They laid Rudolf Formis down on the bench by the stove. The Inspector bent over him and saw the three gunshot wounds in the man's body. Formis was still breathing, but every rise and fall of his chest was costing him dear; it was as if the struggle with death had taken him over. His eyes were open, but the pupils had a distant, feverish glint.

The Inspector gave up trying to talk to him and went over to the telephone. He demanded a line to Prague, then looked at the landlord, who was standing by his side, his face still contorted with pain from the vicious blows to his skull. But he was bearing up: he wanted Formis's killers hunted down ... The connection to the capital took a few minutes to come through. The policeman cursed; then, as if he had suddenly remembered the dying man, he turned to the landlord and his voice was soft, almost gentle: 'Do you have their car number?'

The landlord shook his head miserably.

'What sort was it?'

'A black limousine.'

'What make?'

'A Mercedes. There were two men and a woman ... ' The hotel owner described them as best he could.

Finally the Inspector got national headquarters on the

line and managed to make his report. He knew that the borders would be sealed off within a few minutes, and that anyone with a German passport would be in for a difficult time. His lips curled up in a smile of bitter satisfaction. If he couldn't save this man, at least he could catch his killers ...

The Inspector trudged back over to the bench by the stove. The other policemen were searching the building. Formis's face was drawn, and the features were already marked by death. Then, suddenly, the dying man's eyes seemed to come alive; there was an immediacy, a savage clearness in his gaze.

Perhaps, during those last minutes, Rudolf Formis saw what he had been fighting for. Perhaps he saw naked human beings, herded together in the snow, the smoking crematoria in Poland. Perhaps he saw the skeleton-like prisoners as they were pumped with injected poisons. Perhaps he saw the young women in icy tanks, the girls they used in the 'cold-water experiments'. Or the victims of the 'gynaecological' researches. Perhaps he saw men beaten to death. Or men whose skulls were crushed, who were left to starve or freeze, who had to dig their own graves in the icy ground. Or human beings who had to die because they had the wrong kind of noses, or the wrong beliefs; because they believed in a particular God, or just because they were human. Perhaps he saw tiny children hurled to a bloody pulp against walls by uniformed killers who called themselves 'soldiers' ... and the rattle of Panzer treads ... and the marching ... and the songs ... and the screams of the vanquished ... Perhaps ...

But beyond all that, Formis's eyes seemed to hold one overwhelming recognition: that a whole world would rise against that barbarism and overthrow it.

The emigré knew that he had lived long enough. His eyes closed slowly, calmly, and even in the stiffening of death his mouth seemed to smile. For he had given of his own blood, and the cause was good.

The Inspector got to his feet and took off his hat.

'Dead,' he said simply.

Almost at the same instant, an explosion cut through the majestic stillness of death. The walls shook. On the second floor, the bomb planted by the gorilla had finally silenced Rudolf Formis's transmitter ...

4

All he could feel was the deadening coldness of that night. All he could hear was the harsh singing of the wind and the roar of the engine. The headlights tore crazy gaps in the darkness. The man at the steering wheel stared ahead in bitter silence, clenching his teeth to the vicious rhythm of the pains in his hand. Werner Stahmer had wrapped a handkerchief round the wound; it was the most that he could do. It was four minutes past ten, and the police were already drawing their dragnet tight. In the last village they had seen the patrols out. Every road had been closed. He had even heard his own description over the German-speaking radio: 'Werner Stahmer is six feet tall, fair-haired, with a high forehead and pale, close-set eyes. Be warned: he is armed. To be shot on sight.'

He nodded morosely. Then he hit the dangerous left-hand bend. His foot whipped off the accelerator and he was pitched sharply forward, almost smashing his head against the windscreen. He righted the car. On one of those bends, they were bound to meet a road-block. Sooner or later ...

'Do you want me to take over for a while?' Georg asked.

Stahmer shook his head. Now that Ira had gone, he had the killer in the front passenger seat. A moronic, dead-headed thug who was incapable of seeing what he had done – and Stahmer had to take him with him, now of all times.

'I don't know what you're so sore about,' the gorilla was grumbling. 'If it hadn't been for me, you'd be dead as a doornail.'

'Shit,' Stahmer said simply.

'That bastard would have killed you ... '

Stahmer looked down pointedly at the bloody handkerchief round his hand.

'If Formis had been in practice,' he muttered with a sour smile, 'I'd need a bandage somewhere else. Or maybe I'd be past that.'

'It's all turned out all right,' Georg countered. 'He's dead ... the transmitter's gone sky-high.' He grinned ferally. 'And we're getting the hell out.'

'You knew Heydrich's orders,' Stahmer said harshly, trying to control himself. 'When we get to Berlin, you'll answer for it.' His voice became dangerously soft. 'Do you really know what you've done? If the Czechs get hold of us, or the girl. What do you think the foreign press will do with all this?'

The gorilla thought for a moment. Stahmer could almost hear the primitive machinery of his brain labouring into action.

'The papers abroad are always attacking the Führer, anyway,' the man said with a dull stubbornness.

First the car had to disappear, then they had to cover their tracks, Stahmer was thinking. He was sweating and freezing at the same time: like malaria, he realised, just like malaria. But now he was on his way again, though slowly. At the next crossroads he turned right and onto a farm track. As they bounced along the narrow roadway, he judged the terrain. With snow chains, they might make it. The track led to a single farm building, then narrowed down even further. He could see a small wood ahead of them in the light from the headlamps.

'What's going on?' Georg asked.

'Belt up,' Stahmer said.

There was no chance now that they'd make it to the German border before dawn. If they had left the hotel half an hour earlier ...

It was then that Stahmer saw the snow-covered ditch. He stepped on the brake pedal so hard that the heavy car slid through a hundred and eighty degrees. Then he got out and looked at the damage. With a silent nod, he went to the boot of the Mercedes and got out a spade, gesturing to the miserable-looking Georg.

'Out,' he rasped. 'Get digging.'

'What for?'

One withering glance from Stahmer was enough. The backup man clambered out, and he began to dig like a man possessed. After a while he started panting and wanted to stop, but Stahmer forced him to go on. Finally he took up the shovel himself. The wound in his hand came open, and he had to bite back the pain. He carried on, but much too slowly. Georg seemed still not to have got the point. He just stared stupidly down at the ditch. It was half an hour before they had laid it bare to the sky.

Stahmer went wordlessly back to the car, put it into reverse, then let the Mercedes roll gradually back into the trench they had created. The car subsided. Then he climbed out, rubbing a bruise on his head.

'Cover it,' he said curtly to the gorilla.

By eleven they had finished. Stahmer looked at the spot again. It looked as if the ditch had attracted a big snowdrift, he thought. With any luck, it would be two or three days before they discovered the Mercedes.

He jabbed Georg in the ribs. Time to get out. On foot now. They moved off side by side, tramping through a strange country at twelve below ...

The swift, hard steps echoed like pistol shots across the courtyard of the building in the Prinz-Albrecht-Strasse. Everyone there knew them. The guards pulled in their chins and turned up their collars, as if sensing the bullet in the back of the neck. They breathed a sigh of relief when the steps had passed. The lights were still on all over the office complex. The headquarters of the R.S.H.A. and the Gestapo didn't keep to office hours: the grisly machine operated day and night, driven by the Devil and greased with blood.

Gruppenführer Reinhard Heydrich tore open the doors to his office; the adjutant in the ante-room stood to attention, then followed him into his lair.

'Any news of Stahmer?' the boss asked as he strode through the rooms.

'No ... that is ... '

'Yes or no?' Heydrich cut in coldly.

'We ... We recorded today's broadcast ... ' the adjutant stammered.

'Play it back to me!'

The recording-machine had already been set up. They had made a wax disc, and the needle crackled over the final words of a human being called Rudolf Formis: 'If my voice ceases,' the words came over the loudspeaker, 'then it is because I have been murdered ... '

Three, four shots, and then silence. A chilly smile spread over Heydrich's face.

'Have the German border posts with Czechoslovakia reinforced.'

'Yes, Gruppenführer.'

'We won't get Formis alive,' Heydrich added. 'They have killed him. That's how they carry out my orders.' His voice became venomous. 'Swine ... Stahmer is to report to me immediately on his return. Day or night.' The security chief took a few paces backwards and forwards. 'Make sure the Propaganda Ministry know about this business. They'll have to think of something ... we're washing our hands of it.'

The adjutant sprang to attention again as Heydrich strode out of the room. A few seconds later, he felt confident enough to start breathing once more.

*

The stopping-train pulled into Prague Central Station right on time. It had been almost empty. A young blonde woman hurried past the late night passengers, not looking around her, just keeping on going. The driver was just getting out of his cab, sharing a joke with his fireman. It was half past ten. Time to go home.

But not for Ira Puch. She walked quickly, trying desperately to look as though she had somewhere to go. At the ticket barrier she saw uniformed police; they looked at her closely, but they let her go through without asking for her papers. She made to walk on, and her hands reached down automatically – until she realised that the luggage was still at the hotel on the Moldau.

She felt many things, but fear was not among them at that moment. What had happened to Rudolf Formis? Perhaps he was still alive, perhaps, like Stahmer, he had only been wounded. Ira felt her heart start to beat faster. She had betrayed Stahmer when she warned the emigré ...

But she was new to the business. She still only half-understood that she had probably signed her own death-warrant.

She walked around the streets for a while, until the freezing night air drove her back towards the station building. A hotel? Too dangerous. The third-class waiting room was open all night, and so she took a seat in the scruffy room and ordered coffee. The air was bad, and her only companions were a couple of noisy drunks in a corner, who were carrying on a running battle with the waiter. But still she had to sit there, though the night seemed endless and any minute she expected a police patrol to walk in.

After a while she opened the wallet Stahmer had given her and checked its contents. There was a passport made out in her real name, money, and an air ticket, just as he had said. Just before dawn, she got up and found a hairdresser and somewhere to wash. Then, for all her inexperience, she realised that she had to buy some convincing tourist 'equipment'. Half an hour later she had acquired a suitcase, a few clothes to put in it, and some toiletries. Then she hailed a taxi and headed for the airport.

She arrived with an hour to spare. The terminal had been under heavy surveillance all night, she soon realised – the Czech authorities were watching invisibly, with a skilled discretion. Ira was asked to step into a room, where a police Inspector in plain clothes politely introduced himself in fluent German.

'Frau Puch?' he began.

'Fräulein,' she corrected him.

'My apologies,' he said, with a cool professional smile. 'You are travelling to Berlin?'

'Yes.'

'And you have enjoyed yourself in our country?'

'Oh, very much.'

'A holiday?'

'Yes.'

'Alone?'

'Yes.'

'Why?' Suddenly there was an almost hawklike glint in his clear blue eyes.

'Please, I ... ' the woman said.

Ira could feel herself being overwhelmed by a weary indifference. The policeman was looking at her carefully; the description he had been given was very general, and it fitted this woman only very roughly. The Inspector decided he would have to depend on his instincts.

No, he thought. This young woman was exhausted, troubled, but it was probably some problem with a boyfriend. She lacked the nervous edge that a guilty assassin, even the most hard-bitten, would have at this kind of interrogation.

The Inspector had already noted the details of her place of work and address in Berlin. A telex was already on its way to the German police, who were not yet infected by Heydrich's power-hunger. A few minutes later, Berlin confirmed Ira's personal details. The Inspector screwed the telex message into a ball and tossed it neatly into a waste-paper basket. Then he stood up.

'My apologies for any inconvenience. Have a good flight.'

It was only when Ira was sitting in the plane that she fully realised that she had escaped. Then she forgot everything in the excitement of her first flight.

'We are now flying over the territory of the Reich,' the stewardess announced over the microphone. Ira felt a swift, foolish relief; she put back her headrest and slept so soundly that she had to be woken up when the aircraft landed at Tempelhof.

Now that she was back in Berlin, the whole affair in Czechoslovakia seemed like a bad dream. She would forget it. Ira went home, and in the afternoon she went to work. In the evening she rang her friend Margot.

'Back in Berlin already?' the girl asked.

'Yes, already,' Ira answered, trying to inject some gaiety into her voice.

'And was it nice?'

Then Ira's friend noticed that something was wrong.

'What's up?' she asked gently.

'Come here,' Ira mumbled.

'Better if you come to my place,' Margot said quickly. 'I've got some people over.'

When Ira arrived, the villa in Dahlem was blazing with light. A few good friends had dropped by, and the evening had developed into a party. Margot came out to greet her friend, wearing a simple – though very sexy – dress that moulded itself to the curves of her petite figure. Two or three men were following her as she walked out towards Ira.

Margot Lehndorff dismissed them with a throaty laugh, put her arm round Ira's shoulders, and led her girl friend into the house.

'Take a seat,' said Margot. 'So. How was it?'

'Quite nice,' Ira answered distantly.

'Want something to drink?'

'Please.'

'Your little holiday wasn't that marvellous, am I right?'

'No, not particularly ... '

Margot switched on the radio. She had dark, long hair, green eyes and a mouth that curved up in a relaxed, warm smile. Even when she was enjoying herself, that air of being in control of the situation never seemed to leave her.

There was some big-band music on the radio, and Margot was tapping her feet to its rhythm as she fetched Ira's drink. Why not? She was young and pretty, with money to spend and not a care in the world; one of those girls who made men turn round, then shrug their shoulders and go on, because she had to be spoken for.

'Come on, tell me ... ' Margot pressed.

At that moment, the music stopped. Time for the news. The two woman ignored it; Margot was showing off her new dress.

'Like it?' she said.

'Lovely.'

Suddenly Ira jack-knifed forward, as if she had a pain in the stomach. Her face paled and stiffened. Then they heard the voice on the radio, loud and clear: 'We are dealing with a vicious slander against the Reich. Who has heard of this so-called Rudolf Formis? The authorities suspect that foreign agitators have staged the crime in order to raise the atrocity-propaganda against Germany to fever-heat ... '

The arrogant, rasping words of the radio commentator cut through the room.

'My God ... ' Ira murmured tonelessly.

To get rid of the fear, the pressure, the sudden, wild panic, she made a fatal mistake: she began to talk ...

The commentator was silent at last. And the end of the news brought despair into the cosy room, turned it into an arid no man's land, a hidden corner of the invisible battle front. Ira and Margot looked at each other in terrified amazement. One was blonde, one dark, but they were both young and beautiful, both made to live, love and dream. And now they were both in danger of their lives.

'It's eight o'clock,' the voice of the radio said.

Ira slumped in her chair, and Margot crouched by her side, holding her hand. She still didn't understand what her friend had told her, but she could see the abject fear and horror in her eyes clearly enough. She wanted to help, oblivious of the fact that it could be fatal for her, too. The incident in the hotel on the Moldau had turned into an international political issue. But here in Berlin, someone was popping a champagne cork. A toast was being drunk. The house was filled with music and laughter. The evening was looking promising – and no one there even knew where the Moldau was, still less cared.

'Won't you tell me ... ?' the dark-haired girl began hesitantly.

Ira shook her head violently.

'There will now be some march music,' an anonymous voice announced over the loudspeaker.

The loud martial tune struck up. Four-four time. Steel helmets. Boots. The uniformed dance of death. Boom, boom, boom ...

'Come on,' Margot persisted. 'Sit down.'

Boom, boom, boom ... Secret Reich Business ... boom, boom, boom ... she couldn't tell Margot ... boom, boom, boom ... a man named Formis was 'unknown' in Germany,

60

and so he couldn't have been murdered ... that was the Devil's logic ... boom, boom, boom ...

'I – ' Ira muttered painfully ' – I can't.'

But she talked. She had to get the fear out, exorcise it somehow. She didn't want to involve her friend, but she desperately needed help.

She told the whole story of the attack on Formis, quickly, a little confusedly. Her finely-boned, full-lipped face became a mirror of all the stages on the road to murder. She felt as if she was back in the corridor of the hotel, hearing a shot. Then another, and another ... 'Boom, boom, boom ...' came the din from the radio.

At first, Margot simply smiled and shook her head incredulously.

Then, gradually, she began to understand the seriousness of Ira's situation. She asked, probed, learned all the details of 'Secret Reich Business', without even knowing what the phrase meant. Why should she? Plenty of other people had died without knowing it ...

Margot looked at her friend gravely, then ran a hand through her hair. Why had Ira got herself involved in such a crazy business in the first place? No matter. No point in thinking about that now.

'So you think that this Stahmer knew that you warned Formis at the last moment?' she asked.

'Yes,' Ira admitted miserably.

'And where is he now?'

Ira shrugged her shoulders hopelessly.

'That's your chance,' Margot said firmly.

'What?'

'Maybe he won't get back,' Margot answered. 'They might catch him and put him in prison. Understand?'

Suddenly there was a knock at the door, and the two girls separated, like conspirators caught in the act. A smiling young man in a dark suit appeared in the door-way.

'Where have you been all this time?' he asked Margot. Then he saw Ira, and added hastily: 'Oh, I'm sorry ... I didn't know you had a visitor.'

'This is Georg,' Margot said by way of introduction.

He went up to Ira and bowed politely. Georg ... the name cut into her like a blow from a whip. Georg, the gorilla with the great, spadelike hands, the killer ...

Ira forced herself to look up and offer him her hand. Suddenly her fear evaporated. Here was just a nice young man like a hundred others.

'Why the horrified look?' he asked with a laugh. Then he offered her his arm.

The three of them went downstairs to the living room, where a cheer went up as they made their entry. There was a record on the gramophone, a gentle, romantic tune. A slow waltz. The company were a colourful crowd, and the champagne was ice cold. Even the laughter was genuine. They rolled up the carpet and set to dancing. Ira drank her second glass of champagne; at first it made her feel dizzy, then just pleasantly light-headed. The terror was disappearing in a lovely warm haze ...

The young man bowed again.

'Would you like to dance?' he asked softly.

She nodded. When they were out on the floor, she relaxed in his arms, and her steps seemed to glide over the parquet as if she were floating on a cloud. They were playing the new hit tune: 'I'll Dance with You into Paradise'.

He was a good partner, skilled and gentle. Ira felt his strong hand on her shoulder and snuggled closer against him. One-two-three ... One-two-three ... She forgot time. She was dancing away from fear. In the arms of a man named Georg.

There was another Georg, and he was a ruthless killer, but then he might never come back ... One-two-three ...

*

The cold was pitiless, the path seemed to have no end, and the countryside they were trudging through was pitch dark. Werner Stahmer and his backup man walked side by side. In silence. Bitter. Determined. And weary.

Every step he took sent a stab of pain into Stahmer's injured hand. It seemed to travel up through the sinews and joints, making even his backbone cry out for relief. But there was none. Not until they got over the German border – and that seemed as far away as the moon.

They came to another crossroads. Stahmer's torch glowed into life. They read the distances on the signpost. The road in front of them had been cleared of snow.

'It'll be easier from now on,' panted Georg.

'No,' Stahmer said, his voice grating like the loose gravel under his feet. 'We'll go across country.'

'Fucking stupid,' Georg growled.

'The easier we take it, the easier it will be for them to catch us,' Stahmer muttered. Then he stumped off, without even looking round to see if the gorilla was following him. He waded through the deep snowdrifts by the side of the road, then jumped the ditch. The field lay in front of them like a white shroud, billowing with hillocks and hollows. The snow was hard-packed and knee-deep. Stahmer reached down painfully with his frozen hands and rolled up his trousers.

It was he who tripped over the first time. His shout was drowned in a heap of snow. Georg pulled him out.

'Shit,' said Stahmer.

They pressed on over the endless, rolling snowscape, heads bowed, like plough-horses. They couldn't feel their hands or feet; Stahmer imagined that he was seeing and sensing everything through a thick gauze – it all seemed so unreal, and slowly the idea of just sinking down in that soft bed of snow was becoming more and more seductive ...

Suddenly they saw the shadow of a wood in front of them.

They stumbled on through the early-morning light, shying like frightened animals at every sound. As they lurched through the trees, showers of snow soaked them, and branches scraped against their numbed faces. They ate snow and chocolate. Every car that they saw was a threat; every human being could be a potential hunter; they avoided houses, which could so easily turn into prisons. The whole country was looking for them, for murder.

By the afternoon, they were too exhausted to walk any more. It was then that they saw a forester's hut, a rough log shelter in a clearing. They listened, then crawled in. There was a smell of rotting hay, and tools were stacked in one corner. Both men ignored the signs of human habitation; all they were interested in was warmth and rest ...

Georg fell asleep immediately. Stahmer lay beside him, too feverish to join him. His hand was oozing pus, and his brain was filled with crazy, frightening images. He tried desperately to keep a clear head; they couldn't possibly stay here. Stahmer heaved himself on one elbow and jabbed at the killer that he was supposed to be getting safely across the border.

'Come on,' he said. 'Stand up ... '

Georg gave an irritated, sleepy grunt.

'I want you to organise soap, shaving things, two fresh shirts, and some food.'

'On my own?' asked the gorilla.

'Yes. Alone,' said Stahmer harshly.

'Where?'

'The nearest village.'

Stahmer watched the heavy as he trudged resentfully away from the hut. Sometimes he hoped that they'd catch him ... No. That wouldn't be a good idea. They might have committed a murder, but at least so far no one could prove

64

it. Stahmer looked at his watch. Stopped. He listened and heard nothing. Then, letting himself down onto his belly, he crawled under the pile of hay and fell asleep.

His nap lasted an hour. Some sixth sense of danger warned him, even before he became conscious of his surroundings again, and in seconds he was wide awake, listening to steps in front of the hut. Georg, he thought with relief. Then the door opened, and two men walked in, talking quietly to each other in Czech, brushing the snow off their thick canvas mittens. One of them lit a match. He was so close to Stahmer that the German could feel the pressure of the man's body against him. He thought of the gun in his pocket. It would be easy – but it would be two more killings. Stahmer was breathing so shallowly that his ribcage was starting to hurt. If Georg turned up now ...

Suddenly he heard a strange sound. He realised that they were forking through the hay. Systematically. He felt the pitchfork plunging into the heap he was hiding under. Close. The next one had to pierce his body. If only he had the strength to get up ...

The pitchfork was pulled out, then cut through the air again with a low whooshing noise. Then the prongs sliced into the hay, right by him.

One man's death had become a political issue. An international one. Photographs of the dead Rudolf Formis were plastered all over the front pages of the foreign press. The free world was following the hunt for the killers with baited breath. The German Propaganda Ministry was denying everything, with a rage that smacked all too clearly of hypocrisy. There had already been an exchange of stern diplomatic notes between Germany and Czechoslovakia. But then all that was child's play – so long as two men managed to stay out of sight ...

The dragnet was being drawn together throughout the country. The Czech police was throwing everything it had into the hunt – and failing. In Prague they were already afraid that Werner Stahmer and his henchman had escaped, while, in Berlin they were convinced they had been captured. If they were caught, the whole thing would run like clockwork: presentation at an international press conference; taped confessions; photographs; screaming headlines – and a wave of loathing for the Third Reich and all its works. The Nazis were still trying to appear 'respectable' at this time. Even abroad, people held out vain hopes: maybe this little man from Austria wasn't so bad as he looked, maybe they could come to some sort of arrangement with him? Hitler needed their credulity, to give him time to re-arm. But if the world found out about what had really happened in the Formis case, the Third Reich would be exposed for the gangster empire it was. The world would know what went on in the Prinz-Albrecht-Strasse – and the kind of methods Reinhard Heydrich used …

The Devil was in a raging fury. Every few minutes, his cowed henchmen were landed with another enquiry after the progress of the Stahmer case. Most of them were sure that the operation had aborted – and that it would be fatal for Heydrich's career, just when he was building the R.S.H.A. up into a real power in the land. Everything was still being developed, prepared and accumulated for the day when the Gruppenführer could organise the killings, the mass-executions, when everyone in the Reich would tremble before his untrammelled might. The files at the Prinz-Albrecht-Strasse contained information on thousands of citizens – enough to blackmail anyone, from the humblest small-town official to the most vainglorious Gauleiter. Knowledge is strength was Heydrich's motto, and so he kept on building up his files, his archives. He hated everyone, and that made his task easier. If he had been

66

ordered to, he would have liquidated Himmler, his pasty-faced boss, tomorrow. And if the good of the Party had demanded it, he would have been prepared to uncover the dark side even of Hitler's past.

But now?

There was every chance that the atrocity on the Moldau would set up a trail that led straight to the heart of Heydrich's private empire of blood.

Suddenly the man who was preparing to enslave millions, the crown prince of terrors, was afraid for his own neck.

Heydrich's contempt for his fellow men was boundless, but his power was still limited. And so his henchmen kept on asking the question that their boss was asking, with that cold snarl of his: Where was Werner Stahmer?

Stahmer came to once more, quite suddenly. He took a bemused look around, then shook his head, trying to clear his brain. Then he saw the gorilla's face. He still didn't understand what had happened; he felt himself all over for the wound that had to be on his body somewhere.

In fact, the pitchfork had missed him. Fear had sent him into dead faint and prevented his discovery. The foresters had loaded up a sled with hay and gone about their business.

'Everything's all right,' Georg said. 'I just pointed to things and paid for them. The village is only just down the road.'

'Are you sure no one followed you?'

'Just let up on all that for a minute, will you?' Georg muttered. 'Christ, we've got smokes, food, booze ... What more do you want? I've even got hold of some soap,' he added with a grin.

Stahmer knew that the longer they stayed in one place,

67

the harder it would be to escape. But they were exhausted, and so they had to spend the night in the hut. At dawn they washed themselves in the snow, shaved as well as they could, then put on fresh shirts. They still had 180 kilometres to go to the border, and the whole route would be swarming with police. At this rate, it would take them a week to make it. They struck off across country again. It was slow, but it was their only hope.

After a short while they came to a little country road.

'What's to stop us going down here?' the gorilla grumbled.

Stahmer shook his head, but in the end he gave in. He knew it was wrong, but the searing agony in his hand was stronger than reason. Suddenly he just didn't seem to care any more. He didn't even look up when they met a group of people on the road. He took a route directly through the village, though they could easily have made a detour round it. The curtains in the village police station were still firmly drawn.

So they covered ten kilometres. Then they decided to rest and smoke a cigarette on a heap of frozen snow by the roadside. As they took their break, a milk truck passed by. The driver took them in with one swift, sidelong glance, and travelled on. Stahmer's eyes followed the truck hungrily. Should they steal a car? No, that would be suicide. Catch a train? Impossible. Continue on foot? They would probably be picked up in the next village.

Stahmer got to his feet and walked to the side of the road. A big Tatra saloon was coming towards them from the village, dawdling along in first gear. The fellow must be scared of the sheet-ice, he thought. It was then that he noticed a woman was driving. Stahmer moved out into the middle of the road, without even thinking, and raised one hand. The car slowed down still further. The lady was wearing a Persian lamb coat and she wound down the window and leaned out. A Czech number plate, from

Prague, Stahmer pondered. And a woman. Worth trying . . .

He nodded politely. The trouble was, he didn't speak a word of Czech.

'Pardon, madame, nous sommes des étrangers,' he began in French.

She hesitated for a moment, maybe because she had just caught sight of Georg.

'Madam, excuse me please, but we are foreigners,' he continued, trying English this time.

She nodded and indicated for them to get in.

Georg sprawled in the back while Stahmer took the seat next to the driver, who was lighting herself a cigarette.

'German?' she said to him in his own language.

Stahmer felt a tremor of fear.

'How did you know?' he asked uncertainly.

'From your accent,' she answered with a smile.

He looked at her in profile. A good-looking woman, he judged, maybe thirty years old, with a lot of money – probably married it. He knew instinctively that she was attracted to him. But the fact came as no surprise; he was used to it. Women were no problem for him, just another tool to be used. For love or for escape, according to the circumstances . . .

'I must apologise,' said Stahmer. 'I'm not in the habit of stopping ladies on the road.'

She laughed.

'And I'm not in the habit of picking up hitch-hikers,' she retorted.

She obviously trusted Stahmer. He sat slightly forward and peered nervously through the front windscreen. The woman obviously misunderstood him.

'Don't worry,' she said smilingly, 'I've had a driver's licence for four years now.'

'Oh, I'm not worried,' he said coolly. 'Tell me, how is it that you speak such good German?'

'My mother came from there,' she said. 'My father is Czech. And what are you doing in our country?'

'Just a pleasure trip,' he said with a forced casualness. 'Ran out of money ... You know the problems with foreign exchange ... '

She stubbed out her cigarette and turned on the radio.

'What do you think about Germany?' Stahmer probed. A German mother. She just might ...

'Oh,' she said dismissively, 'I don't understand politics.'

They passed through the next town without incident. This kind of escaping was almost fun. The car had an efficient heating system. Gradually, as they settled into the warmth and the soft upholstery, the two Germans began to lose their fear. Georg was sitting in the back as if he were on a Sunday outing, with an almost childish expression of contentment on his ravaged face. His intelligence was, if anything, even less well developed than his conscience; he was capable of thinking about as far ahead as the next corner.

This time, even Stahmer failed to recognise the new danger. The threat came from the airwaves, when the music suddenly stopped and an announcer's voice, speaking in rapid Czech, came over the loudspeaker.

The announcer was repeating some kind of bulletin. At first Stahmer thought it was just his nerves when he caught what sounded like his own name. Then he heard it again. And a third time ... Stay calm, whatever you do, he told himself. He looked at the woman as casually as he was able, and watched her expression. In fact, she could understand every word of the bulletin. 'Stahmer is about six feet tall, fair haired, with a high forehead, and pale, close-set eyes, Warning: Stahmer is armed. To be shot on sight. Stahmer's accomplice is about the same height, and has a broad, ordinary face ... I repeat ... '

Suddenly her hands tightened on the steering wheel, and she glanced at the man beside her with an unmistakable expression of fear. She dared not turn round to look at the man in the back. She listened to the personal descriptions of the men, and then she knew for sure that she had the two most wanted fugitives in the country in her car. She quickly tried to cover up her anxiety, but it was already obvious that Stahmer had realised what she had heard. The woman swallowed hard and began to slow the car down.

It was then that Stahmer, in turn, knew for certain.

She got her question in first.

'Your name is Stahmer, isn't it?' she began.

He kept up a stubborn silence.

'And you're wanted for murder,' the woman in the lamb coat continued quietly.

Stahmer reached over to the car radio and switched it off.

'Am I right?' she asked.

Still he made no answer.

Georg was stretched out in the back seat, taking a nap. What the hell could they do? Force her to stop, and then take off across country again? No good. Once they got to the next village, she would bring the police down on them. Should they beat her up and steal the car? That would really be desperate measures ...

'Do I look like a murderer?' he asked her.

She shrugged. 'Tell that to the police,' she stuttered.

He grabbed her roughly by the arm.

'Listen to me,' he said.

He forced her to meet his eyes.

She felt the terror – fear of those eyes, and those hands ...

'Nothing will happen to you,' he murmured. 'I'm sorry, but we have to get out of here. And you're going to help us.'

'No,' she said weakly.

His pressure on her hand increased until she could feel it stopping the blood flow, like an iron fetter. His eyes were cold, hard, and his face seemed to radiate a strange, barbaric fascination. She was uncomfortably aware of a brutal masculinity that sent shivers down her spine. And she knew she was weakening.

'Will you help me?' he hissed, in a voice like an angry lover.

She nodded, and loathed herself for it. But then he couldn't be a killer, she thought. It must be a mistake, she told herself again and again. No criminal looked like that . . .

Suddenly the car was sliding towards a road block. Six or seven policemen had sealed off both sides of the road, and it was too late now to turn back. The woman's eyes widened with terror. She slowed down and looked helplessly at Stahmer.

'What now?' she said dully. The woman seemed to have merged her will into his.

'Show your papers and tell them we're friends of yours from Prague,' he rasped.

The game was up, he was thinking. Here, on this stupid little road. It was rough justice: that was what you got when you tried to escape first class.

The car came to a halt, with its engine still revving. The woman handed out her papers and her passport. She was the wife of a well-known Prague industrialist, and the policemen immediately became more polite.

The conversation seemed to last for ever. Rapid, terse questions and answers in Czech. Georg was staring out from the back window with a look of intense confusion; he had only just realised what was going on. Stahmer considered getting out of the car and giving himself up. But he carried on concentrating on the woman, almost as if he was trying to hypnotise her.

Then the incredible happened.

The policeman by their car raised his hand and waved them through. The woman turned once more, as if imploring help, but the cop just nodded affably. Then she stepped on the accelerator, and the car rolled slowly away from the trap.

'Thank you,' murmured a bemused Stahmer.

The woman was silent for the next few kilometres. It was only then that she began to realise just how cool the man next to her had been all through the road block check.

'What would have happened if I had called for help just now?' she asked hesitantly.

Stahmer thought for a moment, then shrugged.

'Nothing,' he said.

5

The tranquillity of the next few days only served to make Ira more nervous. She didn't dare to leave her little Berlin apartment; whenever the phone rang, whenever there was a knock on the door, her skin prickled in terrified anticipation. The war of words over Rudolf Formis in the newspapers had almost stopped. And Werner Stahmer was still untraced. Even his masters seemed to have forgotten him. Sometimes Ira even wondered if the incident on the Moldau had ever happened. Then she would look at the passport, the Czech crowns, and the used plane ticket, and the whole nightmare would come flooding back.

Ira was due to meet Margot and some friends tonight to go to a party. How was she going to summon up the courage? Margot insisted. It was carnival time in Berlin – the season for gala evenings, parties and arts balls, when everyone seemed to be burning the candle at both ends. Even the party bosses took off their brown shirts and slipped into clown outfits, or stood around in wooden bunches in dinner jackets, like tailor's dummies in a shop window.

Margot arrived just before nine that evening. She saw that her friend had not even changed yet.

'Just as I thought,' she said with a smile, tearing open the wardrobe door. 'Come on, get into something. Quick, our knights in shining armour are waiting ... '

The others trooped in after her: Fritz, Jürgen, Georg. Georg nodded to Ira. Still flirting. Eventually Ira went with them, willingly.

It was long, hot night, full of hurrying waiters, music, wine and high spirits. Ira danced, flitted from group to group, smiling, drinking, flirting. There was something feverish about her wild hedonism; she danced and danced, until she had forgotten that three days before she had been dragged through knee-deep snow, petrified with fear and cold ...

At first she didn't notice that Georg had become her constant companion during the course of the evening. He had a nice smile, and he was a good listener. His face was solid and dependable, and he had gentle, soft hands.

'I like you,' he told her.

'Thanks,' Ira answered.

Margot came up. 'Enjoying yourselves?'

'We shall,' Georg said with a grin.

He took Ira's arm and led her over to the bar.

'Champagne!' he called out, even before they got to the counter. The way he pronounced it proved that it was something he only drank on high days and holidays. He pressed a glass into Ira's hand.

'Cheers!' he toasted. 'To us ... '

She hesitated.

'To the party,' she said cautiously.

'From the look on your face, anyone would think it was already over,' he laughed. 'Anyway, tomorrow's another day ... '

Ira felt a shiver of fear. Yes. Tomorrow. Or the day after. Some day for certain ...

'You look worried,' Georg said.

'Come on, let's have another drink,' Ira answered quickly.

Then the room seemed to be spinning in front of her. The faces seemed distorted. The laughter around them had turned into a cruel chorus. She turned on her heel, feeling Georg's gentle pressure on her arm, his breath on her cheek. She became soft, yielding, dreamy.

Sooner or later, somewhere, she had to stop. During a break in the corridor, when no one else was about. He put

75

his arms round her, and he kissed her. But Ira's lips were cold, and she kept her mouth tight closed. Georg felt as if he had a doll in his arms, not a flesh-and-blood woman.

'Look,' he said, his even face puzzled and a little hurt. 'What's wrong?'

'Nothing ... '

All she could think was: If only his name wasn't Georg ...

The man was alone, in uniform. He knew the way, and as he walked he stared placidly into the night. Nothing doing. The border guard would be coming off duty in an hour. He paused for a moment, thinking of his warm room, the dinner in the oven, the glass of Pilsener. Suddenly he heard a sound behind him, and he turned.

Too late. The pistol butt thudded dully into the back of his skull, and the man crumpled to the ground, with a rasping sigh on his lips. The killer they called Georg had done his job again. Beside him stood Werner Stahmer.

They had made their way into the frontier zone. Germany was only a kilometre and a half away now – but still unreachable. They had got one border guard out of the way, but they knew there were probably dozens, some of them with dogs, between them and the border. And they all had orders to shoot on sight.

Stahmer had managed to persuade the woman from Prague to make some detours, zig-zagging in the direction of Eger, near the western border. She had followed his instructions passively, as if she had no will of her own and he was her Svengali. When Stahmer finally got out of the Tatra near Eger, he was convinced that she would go straight to the police. As it turned out, he was wrong. Perhaps she was ashamed of admitting that she had harboured two murderers – of her own free will.

Now Stahmer and Georg were standing beside the body of the border guard, listening into the night. Somewhere very close, searchlights were sweeping, clawing at the darkness. But there was a thick mist; they might have a chance, even if the probing beams picked them out. Too much reliance on the fog might be risky, though – now and again a strong gust of wind swirled a patch of it away, leaving them standing in bright moonlight, naked and unprotected.

They crouched in the snow until their bodies threatened to freeze up. Then they began to crawl slowly forwards. They made quick dashes at regular intervals, then paused when they heard voices. Like now.

Suddenly they saw a dog, a black blur racing towards them. Georg glimpsed its glinting wolf-like eyes and reached for his gun.

'Don't shoot, for Christ's sake,' Stahmer hissed.

The dog seemed to be heading straight for him, then swerved suddenly and attacked Georg, who pushed it away with a hefty kick. The animal launched itself straight back at him and bit him in the leg.

Then they heard steps, the sound of whistles, shouts. Three, maybe four border guards. The dazzling beam of the searchlight began to come closer, until it was only two or three metres from them. Georg hammered the dog with his boots and his gun butt, and it howled with pain and slunk away.

It was the signal for the final dash for freedom. A moment later, the full power of the searchlight was on them.

'Move!' Stahmer panted.

He jumped to his feet, and Georg stumbled after him. To the left, to get out of the fatal light. To the right ... the

77

gleaming eye followed. It had them, and it wasn't going to let go.

They heard another shout, close by this time. Then a shot over their heads. Warning. They lurched on, stumbling, hauling themselves to their feet again. There was the whistle of bullets all around them, and from in front they could see the next searchlight reaching out. But just to the right there was a tiny wood.

'No ... I can't go on!' Georg moaned.

Stahmer grabbed him and dragged him onwards into an insane, lurching run for the trees. Then they were there. Still the whistles, the shouting, the shots. Georg collapsed and lay motionless on the icy floor of the wood.

'Up!' Stahmer hissed at him. No reaction. Then Stahmer coolly began to pummel the nape of his neck with the flat of one hand. He pulled his head up by the hair. There was thick mist beyond the wood – they could be in that in a matter of seconds, and seconds were what counted now. Slowly he managed to haul the backup man to his feet and began to push him along in front. Georg stood still, muttering animal grunts of protest. Stahmer kicked him hard in the backside, sending him careering into a tree trunk. When he stumbled round to stare at his assailant, his face was covered in blood and his eyes were aflame with an unreasoning hate. He bared his teeth like a rabid animal. Stahmer lashed out with his foot again, this time in a high kick that caught the gorilla under the chin, snapping his head back and sending his teeth biting into his tongue.

'Swine!' Georg snarled, and spat blood.

Stahmer could feel the pain in his hand now, worse than before, but he ignored it; his fury gave him strength. He drove the moronic heavy in front of him, with kicks and punches, like a stubborn animal. Whenever Georg paused, he lashed out with his knee or his fist. The killer was crying, but Stahmer didn't let up. Left foot, right foot. Left fist ...

There was a stabbing pain between his ribs now, and both hands were masses of agony, but he kept on.

Georg was bawling like a child, mumbling, begging; he wanted to throw himself to the ground and wait for their pursuers – anything but go on. All that kept him going was his terror of the man with him.

They had covered three hundred metres. The mist was clearing. Suddenly a half-dozen tentacles of light were reaching out for them nearby. They had to get out. Georg collapsed, groaning, one more time, and Stahmer went for him again, booting and striking out with his fists, hammering and pummelling.

'You pathetic, cowardly bastard!' he growled.

Georg hunched his head between his shoulders and raced out and straight into the glare of the searchlights. Stahmer followed. They were running for their lives.

Suddenly shadows seemed to spring out of the darkness. Men in uniform, ten or fifteen metres in front of them. A whistle sounded. A harsh voice shouted an order. Stahmer and Georg stopped dead. It was the end of the road ...

The newspaper headlines about Rolf Formis seemed to have gone the way of all print. It was carnival time, and who cared about politics? Ira danced the nights away and forgot her fear.

Then, one morning, the doorbell rang.

'I'm coming,' she called from the bathroom.

Must be the postman, she thought, or the charlady. She dried her hands unhurriedly, then glanced automatically at her reflection in the mirror over the wash basin. She looked good, despite the late nights. Her face was young, pretty, and fresh. She went through the small hallway of her two-room apartment and unlocked the security chain on the door.

Suddenly she rocked on her heels, as if she had seen a ghost.

'You?' she said incredulously.

'Me,' her visitor confirmed.

Then he walked straight on into the apartment, a man who had never heard of privacy or closed doors. He was tall and slim, with broad shoulders and narrow hips. The kind of man whose looks showed that he had too much courage and too little heart.

Werner Stahmer pushed past Ira without even looking at her.

Then he stood in the middle of the room, a cynical smile on his lips.

'I would guess you're not very glad to see me,' he said with a humourless laugh.

There was a pause, and in those few heavy moments he seemed to go through every stage of the flight from the Moldau – particularly the end, the driving of Georg over the border, the blood, the kicks, the blows. Yes, finally they had run straight into the barrels of machine pistols, they had put their hands up, waited helplessly. It had taken a few seconds before he had realised that they were faced with a German, not a Czech border patrol.

'Listen,' Ira said desperately. But she couldn't go on.

Stahmer had brought the nightmare back into her life. And what could she say? She moved away from him, her face pale and suddenly weary, backing over towards the farthest corner of the room. But Stahmer simply stood where he was, while she waited for the questions, the accusations. He sighed and pointed to his wounded arm.

'I've got you to thank for that,' he said curtly.

Ira shook her head helplessly.

'Yes,' he went on, 'you stabbed me in the back. You warned Formis ... You are a traitor.'

80

Ira sat down, leaned back in her chair, and listened to his words. She knew what had to come now; she had rehearsed the scene a hundred times in her mind during these last few days, despite her hope that Stahmer wouldn't make it back across the border. He was just as she had imagined: big, threatening, icy cold. The game was over, she thought feverishly. The end of the dream.

He strode over to her and shoved his good hand roughly under her chin.

'Why?' he rasped.

'You ... murdered him,' she answered, her whole body trembling.

'We?' Stahmer said bitterly. 'No: you. We would have got him back to Germany alive.'

'And then?' she said softly.

He shrugged his shoulders. 'That's not my department ... none of my business.'

'But you would have been responsible,' she said, firm and accusing now.

To her amazement, she suddenly realised that he was avoiding her eyes.

Stahmer paced up and down the room. He was not particularly interested in making the girl suffer. But how was he going to explain the fiasco to Heydrich? He had reported to the R.S.H.A. straight after his return to Berlin, and had been relieved to find that the Gruppenführer was away on a short tour of inspection. He didn't have to face his boss until this afternoon.

'Who have you spoken to about this?' he asked quickly.

'No one,' Ira said. 'You told me not to,' she said, desperately elaborating on the lie.

Stahmer stopped and peered at a framed photograph that showed two girls on the beach. One was blonde, the other dark. They both wore confident, superior smiles; they were dangling their long brown legs over a breakwater, pleased with themselves, the day and the world. Ira and Margot ...

'Not even to her?' Stahmer asked, pointing vaguely at the other girl. 'Who is she?' he said, without waiting for Ira to reply.

'A girl friend.'

'All right,' he said grudgingly. Then he looked at her, harshly but with a little sadness in his eyes. 'I don't know what will happen to you,' he said. 'You must not leave this apartment.' He shrugged. 'Just remember, you brought all this on yourself.'

'What are you going to ...?'

Stahmer dismissed her frantic plea with a wave of the hand. Then he nodded his farewell. He still had a while until his meeting with Heydrich, a little time to decide the girl's fate.

Outside, Stahmer let himself be carried along by the crowds in the busy street. He was deep in thought. Politics didn't interest him. All he did was carry out his orders. Or so he told himself ...

It was a slack early afternoon in the Prinz-Albrecht-Strasse. Stahmer and Georg were kept waiting outside Heydrich's office long enough to get through ten cigarettes each. Meanwhile, Ira scuttled around her apartment, wondering whether to ring Margot, then deciding that she had involved her friend enough already.

Heydrich arrived just before three. His long, swift strides were easily recognisable, and Stahmer and Georg heard him coming long before the doors flew open. Heydrich walked straight through the anteroom without looking at them, as if they didn't exist. It was a bad sign.

When they were finally summoned into his presence, the Gruppenführer was standing behind his desk, impassive and pale. His thin lips seemed to be smiling over some cruel irony that only he could know. He responded to their smart salutes with a slight, grudging nod.

'Orders carried out,' Stahmer reported.

The Devil raised an eyebrow.

'Which orders?'

'The Formis case,' Stahmer said, trying to stop the fear showing, knowing he had to brazen this one out.

'And where is the fellow?' Heydrich asked, in a dangerous, soft hiss.

'Dead,' Georg said, with primitive pride.

'You killed him?' asked Heydrich. He seemed genuinely interested.

'Yes, Gruppenführer,' Georg grinned and clicked his heels.

'Why?' Heydrich spat out the question.

'He fired first.'

'Two against one,' Heydrich said contemptuously. 'Cretins!'

'But ... ' Georg stammered.

'Shut up,' the R.S.H.A. boss cut in sharply.

He gazed for a few seconds at Georg's face, which still carried the marks left behind by Stahmer's fists. He nodded, as if he had just understood something.

'And where is the girl?' he asked, suddenly turning his attention to Stahmer.

'In Berlin for the past two days,' the agent said. Now Heydrich will keep on asking questions, he thought, and Ira will be finished.

'How was she?'

'Satisfactory, Gruppenführer,' Stahmer answered, just a shade too quickly.

The tall man in the tailored black uniform pondered for a moment. 'So what shall we do with her?' he said to himself. He didn't seem to be able to decide. 'We'll see,' he said finally.

Then Heydrich paced backwards and forwards a little

longer behind his desk, ignoring the other two men.

He swung on his heel and faced them with that smile again.

'You did a first class job,' he said sarcastically. 'A worldwide scandal. You've given ammunition to the foreign press, allowed the name of the Reich to be dragged through the mud, you ... '

He broke off. It was one of those rare occasions when the Gruppenführer was unable to summon up words to describe how much he despised a fellow human being.

Heydrich turned and looked at a large wall map. Then a slow smile spread over his face. Stahmer knew what was about to happen, and broke out into a cold sweat.

The Gruppenführer pointed with his pencil to the map and half turned towards the man they called Georg.

'Dachau ... Buchenwald ... Oranienburg ... ' he recited indifferently. 'Take your pick.'

'What am I supposed to do, Gruppenführer?' asked the killer, his jaw hanging, his button eyes registering genuine amazement.

'I am giving you the opportunity of realising what it means to disobey my orders. I'm going to send you to a camp ... ' The bloodless smile broadened. 'In view of your past services, you may choose which one yourself.' Then his voice became harsh. 'Understood?'

'No, Gruppenführer,' the gorilla answered, his face rigid with terror. Slowly, the full cruelty of Heydrich's game was starting to penetrate his dull brain.

Heydrich strode over to the door to the anteroom and hurled it open. An adjutant came rushing in.

'This man here,' the boss of the R.S.H.A. ordered, 'is to be sent to ... ' He hesitated and looked enquiringly at Georg.

'Come on, man, make your mind up,' he muttered.

'Dach ... Dachau,' the killer whispered, as if in a dream.

'Dachau,' the Gruppenführer repeated. 'Immediately. Until further notice.'

It was the kind of arrangement that pleased him. Heydrich didn't care whether the men he stuck behind barbed wire were the enemies or the pillars of the system. Power was all that really mattered. The capacity to inflict terror. Against anybody.

'But ... ' Georg screwed himself up to a final protest.

The adjutant took him roughly by the arm and dragged him out of the room.

'As for you,' Heydrich grinned, turning to Stahmer. 'You will report immediately to Standartenführer Löbel.'

'Yes, Gruppenführer,' he said.

His voice was thick with a fear that was rapidly turning into relief. End of the meeting. Finished. Nothing more. Just a vague nod. That was all Heydrich needed to set his underlings in motion.

Half an hour later, Stahmer was given the strangest orders that had ever been issued from Satan's inner sanctum.

Five paces forward, five paces back. Ira was in a cell. The silver-grey curtains deadened the noise from the street. The room was simply but tastefully furnished; it was not a cell, but her apartment, which she was so fond of, which she had rented and furnished when her father married again. The real prison was in her head, and her jailer was Werner Stahmer. He was the kind of man who turned up when he was least expected, unannounced – and who liked to keep other human beings dangling on his string.

She had been waiting for hours, and still he hadn't come. She looked out of the window; the fact that there was nothing to be seen outside only increased her fear. She was trying to break out of the vicious circle of thoughts that kept her a slave to that terror, trying to forget the stupid, thoughtless way she had volunteered for this whole brutal business. She had thought of it as a skiing holiday at the state's expense when they had invited her to go on that weird trip to Prague. Perhaps it had been that touch of mystery, even danger, that had finally persuaded her.

And now there was no going back. Still Werner Stahmer hadn't arrived.

She began to fantasise. The young woman didn't know very much about Germany's new masters, but she felt an instinctive fear. Maybe her aversion came through her father, who had escaped into politics from a dull, unsatisfying life. For years, he had been preaching about German greatness, about an end to poverty, about the wonderful new life that had passed him by. Old Puch still worked as an engraver in a gloomy basement, but it had done nothing to change his childish belief in the Great German Mission. He had become a fanatic, and to escape his harsh, droning voice she would have moved out into any old hovel.

Ira had never known her mother, who had died when she was a baby. Her father had married for the second time a few years previously, and her two little half-sisters called her 'auntie'. She got on well with her stepmother.

The doorbell rang. Ira had had hours to prepare herself, but now she was paralysed with fear. She stood up slowly and went to the hallway. Just a second more of uncertainty. She opened the door.

It was Margot. Ira could almost have laughed, but it didn't come. She felt her face twisted in a bizarre parody of a smile.

'I'm ... expecting visitors,' she said.

'Rubbish,' her friend said briskly. 'You're terrified.'

'Go, please go,' Ira pleaded.

'I've thought things over,' Margot continued, ignoring her, 'and there's a way out.'

'He came here,' Ira said weakly.

'And?'

'I think ... he'll come again ... and take me away ... '

'I have a suggestion,' Margot said firmly. 'You go back to your father, and I'll take over this place. If things get nasty, I can warn you. Your father has friends in the right quarters, hasn't he?'

'Yes,' Ira said wearily.

'Fine then.'

Margot would brook no contradiction. Ira moved house, more because of her friend's insistence than out of any great enthusiasm. She knew perfectly well that swapping homes wouldn't do much good, but at least it helped to take her mind off things.

'Have you read the paper?' her father said when she arrived. Old Puch's myopic eyes glinted behind his thick glasses. The gleam of the zealot.

'The Führer is going to build a new, rich Germany,' he added.

'Tell us when you get your share,' Ira muttered sarcastically.

Her father wagged a finger at her.

'You have to look at the whole picture,' Puch scolded. 'You are nothing, but the nation is everything.'

'The family's important, too,' Ira's stepmother chipped in. The two women smiled at each other and looked out of the window.

The children, four and six years old, came rushing in and hurled themselves at their 'auntie'. They gave her a noisy welcome, because they were fond of her, and because she was sure to buy them ice creams.

*

87

Werner Stahmer had time on his hands all of a sudden. It was one of those nights when a man should smother himself in schnapps or girls. He took a shower and began to feel better. Stahmer dressed, hailed a taxi and went into the West End where he wandered around, trying to make up his mind about tonight's entertainment. Suddenly he thought of Ira, the girl on the Czech mission. For a moment, he found himself laughing at his own stupidity. Yes, he was the big, brave agent – and maybe he was a sentimentalist, after all. He had let that girl get away with dropping him in it, almost getting him killed, and then he had covered for her – ready for the next time, when she might do the job properly ...

He would give her a good telling-off, he decided, drink a schnapps with her and give her another lecture on keeping her mouth shut.

Ten minutes later, he was ringing the doorbell of her apartment. Pressing hard and long on the button. Masterful. The kind of man who took control of any situation. By the time he noticed that someone different had opened the door, he was halfway into the hall.

'Fräulein Puch is not here,' Margot said.

'I can see that,' he glowered.

'If you had any manners, I would invite you in,' Ira's friend retorted.

'You have a nice line in cheek,' Stahmer said, 'for someone your age.'

He took a good look at her, and he liked what he saw. For a moment he forgot why he had come, and he smiled. Not a bad exchange, he thought.

She sat opposite him, staring at him with a frank interest. Not bad packaging, she mused, but don't look too closely at the contents.

'Can I offer you anything?' she said.

He shook his head and carried on looking at her, as if he was seeing a real woman for the first time in his life:

'Were you coming ... to take her?' Margot murmured anxiously.

'No, not her,' he said casually. 'You.'

He nodded to her, stood up, and introduced himself.

'I thought we might go for a stroll through the city,' he added. 'If you like.'

'So long as you don't ... bother ... Ira ... '

He looked at her sharply.

'What has she told you?'

'Nothing,' the girl answered.

'It's best that way,' he muttered. Then he became human again.

First they went out to eat. Stahmer gave his charm full rein, playing on it like a maestro on a Bechstein grand. He was no pessimist, but as the evening went on he had a shrewd suspicion that he was going to find it hard to get very far with this girl.

Margot stayed cool, without being unfriendly. She was to the point without being unfeminine, managed to be good company without letting her real self show. Werner Stahmer had thought he knew how to deal with women. They were like days: sometimes they were sunny, the next thing they were dull, and then they were fun again. One after the other. He kept the calendar. And he was the one who threw the used pages into the waste-paper basket.

'And now?' she asked after they had eaten.

'Well, if you see this evening as a tiresome duty, then I'll take you home,' he said.

'Oh no,' she added quickly, 'the meal was very good.'

He noticed that her dimples showed when she smiled.

'You're very pretty,' he said,

'Thank you,' she smiled again.

'But I don't think that I impress you over much,' he stated flatly.

'The thing that I most like about you is that you didn't ...
hand over Ira.'

'You keep talking about Ira,' Stahmer muttered irritably.
Then he gave her a searching look. 'Why?'

'Because of that stupid business in Czechoslovakia.'

'Are you crazy?' he hissed, reaching out and grabbing her
by the arm. 'I'm sorry,' he said, more calmly. 'Then Ira did
tell you ... '

Margot nodded.

'Do you know what that could mean?'

Margot laughed. Throaty, mocking, from the heart.

'From the look on your face, you must have a pocket full
of live hand grenades,' she said.

'What do you know about hand grenades?' he rasped
back at her, astonished at the bitterness in his own voice.
His fingers were fiddling with his collar; suddenly it felt
tight around his neck.

Margot observed him. He was puffing himself up, she
thought. It was really a pity that he had to be such a big
head.

'Listen,' he was saying. 'Ira has done something very
stupid. You must understand ... '

She nodded, but she didn't look him in the eye.

'We're dealing with "Secret Reich Business",' he
continued grimly. 'I don't think that you understand what
that is.' He gestured vaguely. 'I'll explain it in one sentence:
If anyone finds out that you know about this ... this
business in Czechoslovakia, then you'll be silenced. You ...
and Ira and me as well.'

'And who is "anyone"?'

'Headquarters,' he answered.

'What headquarters?'

'That's not important,' he muttered, taking refuge in a
cigarette.

'Margot,' he said then, and his tone changed. 'You

90

must understand. Don't think I'm a fool. But after all, I'm involved in ... '

'All this dirty work,' she finished for him. Her words were brutal.

'If that's the way you see it, yes.'

'It's really a pity,' the girl said thoughtfully.

'How's that?'

'You look as though you could hold down a decent job.'

'Sure,' he scoffed, 'I could be a cosy civil servant, with a pension at the end of it all.'

'That would be better than ... '

'Than what?'

'Kidnapping, burglary, killing people, just carrying out other men's stupid orders.'

Almost against his will, he had to listen to her. Deep down, she was right, he thought. Not that she understood anything about things like that. But then perhaps that wasn't such a bad thing.

'I don't think you've understood my meaning,' he said out loud, with a desperate stubbornness. 'You ... '

'I know,' Margot said, more gravely now. 'I'm the sort of person they silence.'

She gave him a sidelong smile.

'And how do they do that?' she said.

Stahmer looked down at his shoes.

'There are various possibilities,' he muttered, without looking up. 'A concentration camp would be the least unpleasant. Then comes the guillotine. Or they could just ... have all three of us disappear. Have you finally got the point, for God's sake?'

She made no answer, but he could tell from the look of naked horror on her face that his jab had hit home. Still she did not speak. Nothing.

'How old are you?' Stahmer said suddenly.

'Twenty-two.'

'And your profession?'

'Are you a policeman?' she asked with a wry smile.

'Why?'

'This sounds like an interrogation.'

'I'm sorry,' he said. He was really messing this up, acting like a bull in a china shop. Where was his magic touch with women?

'Human beings are curious,' he said simply. 'And I'm one, too, even if you think I'm some kind of wild beast.'

'Let's not quarrel,' she said.

'My autobiography isn't very interesting,' she said then, after a short pause. 'I'm my father's daughter.'

'And what would you like to be?'

'A man's wife.'

'And does that man exist?'

'I suppose so,' she answered. 'It's just that I haven't met him yet.'

He laughed. 'You've set your sights high.'

They went on to a little bar called 'Don Juan'. Stahmer ordered a bottle of wine. He raised his glass and toasted Margot, but she sipped sparingly at her drink. One hand was fiddling with her glass, and her clear blue eyes were sizing up his face. Stahmer forgot all about his job. They were getting closer to each other, but not close enough. For a change, he talked only a little about himself. He wanted to know about her.

'My father owns three shoe shops in Berlin,' Margot told him. 'I don't know exactly how much he has in the bank. I am protestant, I left school at the age of eighteen, and I would like to have two children one day. A boy and a girl, if possible. Anything else you'd like to know?'

He laughed.

'You're a strange character,' he said. 'A girl of your age, and you've already written off your life. No sense of adventure.'

'Perhaps marriage is the greatest adventure of all,' she answered with a smile.

She smelled of lavender water, of peace, and of a kind of honest decency. It was a good evening. He gave up finding ways to flirt with her. He didn't want to impress her any more, just to be with her. When they parted, all he had got was her telephone number, and that only at the second attempt.

'May I give you a ring?' he asked.

'Give it a try,' the dark-haired girl said.

'Do you think I'll succeed?'

'The answer to that will cost you twenty pfennigs,' she said. 'It's available from any telephone booth.'

Then she disappeared, without another word.

The fog was drifting over the city from the direction of the Tiergarten, swirling round the embassy buildings on the edge of the park, then spraying itself out in thin clouds onto the streets of the administrative quarter.

The sentry's steps rang hollow in the clear night air. He moved with a rhythmic regularity: ten paces forward, ten back, keeping his eye on the street while his mind concentrated on the time when he was due to be relieved. The long, low sandstone building threw the echo of his steps back at the soldier. In the windows, table-lamps glinted singly, like glow-worms. And behind them were nothing but files, because this building was full of documents: it was the army archive.

Three strokes of the clock sounded through the damp winter air. A quarter to one. The sentry yawned and stared at the entrance. He was due to be relieved any minute. Anyway, what was there to guard here? Nothing but pieces of paper, from the cellar to the roof. Who was interested in them, apart from retired generals.

A shadow glided silently along the wall behind the

soldier. A man, coming from the blind side of the street, hurrying along the edge of the building until he got to the wall of the inner courtyard. A quick glance at the sentry. A few fragments of blackened snow rustled down into the street from the top of the wall.

The man leaned against the wall, breathing heavily, then listened. Then he went forward, ducking as he ran, checking the building. There it was: the lightning conductor.

One o'clock. Changing of the guard. The shadow had already reached the roof. He started slightly as a flock of outraged pigeons cooed their protest and flapped their wings at his intrusion. For a moment he had to struggle against a feeling of dizzy weakness. Then he managed to heave down his blow-torch and pass key.

The trap door in the roof creaked; it was years since it had last been used. Then he was through, feeling the boards of the attic floor groaning under his weight. He had to head for the stairs.

The burglar took a deep breath once more, accustoming himself to the almost stifling heat of the overheated corridor, and switched on his torch. One hand pressed over the end of the torch, acting as a blind, allowing just a narrow finger of light to flit round, ghosting over doors and on through the empty building.

Second floor. His torch shimmered on a folding door. 'War Document Room O', he read, 'Entry strictly forbidden'. The bunch of keys on his belt rustled. Ancient keys, and the second one fitted the lock. So that was what those army blockheads called 'security'. The light groped over great tiers of drawers, reaching from the floor to the ceiling.

The man knew what he was looking for. Top right, the card indexes. His cold eyes watched as his fingers worked at the cards. Files A 17 to 32 ...

The material was in locked metal boxes. The burglar got to work with his blow-torch, and in a few seconds he had the bundles of documents in his hand. The man read quickly: 'Military treaties between the government of the Reich and the Soviet Union' ... 'Supplementary agreements' ... 'Secret protocols'. Bunches of files went into the rucksack on his back by the blow-torch.

He was ready to leave. Then, suddenly, he heard steps. Heavy, dragging.

The door was pushed open. The burglar pressed himself flat against the wall, remembering the words of the man who had given him his orders: 'If they catch you, we'll say we know nothing about you ... you're on your own. Keep that in mind. You know the stakes involved – so no sentimental nonsense ... And take your gun.'

It was a nightwatchman with a hurricane lamp who shuffled into the room. In a second, the burglar judged, his hands steady, head cool.

Now ...

There was the sound of a choked-off curse in the darkness. Then a sickening, dull thud, and the body of the watchman slumped to the floor. The burglar bent briefly over him. Then he heard whistles, loud and piercing. Steps. Men ...

Christ, someone had set off the alarm ...

Down below, he could hear the tramp of soldiers' boots. He dashed out of the room, for a moment heading upward to the roof. But that didn't make sense. Orders were being bellowed, and still the whistles cut through the night.

As the sounds of his pursuers moved upward, the burglar moved back down, stumbling frantically over the back steps, two at a time. He stopped in front of a lift door and pressed the call button; that should confuse them. A few seconds later, they were storming towards the fifth floor while he crouched on the third, listening. The more chaos the better. The burglar set off the fire alarm, and a siren howled into life. Move ...

The exits were under guard. He heard someone yell: 'He must have jumped out of the window!'

The sound of tramping jackboots was becoming more scattered; they were dividing up into groups and searching the place systematically. He reached the cellar and went straight for the nearest door. The latch gave way under his assault, pitching him into what looked like the boiler room. He hurled himself behind a pile of coal. It was then that he saw the pair of blue overalls lying nearby. They had to belong to the stoker. In a second, he had torn off his jacket and trousers and squirmed into the work clothes. On with the light ... He grabbed a shovel and wrenched open the door of the boiler; then he started shovelling coal, shovelling for all he was worth.

He clattered, scraped and banged, working, spreading coal dust all over his suit and his rucksack.

They came a few minutes later, but he ignored them, just carried on shovelling like a man possessed. There were four of them – three soldiers and a civilian.

'That's the stoker,' said the sergeant-major.

The man working on the boiler half-turned and leaned on his shovel.

'Has anyone come by here?' asked one of the soldiers.

'Not a soul,' the man with the shovel growled.

'Are you sure.'

''Course I am. I'd have seen 'em.'

'Carry on,' the sergeant-major said dismissively. The sooty face grinned at him, and when he left it dissolved into a wide smile of malicious glee.

After a couple of hours they gave up the search. The building was quiet again. The burglar looked at his watch: five o'clock. The real stoker could turn up any minute. He leaned against the door, listened, and caught the sound of weary, shuffling steps coming down the corridor. He braced himself and raised the shovel in both hands.

One blow, and the man coming through the door

plummeted like a sack of potatoes.

The burglar hauled his rucksack onto his shoulders. Time to test those nerves of yours, he thought. Then he strolled casually up and out into the yard, straight towards the sentry. The soldier nodded and waved to him, obviously relieved to have a chance for a bit of human contact.

'Wish I were in your shoes,' the private said, spitting carefully onto the flagstones. 'Nice to be knocking off first thing in the morning.'

'You should have been a stoker,' the other said. Then he wandered on. Slowly. Easily. As if he had a home to go to.

'Hey, mate!' the soldier called out after him.

The burglar stopped. The sentry pointed to his rucksack. 'Bet you've been pinching coal to take home, eh?'

'Get stuffed,' he answered placidly.

The soldier laughed.

Once he was through the exit gate, the man with the rucksack broke into a swift walk. The grey early-morning light picked out his face. It was impassive, finely-chiselled, with close-set eyes and a firm chin.

Werner Stahmer had just carried out the first part of his new assignment: breaking into the army archive.

If he had failed, something like five thousand human beings would have had a chance of staying alive.

6

Ten a.m., and the R.S.H.A. machine was in full flow. The building in the Prinz-Albrecht-Strasse vibrated with the slamming of doors, the ringing of telephones, the chatter of telex machines, the rattle of typewriters.

Werner Stahmer crossed the hallway with swift, confident strides.

His route took him past the offices where the Second World War was being prepared. He passed rooms where they were organising the persecution of the churches. He went through departments for mass-extermination and counter-espionage. He skirted the sabotage section and the administrative offices for the political camps.

Every crime that the Third Reich could conceive of was plotted, organised, and ordered here – in the name of the blond-haired Devil whose name was Heydrich and whose limitless hatred oiled the machinery of death.

Stahmer reached the Department for Eastern Affairs and knocked casually on the door. In one hand he held a fat briefcase containing the stolen documents from the army archive.

Stahmer nodded to the girl receptionist and went straight through into her boss's office. The head of the department, S.S. Standartenführer Hermann Löbel, had been expecting him. Löbel was a typical product of the new Nazi regime: the thug turned bureaucrat. In any other country in the world, he would have been behind bars, but here he dictated policy in a plush office. Most people didn't take him too seriously; he had a tendency to grandiose plans. Rumour in the R.S.H.A. had it that his closest connection with Eastern Europe was a strong fondness for vodka.

Löbel received Stahmer standing up, with a broad smile. He grasped the agent's hand with both of his and shook it vigorously.

'Order carried out,' Stahmer reported. 'Here are the files ...'

'I know, I know,' the Standartenführer said jovially.

'How?' Stahmer asked, mildly disappointed that his thunder had been stolen.

'Well,' Löbel said with a grin, 'I've already got a report from the army archive on the burglary. Through official channels, of course ...'

He jerked a thumb at the paper on his desk top. 'Christ, Stahmer,' he said. 'You should have seen the way I pulled the wool over those idiots' eyes. And that's not all,' he added with a satisfied leer. 'Heydrich has ordered that we're responsible for investigating things. Would you believe it?'

Stahmer nodded.

'You don't look as though you've been up all night,' the Standartenführer continued conversationally, with a hint of praise. 'Was it hard?'

'Not too bad, Standartenführer.'

'Well, it's a good thing that no one got killed,' said the man who had already murdered millions of Eastern Europeans – on paper, for now. 'Now we can really get things under way.'

Stahmer lit a cigarette. His thoughts were elsewhere. With Margot. He could see her in his mind's eye, smiling. He would ring her tonight, get his twenty pfennigs' worth. His hand was already searching in his pocket to make sure he had enough change, and so it was that he failed to hear Löbel's next instruction.

Stahmer didn't take him seriously, in any case. So far as he was concerned, the Standartenführer was a pathetic armchair hero; if anything, he found his wild plans and enthusiasms laughable. How was Stahmer to know that

Löbel's crazy projects would one day become reality? That one day, they would pile up the rotting corpses, send out the execution squads, just as he had always planned?

Löbel's face was glowing with the urge to prove himself.

'Repeat everything,' he was saying.

Werner Stahmer shook his head. All he could think of was the fact that he had enough change for two phone calls ...

'My apologies, I didn't quite get everything you said,' Stahmer answered dully.

'Need some sleep, eh?' Löbel's irritation disappeared, and he decided to be fatherly. 'Of course. I realise you must be dog tired.'

For a few seconds, the head of the Eastern Department showed a brief hangman's mercy. He paused and ordered coffee. Then, after a short interval, he returned to the matter in hand.

'Right,' he repeated. 'You will report to the army archive. Get this character, Inspector Wendland, to hand over the documentation to you. From then on, everyone will dance to our tune.'

'Me?' Stahmer asked, bemused.

'Why not?' Löbel said with a loud belly-laugh. 'After all, who knows better than you who the burglar is ...?'

Not so stupid, Stahmer mused. Heydrich had a sense of humour. Set a thief to catch himself! And all over a few stolen bits of paper. If Stahmer had realised that the 'joke' was leading towards rivers of blood, he might not have thought it was so funny ...

'And then?' he asked again.

'Don't concern yourself with that – not at the moment, anyway,' the Standartenführer murmured. 'We need the stuff to prepare ... some negotiations,' he explained vaguely.

He strolled over to the window, lit a cigarette, then turned slowly and asked mysteriously: 'Can you ride, Stahmer?'

'Yes, sure. Why?'

'First sort out the business with the army archive. Obviously the real culprit won't get caught – maybe the best thing would be to dig up some poor sap and stick him behind bars until the thing's blown over. Then get some rest.'

'I'm not tired,' Stahmer growled.

'All the better! Look,' Löbel continued, 'you're the kind of fellow who can influence women ... I want you to report to a private riding school. Rudolphi, it's called. There's a girl who rides there every day, and she's the daughter of the White Russian general, Denikin. You're to make a play for her.'

The Standartenführer grinned crookedly.

'Make sure you don't fall off your nag ... And make contact with the girl, by whatever means necessary, and as quickly as possible. We need the lady for our project.'

'Very well, Standartenführer,' Stahmer answered. Then he was dismissed. As he walked back through the corridors, he thought of the new assignment in the army archive and smiled to himself. It was the kind of thing that appealed to him. And a bit of horse-riding would be all right, too ... Yes, and he would ring Margot this evening. Everything seemed to be going his way again. The dead Formis was pushed to the back of his mind now; any thoughts he had about that didn't have a chance to make an impression. Georg, the killer, was in Dachau, which was a recompense of a kind. And he, Stahmer, hadn't lost favour with Heydrich. The Devil was all-powerful. What harm could come to his disciples?

*

Detective Inspector Wendland, a young, ambitious police-man, had settled nicely into his investigation at the army archive. He was about to deliver a full, detailed report to Werner Stahmer on the results of his inquiries, but the man from the R.S.H.A. declined coldly and just took the report out of his hand.

'I am sorry,' he said, 'but you must realise that we will deal with the matter from here on.'

'Do you think that's right?' the Inspector said reluctantly.

'I don't ask questions,' Stahmer growled. 'I carry out orders ... just as you do.'

The detective shrugged. It wasn't the first time he had had to deal with the cowboys from the R.S.H.A., but it still irritated him as a professional policeman. The problem was that Heydrich's lads had the power, and anyone who didn't bow to the fact soon got into big trouble.

First of all, Stahmer interrogated the man who had been officer of the watch during the previous night. He recognised him: it was the sergeant-major who had come down into the boiler room.

'The bastard pretended to be a stoker,' the soldier said. 'Unfortunately, we didn't realise it until too late.'

'Unfortunately ... ' Stahmer mimicked, playing the role of the merciless investigator. Inside, he was glowing with satisfaction. 'Idiot. And how did the man get out of the building?'

'We don't know yet,' the sergeant-major answered stiffly.

'I hope you are aware of the consequences of your negligence,' Stahmer said threateningly. While his face showed righteous indignation, his brain was working feverishly. So the sentry had kept his mouth shut, probably out of fear of court martial. It had been the only danger – if the guard had a good memory for faces, he might have been able to recognise him, even without all the coal dust on his face.

Suddenly Stahmer's manner became mild, almost jolly.

'Did you at least get a good look at the fake stoker?' he asked the sergeant-major.

'No ... I mean ... '

'Yes or no?'

'I only saw him for a second,' the man muttered lamely, 'and the light down there's very bad, I can tell you.'

'Put a new bulb in,' Stahmer said good-humouredly. 'And what did this fellow look like, you clown?'

'Tall, slim build, broad shoulders ... a sort of athletic type.' The sergeant-major's hands tried to model the shape of the man. 'Well, actually ... like you.'

'Like me?' Stahmer said with wry amusement.

He stood up and went closer to the sergeant-major, staring at him with a penetrating concentration. The Devil was riding him, and he rode the rest ...

'There you are,' he said ironically, 'take a good look ... '

It took two hours for Stahmer to talk to all the men involved. He made notes, dictated reports, toning down elements that could have been dangerous for him, emphasising witnesses' opinions that he knew to be misguided. The way he doctored the evidence was so skilful that even Inspector Wendland was fooled. The policeman ended up being impressed, despite himself, with the speed and efficiency of the young man from the R.S.H.A.

Werner Stahmer said a friendly goodbye to him.

'Consider yourself lucky that you don't have to worry about this business,' he told Wendland. 'I'll be getting my orders direct from the Prinz-Albrecht-Strasse from now on.'

'Best of luck,' the Inspector said sourly. 'As long as you're sure that we can't ... '

'Rubbish,' Stahmer answered, with a dismissive wave of one hand. 'The less we get involved with all that, the sooner

Headquarters will forget about this whole stupid business. Who'd be interested in those bits of paper, anyway?'

Stahmer had carried out the second stage of his assignment. From now on, the thing would go like clockwork. Fantastic. Weird. Even ridiculous. It was the sort of lunatic scheme that could only have issued from Heydrich's perverted brain. Nevertheless, it was going to cost the lives of five thousand human beings.

The taxi's tyres burned against the kerb of the Elsässer Strasse as the car squealed to a halt. A tight piece of parking. Löbel glanced down at the smokey windows of the workshop in the cellar outside.

'Wait,' he said to the driver.

The Standartenführer could have used an official car, but tonight he had decided to be discreet. In any case, it took very important business to lure him out of the office, and this visit was not only important but risky. He climbed out of the taxi and walked down the steps to the workshop. A plate on the door announced: 'Konrad Puch, Master-Engraver'.

Löbel nodded. The man had been carefully chosen, both from a professional and a political point of view. They had his history on an index-card back at the R.S.H.A. offices: Puch was an old party member, and politically totally reliable.

Löbel pushed open the door and heard the shop bell chime tinnily. Inside, it was perpetual twilight. The place smelled like a burial vault.

Then a curtain was pushed aside, and a pasty-faced man said hastily: 'Heil Hitler! Can I help you?'

The engraver had pushed his nickel glasses back onto his forehead and was peering at his visitor with interested, though short-sighted, eyes that strained in the half-light.

'Are we alone?' Löbel asked.

Puch shrugged.

'My wife and daughter are in the back, but they won't hear us,' he said.

'I have a ... job for you,' the S.S. officer said, slowly, emphasising his words.

The engraver reached for his notebook to write down the details.

The Standartenführer put up one hand.

'No,' he continued. 'Please don't make a record of anything. This is a rather ... complicated business.' He cleared his throat. 'I am a writer engaged in a scientific work. Your task would be copying documents ... and perhaps producing some originals from official stamps. Do you think you could manage something like that?'

'Yes. Certainly,' Puch answered quickly.

'It will be a difficult job,' Löbel said. 'I will put a laboratory at your disposal, along with all the necessary equipment. You will have to remain in ... permanent contact with us.'

Puch swallowed hard. He was beginning to get the point.

'Yes, yes ... ' he muttered, 'but I shan't be able to carry on my usual business.'

'What is your monthly turnover?'

'Five hundred marks,' Puch answered.

'Fine. Your work with us will last two months at the most. Shall we say ... five thousand. Is that enough?'

The engraver's eyes seemed to glaze over.

'Five thousand,' he echoed, with a bemused grimace.

Löbel's face became serious.

'This is a Party matter,' he said quietly.

He examined Puch carefully, noticing how the look of confusion and suspicion gave way to a delighted grin.

'I see,' he said then. 'So the Party hasn't forgotten me after all ... '

Almost as a reflex action he reached and rubbed the Party badge on his grubby lapel, as if it were a magic token.

'Certainly it hasn't,' said the Standartenführer drily.

Even after Löbel had explained things to him, Puch remained a little distrustful, but gradually he was reassured by the fact that the Movement hadn't forgotten him. He stepped into the parlour of his little apartment.

'All right,' he said to his wife. 'You wanted a new coat ... Buy one!'

'Have you won the lottery?' she asked, astonished.

'And you find yourself something nice, too,' he said to Ira. 'And maybe we'll get a pedal-car for the kids.'

Ira and her stepmother looked at him wide-eyed.

'Yes,' he said, puffing himself up, 'good times are on the way. Party business ... a secret assignment. I'm not allowed to say more that that. And it's very good money.'

'It all sounds very impressive,' said Ira. She had to suppress a smile at the thought of her harmless old father involving himself in some new game of cowboys and Indians. Then she thought of Rudolf Formis, and her face hardened. Don't be stupid, she told herself. He was probably going to make blocks for Party cards, or badges for the Winter Aid Fund.

'Yes,' he said finally. 'And I've got the Führer to thank for everything.'

Hearing her father coming out with his old political routine gave Ira a kind of strange comfort. It was the man she knew, and – as far as she was aware – he would always be the same.

Then Löbel took Puch away. They had rented a villa in the suburb of Schlachtensee and fitted it out at short notice. An innocent-looking name-plate had been put up outside. The house stood well away from the street and looked like a typical middle-class home. No one would ever have thought it could possibly have any connection with the R.S.H.A.

Puch, the little pasty-faced engraver, looked around the workshop delightedly.

'When do I start?' he asked.

'Immediately,' Löbel said.

'And where's the material?'

The Standartenführer opened his briefcase, took out the documents and handed them over to Puch, without saying a word. The engraver looked through them casually, then he started when he saw the Reich stamps on the papers.

'No,' he said, with fear in his voice, 'I can't mess around with these, Herr ... Herr ... '

'Herr Möllner,' Löbel said coldly.

'This is ... '

'An assignment of vital importance to the nation,' Löbel *alias* Möllner completed his sentence for him. He took a rough grip on the little man's shoulder. 'You will carry it out ... You will tell no one ... And you will be damned well paid for it. Understood?'

At last Werner Stahmer found the time to phone Margot. She wasn't at home, as it turned out. A sleepy voice asked him to leave his number. He felt like a tradesman being dismissed. But Margot did eventually ring back.

'No, it wasn't anything in particular,' Stahmer said. 'I just wanted to know how you were getting on.'

'Fine, thanks,' she answered, then lapsed into silence.

'Was that all?' Margot said after a few seconds.

'No,' he said. 'It's just that I've got some free time today. Could we ...?'

'Wonderful,' she cut in. 'You've got time on your hands. You don't seem to take my wants into account.'

He felt as if he could feel the cool scent of lavender wafting over the line.

'I'm sorry,' he said irritably.

'You don't like having to ask for things, do you?' she said with a laugh. Then she continued: 'I'm going to the cinema. Want to come with me?'

There was no hint of deceit in her voice, but nevertheless he felt that she was setting a trap.

'Sure,' he said.

By half past eight, he was sitting in the foyer of the cinema with her, feeling overjoyed to be able to escape from duty at last. He didn't even bother to look at what film they were showing; he was far too busy watching her as she walked up ahead of him into the circle. He took no interest in the trailers and advertisements, just sat their feeding his eyes on her face and her body, wanting to reach out and stroke, caress ... For once, Stahmer was in the position of being a spectator, not a man of action.

Then the film started. First the title and credits. Stahmer settled back in his seat and stared indifferently at the screen. When he saw the title, he froze: it was called 'Traitors'.

'Would you like a piece of chocolate?' Margot asked.

Her voice was soft above the rustle of the silver paper.

'I'd prefer a cognac,' he laughed.

He looked suspiciously at her, then back at the screen. Chance? Then the story began. It was an espionage-drama, with the certificate 'politically valuable'; in other words, it was a propaganda film. For ninety minutes, René Deltgen and Paul Dahlke competed with each other to betray the Third Reich's secrets. At the end, the enemies of the people ran dutifully into the arms of the police; one was shot down while trying to escape in a plane, the other went under in a swamp, accompanied by a chorus of police dogs.

Werner Stahmer felt like turning his back on the whole thing, but he had to keep gazing at the screen, with a kind of sickened fascination and curiosity. Margot glanced sideways at him occasionally. He didn't meet her eyes.

When the house lights went up, he headed wordlessly for the exit.

'Did you enjoy it?' Margot asked from over his shoulder.

'Why did you have to choose that particular load of rubbish?' he snapped back at her, blinking in the bright lights of the foyer.

She smiled.

'Now, I think, you can have your cognac,' she said. 'And I'll join you.'

He let himself be led out of the cinema by her, straight into the nearest bar. They ordered two double cognacs, and he shook himself when he had downed his.

'Brrr,' he muttered.

Margot hadn't touched her schnapps yet.

Suddenly he met her eyes, and he swallowed hard. Margot's expression had totally changed. He had never seen her look so gentle, thoughtful and – pitying.

'That was it, then,' she said softly.

'What?' he asked hesitantly.

She looked at him firmly, as if she were trying to read his mind.

'I mean, that's your life, your job ... just like a film, isn't it?'

He shook his head. Now he knew for certain that Margot had only gone to this film because of him.

'For God's sake,' he laughed, 'Margot, forget all that nonsense.'

But she kept her eyes fixed on him.

'Is it like that?' she asked, almost impatiently. 'Or is it worse?'

'More squalid, you wanted to say,' he muttered harshly.

'Yes,' she said.

'No,' he said, forcing himself to look indifferent. 'What we just saw was rubbish, romantic fantasy, that's all.'

Then they both fell silent. He had wanted to use Margot to forget all about the missions, the killings. But she had probed straight into all that, opening up old wounds. And the strange thing was that he didn't even feel angry with her.

'I'm sorry,' she said quietly.

There was no mockery in her now. He touched her slim fingers with his hand, automatically. They both looked almost shocked, like young dogs when they first see themselves in a mirror. After that, neither of them dared move.

All Stahmer could think was: how beautiful. Here was the man who had power over women, who was used to conquest, who took them as they came, dark or fair, and used them. Here was the man for whom women were an adventure that ended on the morning after, when he got ready to return to the service, to his life as the Devil's disciple ...

The waiter approached with a smooth professional smile.

'Another double?' he asked.

Stahmer nodded absently. He was chewing over an idea, trying to frame a question he knew was idiotic. The idea had suddenly shot into his head, without his being able to do anything about it. Then it had grown, pressing at him, turning into a near-obsession, an almost painful longing.

'Listen Margot,' he said clumsily. 'I ... I have to relax sometime. Would you, I mean, could I invite you ... I would be delighted if ... ' The rest was lost in a confused mumble.

Margot looked up at him.

'A holiday,' she said calmly. 'That would be nice.'

'Soon,' he said quickly. 'The two of us ... completely alone.'

He knew he sounded foolish.

Suddenly her smile disappeared.

'Oh, I understand,' she murmured, serious now. 'A holiday like the one with Ira, yes? Duty, with a little bit of private life on the side?'

'But Margot ... '

'No thank you, Herr Stahmer ... I think your idea of a pleasure-trip is too adventurous for me.' Her words seemed to burn into his consciousness like a brand.

'I see,' was all he could say.

He stared down at the table cloth. Could he blame her for thinking that way? And how could he make her understand that things were different this time?

The prison of his existence, which he had hoped to escape from for one evening, had shut its doors on him again.

'So you believe,' he said dully, 'that I would just cold-bloodedly use you for something?'

She shook her head.

'Haven't you already done that once ... with Ira?'

'But that was ... that was ... '

'Different?' Margot said. 'Perhaps ... '

Her forehead wrinkled with thought.

'It's just that I don't want it to come to that.'

'Why not?' he said resentfully.

'I'm frightened of being disappointed,' she said.

Then he reached for her hand once more, with a half-smile on his lips. She stood up quickly.

'Would it matter to you if I were to disappoint you?' he asked slowly.

She looked at him with imploring eyes.

'I must go now,' she whispered.

For the first time, she seemed uncertain of herself,

111

embarrassed. She had flirted with him, and now she was afraid of the consequences. And she couldn't reject him, because he already meant too much to her. And once he had been decent – very decent. He had kept silent, and risked his own neck as a result. Someone who behaved like that couldn't be all bad, Margot thought, trying to convince herself with her own logic. He mustn't be ...

They went arm in arm through the cold winter streets, walking slowly, in silence, leaning slightly against each other. Now would be the time to stop and take her in my arms, make her see reason, Stahmer thought. But he had completely lost his usual bravado. His experience, his seduction routine, had gone out of the window; all he felt was a tenderness that had little passion in it; he did not want to possess, to conquer, but just to wait until the warmth that radiated from her could become a part of him ...

The polished saddles creaked gently. Horses' hooves thudded dully on the forest floor. There was a pale early-morning mist over the parkland. They were a varied, motley assembly of ladies and gentlemen: elderly company directors along with fresh-faced young girls; retired cavalry officers side by side with Nazi high-ups; passionate sportsmen and *nouveau-riche* snobs. At the rear of the column rode Werner Stahmer, who had been a member of the fashionable Berlin riding club for two days now. He was there under the Devil's colours.

Stahmer rode confidently, with enjoyment, but he was here on orders, not for the pleasure of it. Löbel's orders had been quite clear; 'We have to penetrate Russian emigré circles that still have some sort of contact with the Soviets. We're in a hurry, so no mistakes ... '

In the meantime, Werner Stahmer had succeeded in getting to within fifty metres of 'emigré circles'. At the head of the procession rode Natasha Denikin, daughter of an exiled Czarist general. The R.S.H.A. were well aware of his indirect contacts with a group of Red Army officers.

Natasha's white blouse fluttered in front of Stahmer's eyes like a banner. Her blue-black hair bounced fetchingly at the nape of her neck. Her face wore an almost permanent cool, arrogant smile, and her mouth seemed made to mock. She was beautiful, even very beautiful, and twenty-five years old. At this moment, she was hemmed in by four young men, who left little doubt over their intentions.

'She's got natural talent, I can tell you ... '

The riding instructor alongside Stahmer grinned.

'Who?' said Stahmer innocently.

'Fräulein Denikin,' the instructor said. 'She was practically born on a horse.'

'Her privilege,' Stahmer growled. 'What else does she do?' he asked. 'Has she got a boyfriend, a fiancé?'

'There've been plenty who've tried,' the man answered. He had protruding ears and a permanent sly smile.

'And?' Stahmer continued languidly.

'Come a cropper,' the instructor chuckled. 'Usually at the starting-gate. She just gives her horse a lick of the whip and leaves them standing wondering what happened.'

The forest was funnelling into a long, low enclosure. The horses' hooves were biting into fresh turf.

'There,' the instructor said to Stahmer. 'Take a look. You might learn something.'

Natasha had gone into a gallop. Her companions were trying to keep up with her, but the girl was crouched like a whiplash over the mane of her steed. She had the best horse, and she was surest in the saddle. Stahmer watched her as she rocketed forward. Crazy stuff, he thought.

His thoughts were with Margot. And only then with the assignment. Both were going well. In the Schlachtensee villa, the forgeries were already finished. A few details still

113

remained: personal things, little hobbies, the habits of senior Russian officers, like the ones General Denikin knew ...

He had to do it, he mused. He had to get himself an invitation and have a few private words with the old war-horse. He spurred his animal into life.

'Do your stuff, old boy,' he murmured into the horse's ear, 'get those ancient bones of yours into action. Just once ...'

The horse reared up and shot forward. Stahmer's legs were locked round the horse's girth. As a boy, he had learned to ride on an estate in East Prussia. Now he was out of practice. But it was all right now – because it had to be ...

The white blouse ahead of him was billowing up like a sail. Stahmer quickly overhauled Natasha's admirers; his big Hanoverian was old, but he was fast. The agent laughed out loud as he saw the bemused looks of the young men he was leaving behind. Mole-hills flew into the air under his hooves, fences flashed past. Natasha turned, smiled mockingly, then leaned back over her horse's neck again. They had left the others a long way behind now.

Then it happened.

The girl misjudged a ditch. The horse stumbled and fell and for a moment it looked as if the white blouse was going to be crushed under the weight of its body. Stahmer reined in frantically. But the girl was already on her feet.

The agent swung himself down from the saddle. She was all right. And they were alone.

'What's the hurry?' he asked, panting from the chase.

Natasha stood with her arms hanging by her sides, her face pale. When she spoke, she had a harsh Slavonic burr in her voice.

'You ride very well,' she said, almost reluctantly.

'I'm a bit out of practice,' he answered modestly.

Stahmer took out a handkerchief and carefully wiped her face. Natasha allowed him to do it. Her skin was soft, and her eyes glimmered when he touched her.

'Right. Home,' he said,

Natasha Denikin took a deep breath.

'Please,' she said softly. 'I would be grateful if you would not mention this incident, Herr …?'

'Stahmer,' he said with a polite bow. 'Of course not.'

They rode in silence together, keeping perfect pace.

'What do you do, then?' she asked.

'I ride, particularly in the mornings,' Stahmer said.

'And otherwise?'

'Lots of things,' he answered with a secretive smile, avoiding the question.

Natasha glanced at him, taking in the bold, close-set eyes, the broad shoulders, the clean-cut face. She had forgotten all about the fall.

Back at the club building, they dismounted and drank half a bottle of champagne together. The Russian girl returned the compliment with an invitation to tea. Then she offered Stahmer her hand.

'I would be pleased if you could come,' she said. 'But I must warn you about my family. They are numerous, and very inquisitive.'

'I see,' he answered, taking his cue, 'so I shall be a Daniel in the Lions' Den.'

'Goodbye, Daniel!' she called after him.

He turned round to look at her once more. Her eyes were shining. A challenge. Or a warning.

On his drive back from the club, Stahmer was caught up in a Party street-rally. He had to stop the car and get out, cursing. There were banners hanging from almost every window, flags waving in the breeze. The veterans were wearing their medals and the children had a day off school. The street was a mass of brown; Germany was celebrating the Führer's birthday.

Marching music boomed out of the loudspeakers, interspersed with rousing speeches. Laurel-swathed photographs of Hitler were in every shop window, among the knitwear and the sweets, and the Führer's eyes were that same kitschy shade of blue as the postcards he used to paint before he decided to become a politician. By the colour portraits stood placards, with black-red-and-white frames, with the message: 'A German shop'. The system had usurped and perverted the idea: suddenly everything was 'German', from toilet paper to fertilisers, from soft toys to underwear. And it was all supposed to be for the good of the Folk, the Reich, the Führer, the brown 'order'. Everything in its place, for Greater Germany!

All the nationalist groups were out in force. The Society for Germandom Overseas was burning blue candles. Members of the Reich Colonial League were being treated to a lecture on the combatting of malaria. The National Socialist Legal Society was intoning hypocritically about 'citizens' rights'. The League of German Girls was knitting woollen socks for the Fatherland. The newspapers would try to outdo themselves yet again in oily praise for the Führer's remarkable achievement in surviving yet another year.

Werner Stahmer stared listlessly at a detachment of Brownshirts. A Standartenführer with the face of a vicious nonentity was marching at their head. The men behind him were singing loudly and out of tune, right arms shooting up in the Hitler salute, left hands in their belt buckles, covering plump, soft bellies. One of them held a banner announcing: 'Germany Awake!'

Unfortunately, quite a few of the faces in the column

looked rather sleepy. They were marching three abreast, clumsily.

'We'll march ever onwards ... Until the ruins fall around us ... ' they bellowed.

Werner Stahmer smiled contemptuously. The ruins would come after the boozing tonight, he thought. The marchers were ridiculous, even pathetic. Didn't they prove that the system was harmless? It was what Stahmer, Reinhard Heydrich's favourite agent, liked to tell himself. But it didn't stop the unpleasant questions that had started surfacing in his mind.

He had felt those questions coming up that afternoon, for instance, when he had been ordered to report to the Prinz-Albrecht-Strasse. The intrigue was ripening – planned, calculated, secret. The Department for Eastern Affairs had been sober today, despite Hitler's birthday. No day off there. The R.S.H.A. was setting up its first, bloody coup on an international level, and Stahmer was playing a key part, without even knowing what it was all for. It was a bit of a joke, an adventure: first a burglary, as ordered; then a morning ride with a Russian girl, and one he found attractive. Flirting on duty.

Someone else was pleased with the way things were going, too: the little engraver Puch, in the villa at Schlachtensee. He was slaving away, full of gratitude for the Party, which had remembered him after all.

'How are you getting on, Stahmer?' Löbel asked.

'Like clockwork,' he said with a satisfied grin. 'She's already invited me round.'

'Excellent ... But remember, there's no time to lose.'

Stahmer nodded.

'What's it all for, actually?' he asked.

'None of your business,' Löbel said, but in the end he couldn't resist talking about his pet scheme. 'It's a big job ... we're feeding the Russians documents ... false ones,' the

Standartenführer added unnecessarily. 'Come with me,' he said then.

They went to see Heydrich. Löbel walked straight through the reception area without stating his business, which was something he could only afford to do when he had good news.

The Gruppenführer was seated at his desk, with his uniform tunic unbuttoned and his jackbooted feet up. He swiped at the air a few times with a long ruler before he acknowledged their presence. He nodded without any expression of surprise when the Standartenführer informed him of his department's progress.

'Good,' he said. 'So now the business is really under way at last. Stahmer,' he added, turning to the agent, 'when the time is right, I'll make sure the Russian go-between gets your address.'

He got to his feet, then paced around the room with long, impatient strides. His build was as whipcord-thin as his face. His watery eyes seemed small, almost mongoloid.

'You will receive more precise instructions,' he continued to Stahmer. 'You will have to pretend to be a beginner – and a greedy one, at that. Also,' he grinned wolfishly, 'he must think you are shit-scared.'

Stahmer nodded. He knew that the R.S.H.A. was aware of several foreign agents' activities, but protected them for their own purposes.

'Standartenführer Löbel will tell you everything else.'

Heydrich dismissed the two men. Stahmer began to grasp what was going on, and he couldn't help feeling disappointed. It all seemed too harmless, not his sort of assignment.

'When does the action start?' he asked Löbel.

'When the man who's working on the documents is ready ... '

'What man?' Stahmer interrupted.

'Don't be naïve,' the Standartenführer sneered. 'We're having the files ... tidied up a bit. They'll be ready in a few days, then the man will disappear and you start your part.'

Stahmer took his leave. Margot was coming over to his place tonight for the first time, and that seemed far more important than the Standartenführer's little plans.

He had cleaned his apartment until it shone, re-arranged the chairs, got in the best food he could find from the delicatessen, and carefully uncorked the bottles, ready for the evening.

Margot arrived on time. He kissed her hand, front and back, and led her into his living room. She was natural and sure of herself, as usual, as she looked around the room:

'Nice ... though the curtains are a bit loud!'

'I'll throw them out tomorrow,' he said.

Margot sniffed the smell from the kitchen.

'Are we having tea?'

'For starters,' he said with a laugh.

'And then?' the girl asked.

Margot sat down and crossed her legs coquettishly. Stahmer's embarrassed grin didn't suit him.

'Strange,' she said. 'Is it the furniture, or what? You seem a little wooden today ... '

He stood up, walked round the table, and sat down next to her. The gramophone took the place of conversation for a while. Some records he had chosen especially. He watched Margot humming along with one of the tunes, her full lips half-open, soft, inviting. She wasn't aggressive any more, and Stahmer had lost his woodenness. They came closer. The evening went as Stahmer had dreamed it would – even without his usual seduction routine.

After they had eaten, they stood up and danced, close,

119

feeling each other's bodies, their breath. They laughed and drank, and everything was going superbly until suddenly Margot said: 'Oh, I almost forgot ... ' she paused, with a puzzled look on her face. 'You have connections, haven't you?'

Stahmer nodded.

'Do you still remember Ira?' She smiled awkwardly. 'Your companion on the Czech trip?'

'Yes,' Stahmer answered, with some irritation.

'Well, her father has disappeared. He was boasting about some commission from the Party, and now he's been away for weeks ... not a trace.'

'Maybe it's another woman,' Stahmer said with an uninterested yawn.

'Oh, it couldn't be that,' Margot said firmly. 'No. He's such a fanatic.'

'What does he do for a living?' Stahmer asked.

'He's an engraver.'

'And how long has he been away?' Stahmer probed again, suddenly tense.

'Three weeks now.'

The bubble burst for Werner Stahmer. Suddenly he had a sick feeling in his stomach. From now on, he was distant. When he tried to overcome it by drinking, he became loud and forced.

The spell of the evening had been broken, almost before it had had a chance to work its magic.

The next day, Stahmer had his fears confirmed: the man who had been forging documents for the R.S.H.A. at the Schlachtensee villa was called Puch, and he was Ira's father.

'A reliable man,' Löbel assured him, 'a worthy old Party comrade. He'll probably have finished by tomorrow.'

'And what then?' Stahmer asked. There was a slight catch in his voice.

Löbel looked at him carefully for a moment, then shrugged his shoulders.

'Do we need witnesses?' he answered.

'What are you going to do, Standartenführer?' Stahmer said harshly.

'He will be got rid of.'

'You mean killed?'

'Come on, man!' Löbel glowered. 'Let's not pretend we're playing games here. For everything I do, I am answerable to a higher interest.'

'A higher interest?'

'The good of the Reich,' the Standartenführer said sharply, 'and to the interests of people such as yourself,' he added.

'And you're going to have a ... harmless old man ... a convinced National Socialist ... just simply ... '

'Well, that's the way it has to be,' Löbel snapped. His eyes narrowed. 'So you're one of those, are you? A bleeding heart?'

'I'll have nothing to do with it, Standartenführer,' Stahmer retorted.

'Why?'

'Personal reasons.'

Löbel walked over to the window and stared out into the street below. Then he turned back to Stahmer, and his face wore a twisted, malicious smile.

'Not possible,' he said curtly.

Werner Stahmer stood in silent astonishment.

'It is good that we have had this conversation,' the Standartenführer continued. 'After all, every one of us has weaknesses ... and we all have to overcome them.'

Pompous idiot, thought Stahmer. He wondered fleetingly whether it would do any good to appeal to Heydrich, his protector, but before he could think it through, Löbel was giving fresh orders: 'From four o'clock this afternoon, you will take over as replacement guard at the villa. You will be personally responsible to me for ensuring that the engraver Puch does not succeed in making contact with the outside world.'

Stahmer still didn't believe it.

'Repeat the order!' the Standartenführer bellowed.

Stahmer felt his head swimming. He had to gain time ...

7

The world was going to sleep. The last sounds of day were fading into the dark. Veils of mist swirled over the wet tarmac of the roads. The little villa in Schlachtensee was a pale blob in the gloom; deserted, apparently uninhabited.

Ten o'clock.

Puch, the little engraver, bent over his work, straining with short-sighted eyes. He had no idea that his life could be counted in hours; he sat in the first-floor room at the villa, enjoying the knowledge that he would soon be finished. Then it would be home to his wife and children, with a cheque for 5000 marks in his pocket. He pondered and calculated: a school satchel for his youngest, new carpets for the living room, a winter coat for his wife ...

On the floor below, Werner Stahmer paced up and down, feverishly wondering what the hell he was going to do. The thick carpet deadened the sound of his strides. He had made up his mind, but how he was going to carry out his plan he had no idea. Time was pressing, and so was his conscience.

The big man went upstairs. His usual air of animal power had gone; he seemed tired, an adventurer who had suddenly become a human being, with human weaknesses. He took the stairs slowly, almost hesitantly.

The engraver turned round slowly to look at him. His bony, work-scarred hands set down the block he had been working on.

'How are you getting on?' Stahmer muttered.

'Finished,' Puch answered, flushed with pride.

Amen, said the agent to himself. Why the hell hadn't the man taken his time? Why hadn't the little cretin ...

'I can't tell you,' Puch droned on, 'how happy I am. This is a great honour, being chosen by the Party ... '

Stahmer felt his legs turning to jelly.

'I am an old fighter,' Ira's father said, softly, almost solemnly. 'I know what the Führer has done for us.'

The agent's face was stony. Just one more word out of the old man, and he would lose control, lose all caution, self-discipline, capacity for thought. This was all too much.

There was a half-empty schnapps glass on the table in front of him. Without thinking, Stahmer picked it up and weighed it in his hand.

'So,' he said hoarsely, 'the Führer will show his thanks, Herr Puch.'

Suddenly he couldn't stand it any more. He hurled the glass against the wall, smashing it into a thousand fragments, cutting through the stillness of the workshop.

Puch swivelled round on his chair.

'For God's sake, Herr Stahmer,' he said, with one hand in front of his face.

Stahmer looked at him dully, with eyes that were expressionless.

'I'll tell you something, Herr Puch,' he began, going up close to the still uncomprehending engraver. The words echoed in his skull; but still Puch didn't seem to understand.

'You shouldn't drink so much,' Ira's father said, shaking his head.

Stahmer put his face against the little man's.

'I have a clear head,' he said harshly. 'And you should make sure that you see clearly, too.' He took a rough hold of Puch's shoulders and shook him. 'Don't you understand what's going to happen? Wake up!'

He hurled the truth in the little man's terrified face: 'You have forged documents. The business you are working on is one where they don't want any witnesses ... ' Stahmer was breathing heavily. 'By touching that stuff, you're signing

124

your own death warrant! I know that, Puch! As soon as you've finished that work, they'll get rid of you!' He pushed his hand under the man's chin, ignoring his protests, held it in a vice-like grip, and bawled: 'Yes, my friend, liquidated ... murdered!'

But all the engraver's face registered was anger and contempt.

'You don't believe me, do you?' Stahmer thundered.

The agent's eyes glinted with a cold fury. 'Your brain can't manage that one, eh?' He was threatening to choke on his own anger and disgust. 'Listen, I'll tell you how nicely they do it: The man in charge will turn up with two or three friends – you know, the sort who wear big boots and carry guns. No need to get nervous, of course, Herr Puch, these friends are here to escort you to see the Obergruppenführer, or maybe Heini Himmler, or even the Führer in person, so that they can say their humble thanks ... '

The engraver turned away with an expression of nausea. This was blasphemy.

'Yes,' Stahmer went on mercilessly, 'then you'll sit in a car, lovely and cosy between your guard of honour ... and drive ... and drive, and then suddenly you'll think: we're going in the wrong direction. Oh, but Herr Puch, you'll be going in exactly the correct direction – straight to your state funeral – and when they get out their guns, Mister Engraver, you'll finally understand – and it'll be much too late!'

The engraver had gone a deep shade of puce. His mouth was working convulsively, but no words came out. Suddenly Stahmer's anger gave way to pity. For Christ's sake, this man had a block of wood for a brain!

'Listen,' he said urgently, 'you've got to get out of here. Now. I'll get you out, and then you'll have to head out of the country. You can rely on me.'

Puch got to his feet. Slowly. The little man drew himself

up until he was ramrod-straight, peering up at Stahmer like a mole inspecting a tree.

'Thank you for the entertainment,' he said, his voice high-pitched with outrage. 'Aren't you ashamed of yourself, telling such a pack of slanderous lies?' Ira's father clenched his fists. 'And someone like you belongs to the Party, is trusted by the Führer?' His thin voice cracked with emotion. 'That's ... yes ... that's subverting the Move-ment!'

Puch broke off in mid-flow.

'I shall have to report you ... yes. I have no choice, Stahmer. I shall really have to report you ... What you just said is monstrous. When somebody attacks the Party like that ... '

He was shouting now, beside himself with fury, spilling out all the clichés, the slogans he had believed in for the past fifteen years of his life.

'The Führer would never do something like that! Never!'

The central heating was pumping warmth into the house, but suddenly Werner Stahmer felt cold, mortally cold. He looked at the clock, then shrugged vaguely and went downstairs again. What was he supposed to say to the man now? He had thrown the engraver a lifeline, and the man preferred to drown ...

For a minute or more, Stahmer stood still, unthinking, feeling nothing, indifferent. Then his reason began to operate again. What was going to happen now? he thought. Would Puch manage to talk? Probably not. When he knew that it was for real, he would blurt out everything, but by then his killers wouldn't be listening; they would be taking another drag on their cigarettes, or grinning to each other as they gave him another kick in the groin, because his chatter got on their nerves. No, they would be too busy enjoying conveying the Führer's 'thanks'.

Half-past eleven.

Werner Stahmer rolled up one of the blinds and stared out onto the dark street. He felt alone, terribly alone – and he still had to ring the R.S.H.A. and tell them that Puch had finished the work. He had to buy time, he thought. He had to convince this blockhead. Or ... maybe Ira could do it?

Stahmer leafed feverishly through the phone book, then dialled. The ringing tone bleeped faintly. For minutes.

He put down the phone, then picked it up again and rang Margot.

'You?'

'Yes,' he said. 'I have to see you ... '

'Now?'

'Yes, especially now,' he answered, his voice a croak.

'Is something wrong?'

'Do you know where your friend Ira is?'

'Ira was here all day,' Margot explained. 'Then this evening she went off with a group of gymnasts – to Leipzig.'

'She's gone away?' Stahmer groaned.

'Come and fetch me!' Margot said fearfully.

A car came to a stop in front of the door. A second later, the entrance to the Schlachtensee villa was open, and steps echoed through the hall. There were several men. Löbel was giving orders in a half-whisper.

On the first floor, Puch put away his tinting-brush, got stiffly to his feet, and straightened his jacket.

The steps were coming nearer. Then the door was thrust open. Standartenführer Löbel was standing in the doorway, a broad, easy smile on his face. Behind him were two men in uniform, wearing knee-breeches and jackboots.

'Well, Herr Puch,' Löbel drawled. 'How are things?'

'Finished,' the engraver answered proudly. 'An hour ago.'

'Excellent. I'm very pleased with you ... the material is absolutely faultless.' Löbel's face lost its grin and became solemn. 'I have some gratifying news for you ... ' his voice sounded like a recording now, hollow, as if it was something he had learned by rote. 'The Gruppenführer wishes to express his thanks to you personally. I have just come from his office ... to here ... ' The Standartenführer stepped aside and pointed to the men by the open door. 'The two comrades here will take you to him ... '

The old man drew himself up straight. An uncertain smile played on his lips, and his face mirrored pride, delight, and surprise.

So they stood opposite each other: Puch and Löbel, the Standartenführer and the little engraver, the murderer and the victim. With the silent escort in the background.

'Today?' Puch asked quietly.

'Today,' Löbel confirmed quickly.

Suddenly the engraver's eyes began to wander, faster and faster, flitting from one corner of the room to the other, taking in the boots and the uniforms, the holsters and the impassive faces. The smile on his pudgy face began to fade.

'Right, then,' he said hesitantly.

His head sank between his shoulders. He packed his things, and he went.

Slowly the engraver walked over to the top of the stairs. The two silent men followed him. He got into the car. The driver held the door open for him. The other sat beside him in the back. Puch let himself sink down into the luxurious upholstery.

Now he began to smile again, shaking his head over his own stupidity. How had he been able to have such thoughts. He had almost let that Stahmer bloke convince him. It was all so damned close to the way the man had described it ...

'Cigarette?' the uniformed man beside him asked.

'Please,' the engraver said eagerly.

The car purred on through the night, threading its way through the deserted streets of Berlin. It was misty outside, and the glow of their cigarettes was mirrored in the glass of the windows.

'Are we going to the Prinz-Albrecht-Strasse?' asked the engraver, trying to sound businesslike.

'No,' his companion said, 'the Gruppenführer wishes to receive you privately.'

'So ... privately.' Puch's eyes widened. 'A great honour,' he murmured.

The man by his side didn't reply.

Puch gazed absently out of the window. Now the car seemed to be travelling very fast. He didn't rightly know where they were by now. When was it he had left his little shop in the Elsässer Strasse? He could see the vague shapes of street-lamps outside.

'The Gruppenführer must live in Dahlem ... or even further out?' the engraver asked.

The S.S. man mumbled something incomprehensible.

The old engraver shifted position on his seat; but no matter how he sat, he could still hear the voice of Werner Stahmer:

'And then you'll drive, and drive, and drive.'

The street-lamps were getting few and far between.

'We must be in Grunewald by now,' Puch said.

'We'll soon be there,' the man beside him said curtly.

The driver's back was broad, and it seemed to be expanding, blocking out the world. Puch bobbed around, craning his neck, but still he felt smaller and smaller in the big car.

'Just don't worry, Herr Puch ...' he could hear Stahmer's voice echoing in his brain.

'Now I'd really like to know if we're there yet,' the engraver said angrily.

'Sure.'

The words in his head again: 'And then suddenly you think: we're going in completely the wrong direction ... '

The back of his shirt was covered in sweat now, sticking to the back of the seat.

'Hey, mate,' said Puch, turning to face his companion, 'this isn't Dahlem.' There was a shrill edge to his voice now.

'I didn't say it was,' the man in the uniform muttered indifferently. 'That was your idea.'

'Where does the man live then?' the engraver whined.

A hollow voice: 'Oh, but Herr Puch, you're heading in exactly the right direction.'

When Werner Stahmer leapt out of the taxi, a dark shape appeared from the front garden of the villa in Dahlem. Margot had waited for him. She was wearing a dark coat and had pushed her hair up under a black beret. She looked like a good fairy in a tragedy.

'Come into the house,' she begged.

'Best not to,' Stahmer said, 'I'd like to ... '

She said nothing, just nodded and took his arm in hers. As soon as he felt her touch, he seemed to calm down. Margot glanced quickly at him. She noticed how tense and nervous he was, and couldn't suppress her surprise.

'What's wrong?' she asked, as matter-of-factly as she could.

'Is it all right ... I mean, do you mind if I don't say anything? I just wanted to be with a sane human being for a few minutes, understand? I was going crazy.'

'Can I help you?'

'No,' he said bleakly.

They walked together in silence. Now they'll be fetching him, Stahmer was thinking, loading him into the car, driving off on the funeral run. About now, that idiot will be

130

realising what it's all about. He started as a car backfired somewhere in the neighbourhood. The shots, he thought wildly, the end. Goodbye.

'Is it to do with Ira's father?' Margot asked outright.

'No,' his voice was about as unconvincing as it could be.

'You're lying,' she said.

Stahmer nodded listlessly. It was all over. He had come out of cover. It was all he had been able to do, he mused, bitter but relieved for the sake of his own conscience. He could see Ira, happily swinging Indian clubs at her gymnastic display, and he cursed softly.

He mustn't involve Margot. All knowledge, the slightest hint, could be fatal ...

'Are you not very ... happy with your job today?' she cut in finally.

Stahmer kept his silence.

'Bad?' she asked.

'Yes,' he answered harshly.

'Don't you want to stop all this?'

'Sure,' Stahmer said with a bitter laugh.

'But?'

'It's not so easy.'

'You're the one who's making it hard,' she said firmly. 'I would ... '

'What?' he interrupted quickly.

'I would like you so much better.'

'You?' he asked desperately. 'Me?'

Without warning, little Puch began to strike out around him. A strong hand grasped his arm.

'We'll be there in a minute,' the man in the uniform hissed.

The engraver tried to tear himself out of his grip.

'I won't!' he screamed. 'Let me go! I want to get out ...!'

131

A second later, he felt a sharp blow in the back of his head. The driver had suddenly stepped on the accelerator, and Puch had fallen back against the rear window. The car was shooting forward like a rocket. Puch's hands clawed desperately at the door handle.

A fist whipped out, and suddenly his arm was paralysed with pain.

'Shut your trap, swine!' the man beside him snarled.

Then the old man began to howl like a child in pain, with loud, choking sobs. The uniformed thug leaned quickly over and pressed a ham of a hand over the engraver's mouth.

Now there was only darkness, and agony, impotent fear, and that hand, blocking out life. But somewhere deep inside his consciousness, Stahmer's voice droned pitilessly on, angry, mocking, prophetic: 'State funeral ... state funeral ... state funeral ... '

Suddenly the car jerked to a halt. It all happened quickly, as if it had been rehearsed to perfection. Grass under his feet. The smell of pine needles. Up there, no stars in the sky.

The driver was round the back now, helping; they wrenched the gibbering Puch out of the car. A perfect team.

Then a shattering, crimson explosion, and nothingness.

The little engraver, Puch, old Party member and Hitler-worshipper, crumpled slowly, and the earth received him – for eternity. The two killers bent over him for an instant, then nodded contentedly.

Order carried out.

The echo distorted the sound of his footsteps. The night was cold, but Stahmer's face was burning. He stood, hands in pockets, and listened. No sound. They had already taken him away, he thought with a bizarre sense of relief. He felt no guilt at his own cowardice, but still he could see an image of the little engraver, somewhere on the edge of some forest, stiff, bloody, and dead.

One day, he mused fleetingly, we will all end up like Puch.

With a shiver that was only partly due to the cold, he went into the house. It was empty. Stahmer's reason was working again now, and he realised that he should have been there when they came. He would have to supply a convincing excuse, he thought as he went over to the telephone.

'Where the hell are you?' the Standartenführer bellowed down the line at him.

'At the villa,' Stahmer said calmly.

'And why did you desert your post?'

'I can't explain over the phone, Standartenführer.'

'Then be so good as to get yourself round here!'

'I can't,' Stahmer answered, astonished at his own coolness. 'Against Heydrich's orders.'

'You will report here!' Löbel screamed. 'And you'd better do some damned hard thinking on the way!'

Stahmer nodded. This time, the taxi let him out two streets away. He took the last stretch on foot, looking around him with his usual caution. The street was empty and pitch dark. The sentry saluted him stiffly, and a second later Stahmer was striding along the corridor. The building was absolutely quiet – except, he thought, for a very faint groaning noise, like an overloaded machine. Somewhere below him, Werner Stahmer allowed himself to think for the first time in his career, they were kicking, beating, torturing. Picking men's brains ... and tearing out the life from their bleeding bodies.

He pulled his coat tighter around himself as he entered the Department. Löbel was sitting at his desk, with his eastern experience beside him: a bottle of vodka.

'What do you think you're up to?' he yelled.

133

Stahmer took his hand slowly out of his pocket and lit a cigarette.

'I saw suspicious-looking figures in the neighbourhood of the villa,' he said after the pause, 'and I had to check them out.'

'And?'

Stahmer blew a neat smoke ring.

'It was a bunch of youngsters ... harmless ... but I couldn't have known that beforehand.'

'Very well,' the Standartenführer said, slightly appeased. 'Sit down.' He poured out a drink for the agent. The colourless vodka overflowed the rim of the glass. Löbel's eyes were bloodshot, his hands were trembling slightly.

'There you are,' he said. Then: 'I can't stand this quietness sometimes.'

Löbel looked at the clock.

'How much longer are they going to be?' he growled.

Then he got to his feet.

'What are you staring at me like that for?' he snapped.

'Nervous?' said Stahmer.

'Well ... ' Löbel circled the room. 'I suppose it's natural ... '

Stahmer nodded.

'I don't like this kind of thing either,' the Standartenführer went on. 'I mean, the fact that the man's so loyal to the Führer ... but sacrifices have to be made. Puch's dying for the Movement.'

Stahmer felt the vodka in his mouth. Bitter. Fiery. Mixed with the bile from his gullet.

Then they heard the steps. Loud, regular, precise. Two men were stomping through the building like a brownshirt squad. Ruthless, machine-like, brutal.

Löbel stared at then dully as they came to attention and raised their arms.

'Heil Hitler, Standartenführer. Order carried out.'

Löbel nodded vaguely.

'Everything go all right?' he asked.

'Like clockwork,' the killers answered, together, like a murderous pair of identical twins.

Then Löbel and Stahmer were alone again. The agent traded drink for drink with his boss, as if vodka was the staff of life. But still he couldn't rid himself of the thought that was burrowing away in his brain, with the pitiless persistence of a dentist's drill: one day, they'll do away with you, just like that ...

Somewhere, in a dark corner of the room Werner Stahmer fancied he could see a young, pretty girl. She was smiling. Sadly, so sadly.

Stahmer slept long, but it was a restless sleep. In his dreams, he was running the gauntlet between long rows of every terror that his unconscious could find to haunt him. He felt like a human wreck when he got up and grabbed at the morning paper. There wasn't even a single line about the fate of the engraver, Puch. He wondered for a moment how long they would be able to keep it quiet, then dismissed the thought. What did it matter? It was in the past now, finished. Amen. Goodnight. The Party would drop its flags over the open grave; speeches would be made. The widow would be looked after, of course. Even Ira would be all right, so long as she didn't ask too many questions about the 'accident'. Margot had understood, and she would keep quiet. He, Werner Stahmer, had learned his lesson, too. He had thought of himself as an adventurer. Now he realised that he was just another hired killer. He either accepted the fact, or he got out. There was no inbetween way.

He poured himself a schnapps. The alcohol tasted like petrol. Stahmer spat it out and got dressed, still feeling the throbbing pains in his head from the previous night's session with Löbel. Suddenly he longed to throw it all over, to take Margot by the hand and escape. Somewhere. Anywhere. A long way away. Where there were no banners, drums, barbed wire, uniforms, barracks. He wandered aimlessly downstairs. In the hallway he saw a man in a blue overall carrying a heavy wooden garbage bin on one shoulder.

'Morning,' the worker said. 'This the way to the yard?'

'Straight ahead,' Stahmer answered.

The man put down his load, wiped his forehead with one sinewy hand, and pointed to the big tub with a grin. 'I've got to deliver this for those pigs out the back.'

'For who?' Stahmer asked in thorough confusion.

The man grinned again, contemptuously.

'You know,' he said. 'For the Party swine. National Socialist Livestock Breeders' Association.' He rolled the ridiculous title off his tongue, imitating a Party bigwig's voice. 'The glorious struggle against waste. Potato-peelings for Greater Germany. All that shit.' He reached down and heaved the tub up onto his shoulder again.

'Tell you what,' he said as he moved towards the exit. 'The Führer ordered the swill, and those runts'll turn into prize pigs, fat as Goering and snorting like Goebbels.'

He pulled open the creaking door to the yard and mumbled, as if to himself: 'And in the end they'll all be off to the slaughterhouse, along with the rest of us poor bastards.'

Stahmer bit back a laugh and followed the worker outside.

'Listen,' he said. 'I'll give you a piece of advice: Be more careful what you say in future.'

'What for?' the man answered mockingly. 'Are you a Nazi?'

Stahmer turned on his heel and left the man standing. In that moment, he couldn't think what to say. After all, was he actually a Nazi? For God's sake, old Puch had been one. As for Stahmer, he didn't know; at the moment he wanted to be a nobody, just to have peace and a quiet life. And he wanted Margot. Above all else, he wanted Margot. Lastly, he wanted to keep his hands clean – clean of blood and filth. Or was he too late for that?

He walked out onto the street and headed towards a café. He was still slightly hungover, and he had a lot on his mind, but he was professional enough to notice that he was being followed. He stopped in front of a shop window. The man behind him carried on walking. Slowly. Like someone who has time – or money.

By the time Stahmer entered the little café, he was sure he was being shadowed. Either by the Reds or by Heydrich's men. He left his coffee half finished, paid, and went out again. He turned into a quiet side street, and there, suddenly, was a short, stocky man standing next to him.

'Are you in a hurry?' he asked. The man spoke good German, but with a slight hint of a foreign accent.

'Who are you?' Stahmer muttered cagily.

'That is not relevant,' the man said. Now Stahmer could clearly tell that his undertone was Slavonic.

Stahmer turned to go, but the other looked quickly round and then followed him.

'Our meeting could mean a great deal of luck – or misfortune – for you,' the litle man said. 'It's your choice.'

They walked together in silence. Stahmer was relieved; it was someone from the 'other side', not one of their own people. He began to play his role, without even consciously realising that he was back 'on duty' again.

'What's your name?' he asked harshly.

'Also irrelevant.' The man smiled thinly. 'It is a false one – as I should imagine yours is, too.'

'What do you think you're doing?' Stahmer said, with feigned irritation. 'So long as I don't know who you are, or who sent you … ' He broke off suddenly, then looked around nervously. 'Do you think I want to end up on the block?'

'You ought to do something about those nerves of yours,' the Slav said coldly. 'Or change your profession?'

'What profession?' asked Stahmer.

The little man answered with a contemptuous wave.

'I'll go ahead of you to your apartment,' he said briskly. 'You will follow, fifty metres behind, on the other side of the street. J will go into the house first, and you will come after me. Immediately. Ten seconds after me, at the most. You will shut the courtyard gate, then we will go to your apartment.'

'I've got visitors,' Stahmer answered, acting as if he were frightened.

'Rubbish. We've been watching your little nest for two days now.'

He mustn't overplay his hand, Stahmer told himself, otherwise the other would smell a rat.

As if reading his mind, the little man grinned maliciously.

'And you can stop play-acting,' he said. 'Maybe you're a beginner, maybe not. Either we have a nice, reasonable chat in your apartment, or I make sure you never talk to anyone else.'

Stahmer nodded. He understood his meaning. This man was speaking the international language of the spy.

The Russian moved off, with Stahmer following him as ordered. No one saw them as they entered the building. But they were bloody careless, Stahmer mused. Then he thought of the mistakes the R.S.H.A. had already made.

He reached his apartment and locked up. The two of them walked in. Stahmer took in his opposite number with one penetrating glance, and filed the details for future reference. He had a high-cheek-boned face, dark eyes, and strangely wild, corn-coloured hair.

'Let's get to the point,' the Russian began tersely. 'You are in possession of material that was taken from the army archive. I am interested in it.' He looked at Stahmer with an icy smile. 'Providing it's genuine.'

Stahmer nodded.

'What do you want for it?' the little man continued. He was trying to control himself, but there was contempt in his voice. This one was a spy out of idealism, Stahmer judged, a communist, incorruptible.

'Money?' the Russian pressed.

Stahmer nodded.

'How much?'

'A lot,' Stahmer answered.

'I don't buy anything I haven't seen,' the Russian said. 'Let me have a sample, and tell me your price.'

Stahmer seemed to hesitate. 'Perhaps that can be done,' he said.

'When?'

'Immediately.'

'Are you saying that you have a sample here in the apartment?' the Russian said suspiciously, obviously unable to believe the apparent amateurism of the whole business.

Stahmer went over to his writing desk. He rummaged frantically around, deliberately revealing the primitive security arrangements he had set up. A microfilm in a cigar box half-hidden among a collection of newspaper cuttings; the wooden box inside a tin case, locked with a double system, with the keys hidden elsewhere in the flat. The Russian followed every detail. Stahmer couldn't tell whether the bluff had worked as he handed him the photocopy.

The man from the East examined it carefully, taking his

time. For the first time, he was unable to hide his excitement.

'You have the whole series, the whole correspondence?' he asked

'What will you pay?'

'I must have the complete series,' the Russian said.

'An advance payment of five thousand,' Stahmer spoke with slow deliberation, 'in Swiss francs. Can you arrange that?'

'I'll see.'

'That's not all, either,' Stahmer continued. 'I want a passport with a genuine visa ... say for France.'

The Russian nodded wordlessly.

'And the advance in cash. If you can't manage francs, I'll take it in marks.'

'Very well,' the Russian agreed finally. 'I'll give you ten thousand,' he opened his briefcase, 'if you let me have the film.'

'How long will you need to get me the visa?' Stahmer interrupted.

'Perhaps a week.' The man tossed a wad of notes carelessly onto the table. The contemptuous smile was quite open now. 'I shall be in touch,' he said, without offering Stahmer his hand.

'I'll be disappearing from Berlin in the meantime, the place is too hot for me at the moment,' Stahmer answered. 'And you be careful, too.'

The Russian dismissed him with a curt wave.

The trap was pulling shut. They had laid the bait, and Heydrich's plan was really starting to move. From now on, Stahmer had to comply with a mass of precautionary measures. He made his report on the first encounter via a cover-address. All Russian agents known to the R.S.H.A. were put under surveillance.

In the afternoon, Stahmer met Standartenführer Löbel at a secret rendezvous. His chief showed him a series of photographs, and Stahmer was able to firmly identify the man he had spoken to.

'Excellent,' said Löbel. 'Ivanov. We've had our eye on that character for months.' He rubbed his plump hands in glee.

Suddenly Heydrich was with them, too. Stahmer and Löbel stood to attention. The R.S.H.A. boss gestured for them to be at ease.

'I think our fish are biting,' he said. 'I hear that one of them has already flown to Moscow. Perhaps our little practical joke might just work.' He smiled faintly. 'If so, fine. If not, it will have been a useful exercise.'

Stahmer thought of the murdered Puch, and he felt a shiver run up his spine.

Heydrich touched Stahmer lightly on the shoulder. 'And you, dear boy, will take a breather now,' he said. 'A proper holiday ... take a girl or something, and get yourself some sunburn. And take plenty of happy snaps. Those fellows won't let you out of their sight from now on.'

The Gruppenführer signalled for him to leave.

Stahmer drove straight to Margot's house. It was a fine spring day, and the city-dwellers were yearning to get away from the hot tarmac. The parks were packed with sun-seeking Berliners. Stahmer had forgotten all his experience, all his fears. He could only think of the Riviera – sun, sand, an azure sea ... and Margot. He made a quick calculation. Eight days, maybe ten if he were lucky.

She was at home, sitting in the garden reading, and she smiled when she saw him arrive.

'I like you better today,' she said by way of greeting.

He nodded dumbly.

She resisted another question and looked at him carefully.

'Nice day,' he said. 'We should be away from the city. A long way away.'

'That's right,' Margot said ironically. 'Maybe as far as Heringsdorf, where we can bump into all the people from Berlin we were trying to escape from.'

'No,' Stahmer answered with a grin. 'South, to the sea, to Italy. Understand? Red wine and spaghetti?'

She giggled.

'You mean, coachloads of fat "Strength through Joy" tourists, playing skat and complaining about the lack of decent beer.'

'Pack yourself a suitcase,' he said sternly. 'We're going. Just the two of us. Have you a passport?'

'You're out of your mind,' she gasped. 'And what about foreign exchange?'

'We'll rob an Italian bank,' he grinned.

Twelve hours later, they were sitting opposite each other in the train, still light-headed with the joy of it all; the express rattled along, and the landscape outside seemed to zoom past like a conveyor-belt. The two of them only had eyes for each other. What had started off as a holiday trip had turned into a full-scale escape.

A passenger got out, and Margot and Stahmer were alone in the compartment. He moved and sat down by her side, drawing the girl gently to him. Then he saw the mid-day edition of one of the Berlin newspapers, which the passenger had left on the arm of his seat. Stahmer read the front-page headline: Mysterious Death in Grunewald ... The mood was shattered. He got slowly to his feet, with Margot's astonished gaze on him, and picked up the paper carefully, as if it were some unclean object. Then he threw it out of the window. He wanted to, had to forget everything: the little engraver Puch, the Russian, Rudolf Formis. What

142

was important now was him and Margot; the two of them, and their future together.

They changed trains in Munich. As they rolled over the Brenner Pass, they could feel the southern magic. By the time they were over the border, everything seemed lighter, clearer. The gates to paradise were decorated with palms and lemon trees. Late that night they reached their goal, a little place on the Italian Riviera. They went straight to sleep, and were up first thing in the morning.

The sky was impossibly blue. Stahmer and Margot lay together, sunning themselves on the almost deserted beach, savouring the fact that they were alone.

'Fourteen days at the most,' Margot said.

'Almost an eternity,' Stahmer answered. 'Fourteen days: that's ... ' he did a quick calculation ' ... three hundred and thirty-six hours of sun, sea, sand and ... '

'And?' Margot asked gently.

He stared blankly into the distance. He felt as if he was a prisoner of his feelings – feelings that even yesterday he hadn't dared admit to himself. He, a man who had never been at a loss for something to say to a woman, had learned how to keep silence. He had become unsure of himself, and of what was 'good' or 'bad' in his life. In a way, he knew he had to overcome his own capacity for self-discipline.

Stahmer let himself be caressed by the sun, mulling over things in his mind. Suddenly he became aware of how short three hundred and thirty-six hours were. A mirage, a dream, and he would wake from it and be standing there, bolt to attention, in front of the Gruppenführer again ...

'What are you thinking about?' asked Margot.

'Nothing,' he murmured.

She smiled slightly. She knew that he was beginning to wrestle with his feelings about his 'profession', and she

143

approved, for it was what she had wanted. She liked him. In fact, she was more than just fond of him. But she didn't want him as he was now. She sensed instinctively that he was going through a crisis of confidence, and she was glad.

Margot shook the sand from her body and went down to the water. Stahmer followed. They played around like excited children, splashing, jumping, having mock-battles, swimming apart, then coming together. Suddenly they could feel something, both together. For most lovers, it would have been an everyday thing, but for Stahmer it was an unknown land that he was entering now.

That evening, they ended up in a little restaurant. As they chatted and laughed over pasta and Chianti, they completely forgot that this friendly country lay under fascism, too. The little place slowly filled up. An Italian had brought a lute with him, and soon the whole room was alive with the magic of fine tenor voices. Then one of the singers accidentally bumped against the wall, and a portrait of Mussolini crashed to the ground. The singing dissolved into laughter. The lute player came over to Stahmer.

'We,' he said in broken German, 'we no fascist. Nix Mussolini. Nix Hitler.'

Stahmer smiled and poured him a glass of wine. Then the others came close, as nervous as young dogs. After a while, the ten of them were all sitting there drinking Chianti together.

Just before midnight, the landlord led them politely but firmly to the door. There was a fresh breeze from the sea, which was shining in the moonlight. It was all so fantastic, and yet so real. Like Margot, as he drew her to him. They scarcely dared to stir, for fear of somehow disturbing the dreamlike scene. They didn't say a word, but they understood each other perfectly.

They walked slowly back to the little boarding-house at the foot of the citadel. They had rooms next to each other.

When they arrived, the landlady gave them a knowing, approving look. She liked lovers – perhaps because all that was so far behind for her ...

They said good night to each other and went their separate ways. Stahmer found it impossible to sleep; he smoked a cigarette he didn't enjoy, then padded over to the window and gazed out over the sea. He could hear Margot turning restlessly next door. All of a sudden, he didn't have to ask what he should, or was allowed to do. He went to her door and knocked gently.

'Margot?' he whispered.

She lay motionless as he came over to her. Then he reached for her with a sudden, wild hunger, and felt her respond. There was no fear, no death any more, just their bodies, tasting each other with a desperate intensity.

Margot untangled herself from his arms and leaned on one elbow, letting strands of long dark hair tumble over her forehead. She smiled a peaceful, satisfied smile.

'Happy?' she purred.

'Yes. And you?' Stahmer said.

'As well.'

'Is that all?'

Margot stretched herself back among the pillows, closed her eyes and smiled.

'No,' she said softly. 'Much, much more.'

'How much?'

'Words aren't enough, are they?'

'Not enough,' he murmured, reaching out in wonder and running one hand over her glistening breasts and stomach. 'Not enough ... '

Hours later, they sat out on the sun terrace together. The landlady padded discreetly up to them, and her smile was even broader, more knowing. She had cut some flowers for the table.

'Signor Stahmer, *oggi cosa mangiare?*' She mimicked a hearty eater.

Stahmer smiled. 'Something. Anything,' he said.

The telegram arrived towards mid-day.

Werner Stahmer was summoned back to Berlin. By the quickest route.

8

Hitler had been kept informed; he had personally approved Stahmer's burglary of the army archive. Now it looked as if the Soviets had taken the bait. Their agent had flown straight to Moscow and spoken to high officers of the G.P.U., the secret police. Every one of his movements had been observed by the Germans. After a slight delay, the sample copy that Stahmer had provided was forwarded to Stalin himself.

The German army had been working closely with the Red Army ever since the Treaty of Rapallo; the Russians allowed German officers to be trained in the use of weapons that were forbidden under the Treaty of Versailles, using Soviet facilities on Soviet soil. As a result of this purely practical arrangement, personal contacts had arisen as a matter of course. At first there had been no political overtones, because there were no senior German officers who sympathised with communism. Since both nations were 'outcasts' in Europe in their different ways, however, there was some mutual sympathy, and there were those in the German army who would have liked to combine with the Russians against the West. These developments had taken place before Hitler's seizure of power in 1933, and were more or less public knowledge.

Heydrich had gathered from his contacts among White-Russian emigrés in Paris that differences had arisen between the powerful Marshall Tukhachevski, whom some called 'the Red Napoleon', and Stalin. No one was sure of the details, but it had been decided to try and exploit the tension between Soviet Russia's two most powerful men. There were two possible courses of action: to work with the Soviet Marshall for Stalin's downfall, or to give the Red dictator material against Tukhachevski.

After some heated debates among leading German espionage experts, it was decided that a 'purge' of the Red Army, starting with Tukhachevski, would usefully weaken Russian military strength.

The break-in at the army archive was stage-managed. The engraver Puch had the job of doctoring the material, making small changes and additions, using the personal information that Stahmer had got from the Denikin family. At the bottom of the forged documents stood genuine signatures of Hitler, Himmler and Ribbentrop, the Nazi Foreign Minister. They gave the appearance that a group of Russian generals, led by Marshall Tukhachevski, was conspiring with Germany to overthrow Stalin.

The Soviet reaction to the documents was awaited with baited breath. When it became known that the Russian agent was already on his way back to the Reich capital, Werner Stahmer was called back from leave to Berlin. He was ordered to stay in his apartment and wait, cut off from the outside world, unable to see Margot. He was back in his role as the 'amateur spy'.

Two days went past. Finally the telephone rang, in the middle of the night. Still half-asleep, Stahmer picked up the receiver. He knew the voice straight away, and his face tensed.

'Are you alone?' the harsh Slavonic voice said.

'Yes,' Stahmer said.

'I'll be with you in a minute ... I'll ring three times.'

Before Stahmer could say anything, the connection was cut. He got up, threw on a bathrobe, and went over to the window. The street seemed empty, but Stahmer knew that appearances were deceptive. He knew too much, whichever way he looked at it: he was a conspirator who wanted to climb off the bandwagon and, in the espionage jungle, witnesses are not popular. On either side. Werner Stahmer was a double agent, and his life was doubly threatened ...

The Russian came on foot, alone, though Stahmer was sure that he must have accomplices hanging around somewhere in the vicinity. The whole thing was like a scene from a gangster film: the little man walked past the house, round the corner, and then slowly back, with his raincoat collar pulled up and his hat over his eyes.

Then the doorbell rang, three times, and the Russian stood in the doorway.

'Have you brought the money?' Stahmer asked.

'Forget the play-acting,' the man answered coldly. 'We can be open with each other.'

'What do you mean?'

'You have your masters,' the Russian said, 'and I have mine.' He smiled sadly. 'Most of the time, we work against each other, but this time we have a common interest.'

'I'm only interested in the money,' Stahmer persisted, ignoring the man's challenge.

'Come on. You'd pay me to get rid of the stuff.' The other man laughed humourlessly. 'But you're in luck ... I'm offering you three million gold roubles. One of your people will come to Berlin on diplomatic business, and he will exchange the money pro rata against the material. You will specify the time and the place ... and after that, I wish to have nothing more to do with you. Is that clear?'

'That sounds satisfactory,' Stahmer said with a shrug. After that, he couldn't get rid of the little man fast enough.

He should have asked some questions, of course. Three million, he thought – was it worth that much to them? They were in too much of a hurry, too eager. There must be something wrong ... Perhaps Stalin had realised that the documents were false, and was pretending that they were genuine, so as to strengthen his own position – at the cost of other men's lives.

No one in the R.S.H.A. was sure of the deeper motivations, either. The business carried on, all according to plan. A man came from Moscow with the money. Then, for a while, there was a silence, an unnerving silence ...

Suddenly, on June 4th 1937, there were sensational headlines in the world's press: Marshall Tukhachevski had been arrested, after a failed suicide attempt. He was tried in secret, on Stalin's orders. The Tass press agency reported that the 'Red Napoleon' and the seven officers accused along with him had made full confessions. Four hours after the death sentence had been pronounced, the executions were carried out under the supervision of Marshall Blücher, himself to be liquidated in a later 'purge'. The first eight were followed by about five thousand other Russian officers who had displeased Stalin in some way or another.

On the German side, however, this incredible coup had a later repercussion: the three million roubles of blood money did not bring good fortune. The Soviets had noted the numbers of all the bank notes; later, when war broke out, they were able to pick up the entire German agent network in Russia by tracing the money.

At last, Werner Stahmer went directly to Heydrich. 'Patience' he had been telling Margot, almost every day for months. It had become a bitter joke between the two lovers. Stahmer had carried out all his orders to the letter, and he had performed his assignments wholly to his boss's satisfaction. He felt sure he was in favour, but he still had illusions about what that meant with a man like Heydrich.

He was told to wait in the reception area. He had lost his old arrogance, but he was determined to push this through. Stahmer thought of Margot, and immediately he

150

was in another world. He could see now how mean-spirited and cold he had been before; he had been a man who treated women like pleasure-machines. Now he had experienced what it was like to throw self-interest to the winds and just feel a total commitment to a woman. Since their all-too-brief holiday on the Italian Riviera, they had been like conspirators, understanding the need for caution, but knowing the ultimate aim ...

Then Stahmer was ushered into the Gruppenführer's presence. He seemed to be in luck; Heydrich was obviously in a good mood. He spent some time telling Stahmer stories about his latest project, the 'Salon Kitty', a sort of state-run brothel, where ladies from Berlin society, reinforced by professional whores, met members of the diplomatic corps – and made sure they had a good time.

'Ribbentrop is a regular client,' Heydrich said with a dry laugh, 'and when Count Ciano, the Italian Foreign Minister, is in town, we have to get extra girls in ... '

The 'Salon Kitty' was fitted with two-way mirrors and thoroughly bugged. A special monitoring group from the R.S.H.A. did twenty-four-hour duty in the cellar.

Heydrich, obviously greatly taken by his new scheme, went into great detail, and Stahmer smiled dutifully.

Suddenly the Gruppenführer became more serious again. He looked searchingly at Stahmer, his chilling eyes boring into the man's face.

'What precisely is it that you want today?' he asked baldly.

The agent hesitated.

'Come on, out with it!' Heydrich said expansively.

'Gruppenführer ... ' Stahmer decided to jump in with both feet. 'I ... I would like to give up my duties here ... '

'What?'

'I would like to ... ' Stahmer stood to attention. '... I would like to take up another profession.'

For a moment, Heydrich's angular face was expressionless. Then he smiled, went over to his desk, and fished out a document. He read quickly through the paper, then turned to Stahmer.

'The girl's name is Margot Lehndorff,' he said. 'She is twenty-two years old. Fortunately she is of pure Aryan stock. Her father owns three shoe shops – and is considered politically unreliable.'

Werner Stahmer stood as if turned to stone.

'I have an understanding for your private life, of course,' Heydrich added, with a dangerous smile that didn't reach his eyes, 'so long as it accords with your duties here. Understood?'

'Yes, Gruppenführer,' Stahmer parroted, instantly despising himself.

'I am not without human feelings,' Heydrich said then. 'We'll discuss the girl some other time.' He paused, drumming his long, thin fingers on the desk top. 'Don't be naïve, Stahmer,' he muttered. 'No one leaves my outfit. Perhaps we can agree on some other arrangement. How is your English?' he asked suddenly.

'Good, Gruppenführer,' Stahmer said mechanically, feeling as if he had just run into a brick wall.

'Excellent,' Heydrich said airily. 'I have had a special camera made. You will travel to England immediately and photograph the coastal areas.'

Werner Stahmer was away for several months. He reported back: order carried out. And he asked Margot to be patient. He was sent to observe the German takeover of Austria, returned: order carried out. He asked Margot to be patient. He was ordered to go to Czechoslovakia again, to Bratislava, to stir up separatist feeling among the Slovaks. Order carried out. And another appeal to Margot's patience ...

It was late autumn of 1938 by this time, and Heydrich was busy with preparations for the war that had to come.

He merely clapped Stahmer on the shoulder and said: 'We'll talk about the other business later ... '

In the first days of November 1938, the atmosphere in the Prinz-Albrecht-Strasse was hair-trigger tense. Something was coming; it was in the air, heavy and oppressive. It was just a matter of pressing a button; no one knew the exact details, but everyone felt it.

Werner Stahmer received an invitation from his school to attend an old boys' reunion in their Bavarian home town. He asked for time off, and it was granted. Heydrich could be generous in small things.

When, with Margot at his side, he arrived in the ancient city, seat of emperors and archbishops, its narrow streets were festooned with screaming swastikas. The loudspeakers were celebrating Hitler's attempted coup d'état of fifteen years before – when the Führer had broken and run away when confronted with armed resistance.

Werner Stahmer had always cared as little about his old school as it had about him. But the next day he found himself greeting long-forgotten school friends, standing smiling in the great hall.

The reunion was packed. On the walls, the names of famous Germans were picked out in gold letters. Dr. Schütz, the headmaster, had had a few of them changed, because nowadays they had to be both Aryan and politically 'safe'. The half-Jewish poet, Heinrich Heine, had been replaced by the patriotic bard, Theodor Körner, and the composer, Mendelssohn, had lost out to Bruckner. Goethe was still proudly in the middle, flanked on the right by Schiller, who was considered a good thing, and Lessing, who was suspected of not being 'national' enough and was already in danger of disappearance.

Stahmer gave Margot a poke in the ribs and pointed to the names. He still thought himself to be unpolitical, but the way they were messing around with the celebrities was just too ludicrous – and sinister – for words.

The man who stood up in front of them to give the speech of welcome was just as unpleasant. He climbed onto a swastika-adorned pulpit and coughed for silence.

'Honoured colleagues, dear scholars,' Dr. Schütz began. 'Today is a proud day in the history of the German nation ... the Führer has laid yet another foundation stone of the Greater German Reich ... '

The man's voice was somehow too emotional, the words were dripping with patriotism, with clumsy phrase-making. It was the voice of a hypocrite and a liar, who didn't believe his own slogans, Stahmer mused.

The headmaster started off with the Spartans, went through the Goths and the great German chieftains, finally reaching the greatness of Adolf Hitler via the Emperor Barbarossa's leadership of the crusades.

'Come on,' said Margot.

'Brrr ... ' Stahmer shook himself, as if something loathsome had just walked across his bare skin.

'Now I understand why you were so bad at school,' the girl said. 'With a headmaster like that!'

'He's new,' Stahmer retorted sourly. 'The old one was sent into the wilderness, and they put this time-server in his place.'

'Well, he certainly knows which side his bread's buttered on,' Margot murmured.

'You're right there,' Stahmer agreed. 'Who knows what he was before he came here ... or what he'll end up doing ... '

For the rest, they were determined not to let Dr. Schütz ruin their day. He left a bad taste in their mouths, though they didn't see it politically; at the worst, it was a sign of the times when empty-headed careerists like that could rise to positions of power and responsibility.

Stahmer showed Margot all the scenes of his mis-spent

youth. He managed to avoid the people he knew, and in the evening he strolled with her over the sandy heath on the edge of town. It was known as a place for lovers, and at the moment it was deserted. The air was cool, and heavy with the sadness of autumn. They went arm in arm, with the sandy pathway crunching under their feet.

'It will snow soon,' Margot said.

'Do you like snow?' asked Stahmer.

'No ... not especially.'

'Why not?'

'I don't like things that run through your hands ... ' she said softly.

'Like us ... like our future,' Stahmer muttered sadly. 'I know what you're saying,' he went on. 'You think I'm a weakling, a ... '

Margot stopped and looked at him.

'No,' she said thoughtfully. 'I know you have no choice.'

'But we must have a future!' Stahmer said with sudden, passionate force.

'The most important thing is that we have each other ... and never mind the circumstances,' Margot said firmly, though she, too, often felt that things couldn't go on like this.

Reason told them that their situation was impossible. But Stahmer was too weak to give Margot up, and she was too strong to leave him. It was a fragile balance, but it had held so far.

They sat down on a bench, holding hands and saying the things that lovers say. The city in the distance was dreaming the dream of centuries, of the history that lay in every brick, every corner, every little cobbled street and church.

The loud-mouthed brownshirts paid history no heed.

'One Folk! One Reich! One Führer!' they bellowed.

One pot of beer. One swallow. One loud belch ...

Stahmer and Margot couldn't hear them, and they didn't want to. On the heath it was misty and cold, but they didn't

155

feel it – they had their own special warmth inside them. Time seemed to have no meaning. Outside, though, the night was coming.

A night of shame and horror.

Together, they saw the blood-red reflection against the sky.

Something was burning, close by.

They left the heath quickly, along paths that were lit up like day by the flames. As they came closer, they could hear the dim sounds of screams and shouts. They passed the Ottostrasse, where the two arms of the Regnitz river came together, and turned into the Herzog-Max-Strasse.

'The synagogue!' Stahmer said, with mingled horror and awe.

They moved closer, hesitantly, and saw forty or fifty uniformed shapes standing by the fire. Margot couldn't help but laugh.

'Did you ever see anything like it?' she said. 'The brownshirts putting out a fire in a synagogue ... '

'Putting it out?' Stahmer asked.

Suddenly he understood. At that moment, he knew what plan the Prinz-Albrecht-Strasse had been working on all that time ...

Now they were standing directly in front of the burning Jewish place of worship.

'Get out of here!' bawled an S.A. man.

But they carried on standing there, in absolute astonishment. The fire was clawing crimson at the night sky, casting a flickering reflection on the façade of the nearby law courts, reaching out towards the statue of 'Justice' on the roof, as if warning it not to interfere.

'Come on,' Margot whispered. But after a few hesitant steps, she stood rooted to the spot.

There was a man standing in front of the synagogue: Commercial Counsellor Lenz, a well-known philanthropist and an honorary citizen of the town. And a Jew. He was heading towards the arsonists now, ready to use all his influence and power as a respected citizen to stop the crazed terror. He came closer to them, raising one hand, a bent, white-haired Moses, trying to part the Red Sea, and about to drown in the tide of brown shirts.

A young thug in mustard-coloured knee-breeches, who had grown up in an orphanage that the Commercial Counsellor had helped found, grabbed hold of the old man and smashed him head first against the charred wall of the building. Again and again. Slavering. Shrieking with animal glee. Until Lenz, who had used all his wealth for the good of this city, was a bloody, twisted heap on the cobbles.

The fire brigade was standing helplessly by; they had been officially forbidden to extinguish the fire.

'More petrol!' a Party official roared. 'You stupid bastards can't even set a Jew-heap on fire!'

New drums of fuel were brought and tossed through a side window. A young boy in a brown shirt cupped one hand around his mouth and yelled in feverish delight:

'Jehovah is sweating!'

Margot's eyes were filling with tears – and not just from the smoke. She was leaning against Stahmer, shuddering. The arsonists were drunk to a man; they had gone on a crawl from bar to bar before the attack, bolstering their 'political will'. Tonight the Führer was paying – in more ways than one. At last they could give full rein to the instincts that the Nazi movement had been built on: the howling lust for mass violence, for vengeance, for plunder.

So they had headed for the synagogue. They had stood uncertainly in front of the entrance for a few minutes – not out of respect for the house of God, but because they had to remove the heavy iron railings. Then one of them forced a way in, and swung himself through. The others followed like rabid sheep – those that could manoeuvre their bloated bodies through the narrow gap. The brownshirts played football with silver lamps, put on ceremonial top hats and minced around the building, roaring with beery laughter. Others rolled up the valuable carpets – not to save them, but to steal.

Then flaming fountains of petrol leapt skywards, tearing at the house of God ...

Meanwhile, the incendiarists' cronies were standing in front of the building. Their faces were uncannily like those of the men in the Prinz-Albrecht-Strasse, Stahmer thought suddenly. As he stared at the blasphemous scene in front of him, he realised with a shock that he was no longer 'unpolitical'. He gazed into the flames, and he imagined he could see Dr. Schütz's head, nodding. Of course, the worthy headmaster wouldn't be present at such a vulgar event; he would be tucked up in bed, like any 'respectable' person, sleeping dreamlessly, without having to watch and wonder while his pupils were violating a holy place. Every country has its evil-doers; they are caught and punished. But in Germany, men like Schütz got down in the dirt with the thugs and the sadists, because they had only one aim: to make a career, even at the price of murder and ruined synagogues.

The brownshirts were passing the time now by attacking passers-by, drinking, throwing up, singing the Horst-Wessel Song. They set on a Jewish couple, and the man, a venerable old gentleman, was forced to stand on a pile of bricks and repeat three times: 'I am a Jewish pig!'

Then some of them were about to let him go. But a troop-leader took out his knife and launched himself at the man – whose wife stepped in front of him and took the stab straight in her arm.

Blood ran, the synagogue burned, they passed round the schnapps bottle ...

Now the bells of the cathedral tower were announcing the second hour of the new, terrible day.

Werner Stahmer led Margot away. They walked unsteadily, in silence, hardly aware of where they were going. Suddenly they knew that something more than just a synagogue was being consumed by that fire; they could see the feelings, their future together being destroyed by the same pitiless flame of evil.

Stahmer and Margot didn't talk about it the next morning; neither of them wanted to admit the truth of what they had seen and realised. They travelled back to Berlin the same day, and Stahmer was determined that he was going to finish this time.

He came back from the decisive meeting with Heydrich under orders to prepare the unleashing of the Second World War ...

9

The August of 1939 was oppressively hot. The burning sun seared the streets of Berlin; even nightfall brought no relief from the sweltering temperatures. The sky would suddenly go overcast from time to time, towards evening, but nothing happened. It was as if the black walls of cloud were only a pretence, a feint, and the real storm was waiting its chance.

People were preoccupied and irritable, and not only in the city. It was holiday time, but hardly anyone was travelling far. In the streets, loudspeakers blared out messages of peace; the people talked of war.

The post office was working overtime, sending out mobilisation orders. The Wehrmacht had already started to requisition private businesses. Slowly but surely, there were more uniforms on the streets. Radio stations brought dramatic, near-hysterical bulletins, along with constant march music. The theme of those weeks was brass bands playing the 'March of the Germans in Poland'. And one man's words dominated the airwaves.

Because Adolf Hitler was speaking. The Führer's voice was everywhere, as oppressive and inescapable as the heat wave, screaming, rasping and barking its message into every home, every bar, throughout Germany, down to the most remote corner ...

'My one aim is and remains the preservation of peace ... '

Anyone who believed that was stupid, and anyone who didn't could only despair. But millions hoped, because they had no choice; they stared at the loudspeakers in the streets as if all that wire and equipment provided some guarantee of reliability, of a future, a freedom from fear. Only the women, unpolitical and instinctively aware of the way things were really going, took action. They started hoarding – buying chocolate, oatmeal, cigarettes, as much soap as they could get hold of.

The heavy truck that rolled through the streets of the Reich capital was as heavily guarded as a gold consignment. An armoured gun-carrier roared ahead of it, with motor cycles on its flanks and a police car bringing up behind. It was headed for the training school run by the S.D., the security section of the S.S., at the little town of Bernau, twenty kilometres north of Berlin. Another little corner of Heydrich's empire. The guard there had already been warned of its coming; when the truck arrived, he nodded and raised the barrier. The dirty tarpaulin flapped like a sinister flag. The truck stopped in the parade ground. A group of young S.S. soldiers stood around in the yard and watched the unloading.

The truck's load consisted of uniforms, green and yellow, along with trousers, boots, battle dress – and Polish insignia. All the stuff was genuine, taken from the other side. Admiral Canaris's counter-espionage department had done a brilliant, painstaking job in collecting the Polish kit, from defectors and from Polish border troops captured on the German side of the border. There were enough uniforms to kit out a whole company. Nothing had been overlooked; they even had up-to-date pay books.

The S.S. soldiers watched the unloading with growing outrage.

'They want to turn us into bloody Polacks,' said one.

'I'm not putting on that fucking fancy dress,' muttered an Unterscharführer.

Others came out of the barrack huts and stood there, whispering to each other, cursing, poking each other in the ribs, spitting on the floor. They had volunteered for this course at the S.D. school. If they had known what it was about, they wouldn't have stuck around. After all, who volunteers for suicide ...?

The first thing the members of this special unit had established was that they were all from Upper Silesia, on the eastern border, and that they had all been selected because they could speak Polish. And when they had drill, they also learned something strange. It wasn't 'Ten-Shun!' any more, but '*Stoj cico!*'. 'Quick march!' became '*Lez koku-masz!*'

They were all members of the Waffen-S.S., eager for action. They were young and they were stupid, and they could still pride themselves for a few weeks on being Hitler's 'special' soldiers. At first they laughed at the strange training they were having to undergo.

It was a grotesque scene: S.S. officers with death's heads on their caps and swastika armbands hissed at them in the language of the 'sub-humans'. Only twenty kilometres from Berlin, German recruits were drilled in Polish; at the shout of *Polozic!*' they learned to bury their sweating faces in the sand of the March of Brandenburg.

'What the hell's going on?' asked an Unterscharführer. The company commander heard him, and rasped at the corporal: 'Leave thinking to the horses – they've got bigger brains than you ... '

The fact was that the officer didn't know either. All he knew was how to stand in front of his men and bawl out the old message: 'You are soldiers of the Führer ... and a soldier doesn't ask questions, he obeys.'

That was the language they understood. It was modern German. The only thing that really got to them was the fact that they were confined to barracks and couldn't write home.

Now, though, when they saw the Polish uniforms, they decided they had had enough of the whole bloody pantomime.

Suddenly the yard was full of men, moving about,

talking loudly, casting ugly looks at any officers who tried to intervene. Slowly, a kind of panic was growing.

'This is mutiny!' the company commander roared.

But he couldn't make himself heard above the noise. With an angry shrug, he went back to the orderly room and asked to be put through to Berlin, to the R.S.H.A., Prinz-Albrecht-Strasse ...

The Gestapo boss, Heinrich Müller, took the call. He was a small man, in every possible sense of the word; shaven-headed, with eyes that were as dull and lifeless as glass and hands that were strangely hairy, almost ape-like.

'What?' he bellowed down the line. 'Your men won't do it? I'll have their arses ... I'll ... '

Müller had to stop to regain his breath. Here was something unconceivable: mutiny, among Satan's soldiers, open disobedience in an S.S. unit. If Heydrich got to hear about it, or Himmler ...

'Swine ... round them up, stick 'em against the wall!'

His hand was sticky with sweat as it clutched the receiver. Müller's understanding of human nature was on about the level of a thuggish street cop. Before 1939 he had been a lowly official in the political police, and he had persecuted the Nazis just as brutally as he tortured their opponents now that the brownshirts were in power. Heydrich knew about his past, and it was precisely because of it that he valued Müller – because he was 'unpolitical', and would do anything at a glance from those cold, mongoloid eyes.

'I give you a binding order,' the Gestapo boss hissed down the phone. 'Confirm action in ten minutes. Anyone who refuses to put on one of those uniforms is to be shot!'

'Very good,' the officer on the other end of the line answered, swallowing hard. 'But I think we must consider ... '

'Consider what!' Müller exploded.

'The ... the consequences, Gruppenführer.'

'I'll be responsible for those. Sort those bastards out, kill 'em if you must!' He banged the receiver down and kicked the desk leg, hard.

Then, sensing another presence in the room, he turned round.

It was Heydrich.

'What's all the excitement about, my dear fellow?' he said softly.

'The ... in Bernau ... a scandal, Obergruppenführer.' Heydrich had recently been promoted.

'Rubbish,' the R.S.H.A. boss said with an urbane smile. He pointed to the phone. 'Come on, make an emergency call.'

Müller looked at him stupidly.

'Can't say I blame them,' Heydrich commented drily. 'They don't know what it's all about. How would you like to dress up as a Polack?'

Then the connection to Bernau was ready. Heydrich took the phone and spoke to the company commander.

'Calm your men down,' he said. 'Tell them what the uniforms are for ... Müller's order is, of course, ridiculous.'

He hung up.

'Come with me,' he said to the Gestapo chief.

They went off together to Heydrich's office. Whenever Müller felt the Obergruppenführer's eyes on him, he automatically stood to attention. Throughout their conversation, he had been standing like a dog waiting for some sign of his master's approval, for a chance to wag his tail. There was no dog more obedient than Heinrich Müller.

'You know Stahmer?' Heydrich asked.

Müller quickly offered Stahmer his hand. There were a few men there from another department as well; the curtains had been drawn, and the reception room had been cleared. Stahmer could sense a sick feeling of anticipation in his stomach as he watched the preparations: this was the big

164

one. Heydrich looked at the tall Stahmer and the dumpy, panting Müller, and a thin smile of satisfaction played around his arrogant mouth, as if he was pleased with the idea of putting this strange couple together in the same harness. The Obergruppenführer paced up and down a few times, then spun round suddenly and spoke. His voice was clear, his eyes diamond-hard and calculating.

'Gentlemen,' he said. 'The time has come.'

Heydrich sat down on a chair and began to play with a paper-knife. Without looking up, he continued: 'Here in this room, we have planned many a coup for the good of the Reich. Compared with what I am about to reveal to you today, all those count as child's play.'

The Gestapo boss nodded. The words 'child's play' echoed in Stahmer's head. Another blasphemy. In his mind's eye he could see an execution-yard, hear a scream, watch a falling man ... and another five thousand Russian officers following him. 'Child's play' ...

'In a few weeks, the battle will begin,' Heydrich continued matter-of-factly. 'We have been ordered by the Führer to provide a decent cause for a declaration of war on Poland.'

Werner Stahmer looked up at Heydrich's expressionless face. The R.S.H.A. boss's words cut into him like a whiplash. The more he tried to take it in, the more unreal the whole scene became: Müller, nodding obediently, the others, standing stiffly all around him. Like a puppet theatre. But the stream of atrocities flowed on.

'We'll do it,' the Obergruppenführer said with a crooked smile. 'But it will have to look as if the Poles attacked us.'

Gestapo-Müller was frowning in his attempts to follow his boss's line of argument. He had plenty of imagination when it came to dreaming up ideas down in the torture-chambers, but when it came to abstract reasoning ...

'It will involve two separate operations,' Heydrich

rasped. 'First we shall attack a German village, using our own soldiers dressed up in German uniforms.'

He turned and jabbed one finger languidly at a spot on the wall map of the Reich.

'And then,' he said. 'We shall attack the Reich radio station at Gleiwitz, just on the German side of the border. There is a distinction to be made, gentlemen: the first attack will be mainly for the record ... but the assault on the radio station has to be so arranged that half the German people actually hear it – live. We have to have shots in the studio, calls for help; it has to be something people will never forget. We have to have some corpses, Stahmer, it doesn't matter how. Don't forget. Well, we'll deal with the details later ... '

Stahmer stiffened. Heydrich's tiny slit eyes were glinting like coals. There was no trace of human life in them; just a frightening energy, like a furnace fire.

'Gentlemen, you can forget sentimentality. The more people get killed in the shootouts, the better for the Führer's plan.'

Müller cleared his thoat. His brain was functioning again now. His brain was ticking over like an adding-machine. When the Reich's bloodhound got on the trail, he didn't stop until his quarry had been torn to pieces.

'How are we to keep all this secret?' he asked hesitantly.

Heydrich looked at the Gestapo boss with something deceptively close to affection.

'Müller,' he said gently. 'That's why I invited you to join the game. In Oppeln, which is where we'll be organising the attack, there'll be dirty business between Germans and our "Polacks". We'll get ourselves some bodies, as I said, all nicely photographed for the press ... and then it will be your job to make sure that no one's around afterwards to blabber about it.'

Müller nodded. He'd got it at last. Of course. Heydrich was a genius. Then he started: 'Am I supposed to kill our

166

own S.S. people?' he asked, shocked. But his sense of guilt was only momentary. When it came to it, he didn't care who he liquidated.

'You have no imagination,' the Obergruppenführer answered with a condescending grin. 'Only one lot will be our own S.S. people. We'll send them to the front straight after, as special commandos. That way we make sure that the enemy does our job for us. "On the field of honour", you know ... '

'And what about the others?'

'We'll talk about that later, alone.'

Heydrich grinned satanically.

'Well, Stahmer,' he said expansively. 'Having the same trouble getting to grips with things?'

'No, Obergruppenführer,' he heard himself say, right on cue. Christ, he was a cowardly bastard, Stahmer thought. Obedience again ...

'Your part will be the hardest,' Heydrich said. 'Pick yourself a few assistants. But only really reliable ones, otherwise they'll have to be off to the front along with the rest.'

Heydrich dismissed everyone except the Gestapo boss. Before Stahmer even had the chance to try to protest against his part in the operation, he had found himself landed with a plan of the Gleiwitz radio station.

It was the 5th August 1939. Stahmer repeated the date to himself, over and over again, as he drove dazedly through the sweltering city. He drove down a dark side street, and had to fight hard to resist an impulse to drive straight at a wall and end everything.

The barrack yard echoed to the shrill shrieks of the morning whistle. The prisoners stumbled out of their huts, heads shaved, striped fatigues, undernourished bodies. They lurched, forced, kicked their ways to the front. Anyone who didn't kick got a hefty booting from the guards, and that was something that the S.S. men at Dachau concentration camp had got very good at. Then the guards stood, hands on hips, glaring at the pathetic wrecks of human beings in front of them. The caged dogs on the camp perimeter went berserk, tearing at the wire of their 'kennels'. They had been well trained, too, but today they weren't going to be let out for some practice.

'Something's going on,' said Hans Mersmann to the prisoner next to him, the man he had lived with in the same barrack for two years, the man he had watched, hoped, prayed and despaired with. And the man with whom he had shared the beatings, the kicks, the insults. The second prisoner's name was Herbert Rosenstein, and he looked almost uncannily similar to Mersmann. One was in Dachau because of his politics, the other because of his race.

'Careful,' Rosenstein whispered back at him. Out of habit, he glanced at the punishment blocks on the edge of the camp.

The prisoners stood in silence. Whenever one of them was asked to step out of the ranks, it meant something terrible was about to happen. A public punishment. Because one of them had been caught smoking a cigarette. Or because a prisoner had stolen a piece of bread from the dustbin outside the guards' canteen. There were all kinds of offences a man could commit, but there was always the same punishment: twenty-five lashes on the block. Or death through hanging. And the others had to stand, and watch, and wait, knowing it could be their turn next ...

'They're not hitting anyone today,' said Rosenstein incredulously.

'That's what's worrying me,' muttered Mersmann.

Across the other side of the yard, someone yelled for the prisoners to come to attention, and the call was taken up until it was being roared out all over the barracks. The men in the striped fatigues heaved themselves together and tried to stand straight. Anyone who failed would get a lick of the whip.

An inspection. By S.S. officers. The prisoners looked anxiously at their usual tormentors, and there was fear in their eyes. In the middle of the group of visitors was a short, dumpy man. He ran his cold eyes over the ranks of the concentration camp inmates with an obvious satisfaction and a leering curiosity, as if he was drinking in their suffering, feeding off it. Mersmann sneaked a look at his insignia of rank. Gruppenführer, he thought; best to keep their heads well down ...

Gestapo-Müller heard the reports of the various camp N.C.O.s with a show of indifference. He was hot, and his forehead was shiny with sweat. He had decided to take this job on himself, despite the heat; something like this was too important to be left to underlings.

'Men,' he shouted across the yard.

The prisoners tensed. Men? They'd never been called that before. Here it was always swine, bastards, shit-bags.

'I am looking for volunteers,' the Gestapo boss intoned.

So that was it, they thought. Volunteers? They'd heard that one before! When they heard that word, they made themselves scarce as quickly as possible. Volunteer ... that meant work on the corpse parties, the *Sonderkommando*.

'A hundred men,' Müller bellowed. 'Come on, hands up!'

No one moved.

'Don't all do it at once,' Müller growled humourlessly.

'I'll get you swine to shift yourselves,' raged the camp official behind him. The Gruppenführer looked round in irritation. He had helped develop the theory of these places, but the practice still confused him.

'I think we shall have to get our volunteers by the whip,' the camp commandant explained. 'I'm afraid that is the usual method, Gruppenführer,' he added primly.

'Very well,' Müller growled.

The Gestapo boss and his entourage wandered over to the ranks and paced along, staring at the fearful eyes of the prisoners, looking distastefully at their wasted bodies.

'These boys aren't exactly a credit to you,' Müller muttered to the commandant. 'They look to be in a pretty shitty state.'

His mind was, of course, working on the principle that he had to provide a hundred well-fed corpses for duty in an Upper Silesian village in the very near future ...

'This is not a sanatorium, Gruppenführer.'

Müller smiled thinly and turned to the prisoners.

'You're a dumb lot,' he said jovially. 'Because anyone who volunteers gets as much to eat as he wants.'

A few skinny arms were hesitantly raised. Like stubble being battered by the wind.

'That's better,' the Gruppenführer grinned.

The prisoners' eyes widened, their hearts beat faster. Suddenly, a senseless, wild hope started to spread among them.

'It couldn't be worse than this place,' Mersmann muttered between clenched teeth.

'Don't be crazy,' Rosenstein hissed back at him.

Now the Gruppenführer was coming closer to them. He had his 'volunteers', but he was choosy. By what standard he was selecting them, the prisoners couldn't tell. As it was, he would have preferred men who looked suitably 'Germanic' for this operation. 'But if there's not enough of those,' he had snarled earlier in the day, 'I'll take what I can get.'

Suddenly Mersmann put up his hand.

Rosenstein moved to pull him back. Müller saw him do it.

'You can go with your mate,' he said with a leer. Two Unterführers dragged the two friends out of the front rank. A quick jab in the ribs, and Rosenstein and Mersmann were staggering towards the group of 'volunteers'.

There were a hundred of them standing there, in hope

and in fear. Their hunger was stronger than their terror. And whatever happened to them couldn't be worse than the death that awaited them in Dachau. At least it would be quicker ...

The prisoners were dismissed.

Müller accompanied the camp commandant to a snack in the guards' mess. The champagne had been laid in ice. The Gruppenführer raised his glass.

'I am highly satisfied with you, my dear fellow,' he murmured. 'Just make sure you feed up these hundred men as quickly as you can.'

'Why?' the commandant asked dully.

'Ever heard the story of Hansel and Gretel?' Müller asked, with a twinkle in his eyes.

'I don't understand ... '

Müller sighed in good-humoured exasperation.

'It's easy – you're the witch with the gingerbread, and they ... ' The Gestapo boss broke off with a wheezing laugh. Then he became solemn again.

'You'll keep those hundred prisoners ready for me,' he said. 'When I give the code word,' he thought for a few moments, 'let's say ... "canned goods", then you send them to me.'

'Very good, Gruppenführer,' the camp commandant answered automatically. He would have liked to ask more questions, but he dared not. Müller watched him, amused.

'Code word: "canned goods". I like that,' he said slyly.

'So what do you want them for?'

'I need them for the Polacks,' Müller answered.

'How?'

'Sure ... as living targets.'

Then the Gruppenführer put one finger to his mouth.

'Mind you,' he said finally. 'If you mention a word of this to anyone, you'll end up in a shooting-gallery, too.'

'Yes ... yes, Gruppenführer.'

The same day, the Gestapo boss travelled back to Berlin.

The plan was moving well. That was the way the Second World War was to start: with an operation worthy of Al Capone. S.S. men in Polish uniforms were going to murder concentration camp prisoners in Wehrmacht kit.

And the weekly newsreel was going to show it all to an astonished world.

The express was rattling along. Towards Gleiwitz. Wires hummed, telegraph poles whizzed past. Werner Stahmer put aside his newspaper and stared out of the window. He was sitting in a train again, but this time he wasn't going to the Riviera. He was on his way to war; and he, the Devil's right hand, was going to light the flame that would rage across three continents.

At first he had toyed with the crazy idea of escaping abroad. Then, when he had rejected the idea, came the fear of telling Margot that he was going back into the shadow-world again. But she had seen it in his face.

'You have to go away again?' she had asked. Sadly, without any hint of anger or accusation.

Stahmer had nodded.

'I'll pack your things,' she had answered, a little too quickly.

Stahmer shook his head. His 'luggage' was supplied by the Prinz-Albrecht-Strasse. All genuine Polish, from the crumpled zloty notes to the matches from Warsaw and the made-to-measure suit with the Polish label. They had even given him a medallion of the Madonna of Czenstocaw to complete the image. Satan used everything, left nothing to chance.

The train stopped. Two or three stops to Gleiwitz. Stahmer's accomplices were on their way, too. Seven of them. They were travelling seperately, in accordance with a carefully-considered plan. The R.S.H.A. didn't believe in putting all its eggs in one basket. Particularly poisoned ones.

There was a judder, and the train moved off. There was a slim blonde sitting opposite Stahmer. She kept trying to catch his eye, but he managed to avoid her. She was smiling, and her skirt had ridden too far up her silk-clad thigh. But the agent ignored it.

'Are you travelling to Gleiwitz as well?' the woman asked at last.

Stahmer nodded, but still didn't look at her. She was expensively but tastelessly dressed, and the look in her eye said: 'I'm easy ... '

'Boring dump,' she chattered on. 'Are you staying there long?'

'I don't know yet.'

Stahmer stayed uncooperative. The blonde pouted, but he could see that she didn't intend giving up.

'Gleiwitz!' came the voice on the empty platform. Stahmer took his suitcase and nodded to the woman. A porter tried to take his bags, but Stahmer shooed him away.

He got into a taxi and gave his destination. Sure, this was a 'boring dump', he mused. Then he was lost in other thoughts.

When he had settled into his hotel, he took out the list they had given him of all the people who worked at the radio station in Gleiwitz. Stahmer knew everything there was to know about the way the station functioned: anyone who wanted to enter it had to fill out a form, and the doorman always checked with the department they were supposed to be visiting. There was no point in just overpowering the man, because getting into the studio itself would cost too much time. So one man at least had to be smuggled into the building beforehand. It had to be himself, Stahmer thought sourly. And he knew he had just a few days to make friends with some fellow who worked at the station, or at least to get to know one well enough to have an excuse to be in the place when his accomplices came storming in.

Stahmer ran his eyes over the list. Job description and short personal details. There had to be some deaths, Stahmer thought bitterly, remembering the Obergruppen-führer's words. But that would be no problem – deaths would come automatically, on both sides. He shivered for a second: what guarantee was there that he wouldn't be one of them? Then he drove his mind back to work on the mission.

Suddenly he had a thought. Why did it have to be a man? Why not a woman? He came across the name Sybille Knapp, twenty-one years old. He made a note of it. Before he made contact with his accomplices, he tracked down the girl. He found out that she went dancing with a boy friend every Wednesday in a bar in the town centre. And he was in luck. It was Wednesday today.

He recognised the girl without any trouble. Heydrich had supplied a photograph. He considered tactics: it shouldn't be too difficult, though the boy friend might present a few problems. Stahmer took a seat at the bar and started to drink. He'd need schnapps to help him with this one, he thought. 'Romantic interlude' in Gleiwitz, maybe a last one. Then all hell would break loose. War. Then they would take the camouflage off the Panzers, and the Stukas could rain howling death, while loudspeakers blared out the story of Polish war guilt to the world. And if he didn't light the fuse, then someone else would, and his head would be on the block, because Satan didn't make light of things like that. He could well end up in some 'special unit' anyway, being sent on a suicide mission at the front. Such things didn't frighten Stahmer any more; he had learned to live with the fact that he knew too much, and that one day the R.S.H.A. would do something about it ...

Sybille Knapp was alone at her table for a moment. She was wearing a pretty blouse with a simple skirt. An attractive, pleasant-looking girl. The three-piece band up on the stage was making an attempt at a fox-trot. Stahmer got to his feet and went over to the girl.

174

'May I have the pleasure?' he said formally.

The girl looked at him for a moment, then nervously in the direction her boy friend had disappeared. She stood up, obviously against her better judgement.

'You dance well,' she said in the middle of the second number.

'Kind of you to say so,' Stahmer answered.

'You're not from here?'

'No. From Berlin.'

Stahmer brought all his charm into play. He had always been successful with women. And after the society ladies he had managed to bed in Berlin, what trouble was he going to have with a little girl from Gleiwitz? There was no lust there, only duty. His duty to the Devil. He drew his partner closer.

The musicians took a break.

'Could I invite you to a glass of something at the bar?' he asked.

'Yes ... but just one,' she murmured hesitantly. Because of her boy friend. She wasn't to know that she had just allowed herself to become a cog in the machinery of world history.

As they seated themselves at the bar, they overheard a conversation between two young men, one that was typical of the time. Would it be war – or peace? The girl turned to Stahmer.

'What do you think, will we stay at peace?'

The Devil's disciple shrugged. He knew that the grenades in his suitcase would provide the first explosions of the Second World War, and that its first battle would take place inside the radio station at Gleiwitz. And that he could be setting up the first death here ...

'Cheers!' he said, raising his glass of wine.

The girl smiled and looked round anxiously. Her companion hadn't come back yet.

'What are you doing in Gleiwitz?' she asked.

'Holiday,' Stahmer said.

'Alone?'

'At the moment.'

Werner Stahmer thought of his six fellow-conspirators, and felt like spitting out his drink. He forced himself to smile at the girl, with the practised ease of the Berlin ladykiller, to go through his routine: a deep gaze into her eyes; an apparently accidental brush against her hand; more drink; the first kiss; his arm round her shoulders; and then home, for the final seal on the job.

'So what do you do in Berlin?' the girl probed.

'I'm in films,' Stahmer answered casually.

'Oh ... '

'Yes. Production manager. Do you know what that is?'

'No,' Sybille said breathlessly.

'Oh, he's the man everybody knows nothing about, even though he puts the whole film together. Let's have a drink, not talk about my boring job. And what do you do?'

'I'm a sound assistant with the radio.'

Werner Stahmer put his glass down hard on the counter, feigning astonishment.

'Oh,' he said. 'So we're just about in the same business.'

He could see from the mirror behind them that the girl's boy friend had come back and was staring sullenly towards the bar.

'I must go back to my table,' she said.

'No, stay here,' Stahmer said affably. 'I'll fetch your friend.'

He walked confidently over to the young man.

'Come over,' he said calmly. 'We're having a drink.'

'What do you mean by ...?'

'Stahmer's the name. I'll explain everything over a glass.'

The boy came with him to the bar, reluctantly. Stahmer gave him a glass and made a sign to the barman. The music started up again.

'Please feel free to dance,' Stahmer encouraged the pair of

176

them. There was no more than a hint of arrogance in his easy smile.

He had to give the girl an opportunity to tell her boy friend what a great man this Stahmer from Berlin was. Because then they would come back. And then the wine would flow, paid for by Reinhard Heydrich. It was sickening, he thought as he made eyes at the girl across the room. Here he was coming between two human beings, probably messing up both their lives. But then he danced to the tune of the Prinz-Albrecht-Strasse. The Obergruppen-führer called the shots, and the shots went straight to the heart – that was the Devil's method.

The dance-bar's windows were open, but the air inside was almost unbearably close. Somewhere out there, columns of troops were tramping under a heavy sky, to the East. Hermann Göring, the Luftwaffe chief, had already informed the people that 'No enemy aircraft will ever fly over the borders of the German Reich', and civil defence units were rehearsing the blackout.

Hitler was drivelling about peace. His tailor was measuring him for a uniform that was intended, not for the front, but for his Reichstag speech. The farmers were cutting their corn; soon the scythe of war would bring home a bloody harvest. The August days of 1939 were like a dazed calm before the storm.

'Champagne!' called Werner Stahmer. A man could get thirsty in hell.

'I see you feel a need to play the big-shot,' the young man said sourly.

'Each to his own,' answered Stahmer with a laugh, clapping him on the shoulder. 'Can't you understand that I'm a stranger here, and that I get bored?'

'So why come here?'

'To relax,' Stahmer said. 'What's your name then?'

'Horst,' the young mumbled sullenly.

'Good lad,' boomed Stahmer, determinedly hearty.

He put out his hand, and they shook on it. A truce – with free drinks. Behind them, a Wehrmacht party appeared. The band struck up a military march, though it tried to compromise by putting it in fox-trot time.

'May I?' Stahmer asked.

Horst nodded.

The agent offered Sybille his arm, in true gallant fashion. Then he pushed her gently towards the dance-floor. Left, one, two, three, four ... In the August of '39, they were even turning dance-floors into parade grounds.

'Are you engaged to him?' Stahmer asked.

'Not really ... ' the girl answered.

Stahmer smiled.

'That doesn't sound very convincing,' he jibed.

'I haven't known him that long.'

'Do you have to know a man for long?' Stahmer was in command now, moving effortlessly through his routine.

'That depends on how I feel,' she said evasively.

'And how do you feel today?'

'At the moment, not bad at all,' the girl whispered throatily.

The champagne was loosening her inhibitions, as it was supposed to.

'What was your last film?' she asked.

'The Road to Tilsit,' he answered without hesitation, blowing a strand of hair off her forehead. She giggled. 'Have you seen it?'

'Yes, it was lovely,' she said admiringly.

'Shall I give you a ring sometime soon?'

'Why not?'

'But I warn you,' Stahmer said, looking straight into her big brown eyes, 'when I promise something, I carry it out.'

'How long are you staying here?'

'Long enough to see you. Often ... '

He took her arm and led her back to the table, where

Horst was sitting brooding, staring into space. Stahmer clapped him on the shoulder again.

'Don't plead tiredness,' he said with a laugh.

The young man reached for his glass, just as obediently as he himself carried out Heydrich's orders, Stahmer thought. Bloody fool. They had a lot in common. Except that Horst had it easier. He could give Stahmer a thump in the mouth, but try doing that to Oberführer Reinhard Heydrich ...

Just wait, Stahmer thought bitterly. I'll soon be out of the way again. But first I have to take a radio station by storm, kill a few human beings, and start the Second World War. Then you can have your girl back, all to yourself. At least until they stick you in a uniform and send you off to die for Greater Germany.

Hands in pockets, Werner Stahmer walked through the sooty streets of Gleiwitz, staring at the factory chimneys that scarred the horizon of the little industrial town on the Polish border. Most of the lights were already off; this was the kind of place that closed down at eleven p.m. Everyone here knew the building that housed the 'Reich radio station Gleiwitz' – a grand name for a place that was little more than a single local studio wired into the national network.

The programmes came from Berlin: a torrent of anti-Polish hate-propaganda and tales of border incidents. The people of Gleiwitz didn't take the news accounts too seriously. They knew the Poles better than that, whether they liked their Slav neighbours or not. The Polacks would have to be idiots to cross the border ...

Stahmer strolled cautiously around the radio station area. He would have to hold the place for four minutes, he pondered. A proclamation in Polish. Some shots. Explosions. And get the hell out.

Hitler had told the R.S.H.A. to organise an incident. Heydrich, who was never one to give short measure when it came to murder and mayhem, had worked out the plan. And Werner Stahmer, who didn't dare oppose the Devil, would carry out the attack.

With or without scruples: what difference did it make?

Stahmer's thoughts took him to Berlin. To Margot. She had no idea where he was. He hadn't told her what he was going to do. Not this time, not ever. He saw her sad eyes in his mind, and knew how hard she fought not to reproach him for what he did. He hated himself, because he loved Margot – and because he was too weak to free himself from her.

So he trudged on through the night, back to the hotel they had booked for him. As soon as the code word came, the bandwagon would roll. The word was: 'Canned goods'.

By that they meant the human beings whose lives were being 'preserved' so that they would make fine, convincing corpses.

The howl that tore through the dusty exercise yard was not that of an animal, but a human being's. It was a man, spreadeagled on the block, counting the strokes. The whip had torn the skin on his back into bloody, oozing shreds. With each new lick of the hide thong, tiny spots of blood showered over the onlookers.

'You swine!' the Oberscharführer roared.

'Thirteen,' the victim's voice rattled feebly. 'Fourteen ... fifteen ... '

Then it was only his body that moved, jerking convulsively as the whip descended again and again. He had been flogged unconscious ... a Dachau anaesthetic ...

The block was wooden, and the men wielding the whips wore S.S. uniforms. The death's heads they wore on their caps were the symbols of the real human heads they trampled on every day. Because they felt like it, because they were bored, because they were ordered to – or just because they had eaten too much at their last meal.

Hundreds of prisoners stood in line, staring at the torment. Their eyes seemed to be covered by an invisible film, their ears blocked by a wax no man could touch. Not me, not me, not me.

The hundred chosen prisoners were bunched separately on the edge of the camp, counting the strokes along with everyone else. The special treatment they had been getting after Gestapo-Müller's visit had given them back life, a capacity to feel. A miracle. Miracles in a concentration camp were modest: they were made of food, leisure, days without beatings. Even Herbert Rosenstein, who had lost his final illusions about his fellow men in the camp, was astonished at how much the little miracles meant.

They first experienced it when the guards stopped caring about the way they made their beds. The morning roll call was a slapdash affair, almost non-existent; the S.S. men just counted heads. They had to get their hundred men, the hundred 'canned goods', and they had to provide a hundred well-nourished corpses.

The duty officer strode quickly through the camp and entered the hut where the prisoners were sitting and eating schnitzel – as much as they could stuff into their shrunken stomachs.

'Well, you pigs,' he said affably. 'How does the menu suit you?'

They all jumped from the seats, so abruptly that the tiny trays they were eating off fell onto the floor. That could mean solitary, or the block. But the N.C.O. just smiled.

Hans Mersmann decided to jump in head first.

'Herr Hauptscharführer,' he asked, 'what are they going to do with us?'

The others moved away. An outright question like that could mean death. But the uniformed thug just carried on smiling.

'Hm. That's your guess, boys,' he snarled. He looked along the row of tables, and saw that the prisoners were still standing to attention. 'Don't just stand there like graven bloody images,' he roared. 'Come on, get on with the troughing!'

They sat down again, awestruck. Their world had been turned upside down.

'Just feed your faces,' the man in the jackboots said. 'You've made it ... a rest-home.' He laughed until he had to catch his breath. 'Do you morons still not understand?'

'No, Herr Hauptscharführer,' Mersmann answered, on behalf of all of them.

'Christ, you're stupid,' the S.S. man grunted. 'The fact is that the foreign press is spreading lies about the Führer ... so we're putting on a press conference, and we don't want any lame dogs turning up there ... You're going to be so fat that the whole world will know what a soft time you bastards have.'

They heard his mocking laughter far down the corridor as he disappeared back in the direction of the guards' canteen.

'Do you believe all that?' Rosenstein said.

'I don't know,' Hans Mersmann told his friend. Hope had a way of being very convincing, particularly when a man was full of food.

The chosen group was kept away from the other prisoners. They were even given cigarettes and chocolate. The world of Dachau became stranger by the moment. One evening, Herbert Rosenstein tried to hand bread and cold meat to comrades in the main camp, but as he reached his hand through the wire a dog leaped at him, knocking him over.

He was finished, the prisoner thought.

Then the dog was wrenched off his body.

'Stand up, you cretin!' a Rottenführer bawled at him.

Leaving the meat to the dog, the S.S. man booted the half-loaf of bread over the fence like a football.

'Don't let me catch you at that game again,' he said. At any other time it would have meant the whip – maybe even the gallows.

So the days went by. The hundred men were weighed. Many already had some colour back in their faces. Almost all had contracted diarrhoea. In some cases, their digestive systems, unused to such good, wholesome food, were threatening to collapse. The camp doctor shook his head, and it meant back to the main camp for them. They walked at a comfortable stroll, which was what they had got used to in the last few days. That was when the 'miracle' ended for them; there were kicks in the behind, the shriek of whistles, and they were greeted by emaciated comrades, by the block, hunger, and the gallows. They cursed their luck and their ruined stomachs, without realising that their lives had been saved – for now ...

After fourteen days, the telegram came from Berlin. A hundred men began their journey of no return. In a real railway carriage, not in a cattle truck. The food they were given for the journey was good and plentiful. Their old tormentors watched them leave with faces that were a strange mixture of hate and satisfaction.

'And now?' Mersmann said softly.

'The end,' sighed Rosenstein.

They were sitting next to each other. Mersmann noticed that Rosenstein had folded his hands on his knees, as if in prayer.

'But what can they do?' his friend persisted.

'They can do anything,' Rosenstein murmured, staring straight ahead. 'Or do you doubt it?'

'Why do you always have to look on the black side?'

Rosenstein said nothing, just shook his head sadly,

listening to the rattle of the couplings as the train picked up speed. Heading, though none of the men knew it, for Oppeln, close to the Polish border. According to the Devil's plan, the Second World War had to be given a good launching party. The first hundred guests at the orgy of death would be put in Wehrmacht uniforms, well fed, to look good for the newsreels, ready for the quick way out of Dachau ...

10

Another full run-through of the Gleiwitz plan. It went well, as it should after so many rehearsals. The men knew their code word: 'Operation Himmler'! They had to sit in the hotel every evening and wait for the telephone call. Then, when it came, they would approach the radio station by various predetermined routes. Werner Stahmer would wait for them inside the building. At exactly two minutes past ten, they were to overpower the doorman. Anyone who resisted in the studio was to be shot down immediately; only the engineer was to be kept alive at all costs. In case of emergency, the 'Poles' would bring a portable transmitter with them. The proclamation to be broadcast was calculated to last exactly three minutes and twenty-four seconds, and the man who was to read it out in Polish had learned it by heart. They judged that by about two minutes after the break-in, someone from the station would have managed to get to a telephone and inform the police. From then on, hand grenades and machine pistols would decide the outcome. It was particularly important that no one from Stahmer's squad fell into police hands alive …

'Got that?' Stahmer asked.

The men nodded. They were from nowhere in particular; they had come from nothing, and they would go back to nothing. They had broad shoulders, stupid, gorilla-like faces. They could count just about far enough to pull the pin on a grenade.

Their meeting took place at a hotel in the city centre. No one was paying any attention to the seven men in the lounge as Stahmer gave them their last instructions in a half-whisper, keeping his tone of voice as conversational as possible. He was due to arrive at the radio station ten minutes before the others. Sybille Knapp would be waiting for him, with her smile and those big, brown eyes. Yes, Obergruppenführer ...

'When do we pull out afterwards?' one of the S.D. men asked.

'When I give the order,' said Stahmer, lighting a cigarette.

'And if you're not around?'

'For God's sake, man,' Stahmer muttered coldly. 'You'll soon notice when you're supposed to be getting the hell out.'

Stahmer went back with the 'announcer' to his own hotel. The man who was to make the proclamation went through his paces, repeating the text in a rich, hissing language that Stahmer didn't understand.

'Poles!' the man was saying. 'The hour of liberation has come. Upper Silesia belongs to Poland ... Rise up against your German oppressors. Kill them wherever you find them ... The English and the French will not desert us in this heroic time ... '

Stahmer looked at his watch when the man had finished.

'You're speaking too quickly,' he said. 'Go through it again.'

He went to the door and wrenched it open. No one about; the corridor was empty. This was going to be a crime where there were no witnesses. Heydrich would eliminate them with the same thoroughness he had brought to bear on the birth of 'Operation Himmler'. No one would escape – from the men who were earmarked to attack the Gleiwitz radio station to the S.S. soldiers in Polish uniforms and the concentration camp inmates in Wehrmacht kit. Knowledge was fatal. A simple motto. It suited the Devil.

This time, the proclamation lasted a full four minutes.

'Too slow,' said Stahmer curtly. 'Be careful, man ...
those extra thirty-six seconds while you burble away there
could cost us our lives.'

The two men parted. No handshake.

In the middle of the night, a phone call came through
from Oppeln. Müller, the Gestapo boss, was sending a car
for him. The bloodhound was proud of being privileged
to command the whole atrocity himself.

'Well, Stahmer,' he greeted the agent. 'How are things?'

'All in order, Gruppenführer.'

'Just make sure none of your people take off on their
own afterwards, that's all,' Müller said. 'None.'

Stahmer nodded wearily. Where was it going to stop?
How high did you have to be to know about all this and
live? He himself was probably a borderline case, he
thought with a shiver of realisation.

Gestapo-Müller was rubbing his hands.

'That was a good idea,' he said benevolently. 'I mean,
the business with the girl.'

Stahmer said nothing, just inclined his head to
acknowledge the compliment.

'Just make sure she hasn't got this particular evening
off,' Müller added.

'When does the operation get under way?' Stahmer
asked.

'Tomorrow, maybe the day after,' the secret police chief
lowered his voice confidentially. 'I've been told quite
firmly from Berlin.'

Stahmer stood to attention, then gazed into the empty
eyes of Germany's chief torturer. With something close to
astonishment, he realised that he was not afraid in that
moment, that he had thrown off all that remained of his
cowardice.

'Gruppenführer,' he began. 'I request that I be relieved
of my post.'

'What?' Müller cupped one hand to his ear, as if he

couldn't believe what he had heard.

'I am asking to be returned to Berlin.'

'Christ,' Müller answered, still terrifyingly calm, 'what a thing to say. Are you sure you're in your right mind?'

'I'm sure, Gruppenführer!'

'Then why do you ask such a stupid question, if I may be so bold?' Müller snapped.

'I cannot go through with this ... I request transfer to the front or somewhere else at a later date,' Stahmer said.

'Somewhere else?' The Gestapo boss's eyes narrowed. 'You must be tired of life, some sort of bloody suicide. Are you drunk?' he growled, building up a head of steam now, pacing around the office with a clump of jackboots, faster and faster. 'Moron! Do you think the war can't start without you, eh? You think we have to call the whole thing off because of your weak-kneed, lily-livered ... '

Slowly the Gruppenführer managed to get himself under control. He subsided into a chair and put his legs up on the desk. Suddenly he was calm again, cold and calculating.

'If it was up to me,' he said matter-of-factly, 'I would have you killed. Unfortunately I need you at the moment.'

Stahmer stood like a statue in front of him, impassive, silent.

'Look, Stahmer,' Müller continued, 'you've got a very good record.'

His tone was changing now, as suddenly as before, and it now held a hint of perverse humanity.

'Look, we all have nerves,' he said. 'Go and have a drink. Get yourself a girl. Do anything you like, if it makes you feel better. For God's sake, this is an honour, this assignment! And you're playing hard to get.' Suddenly his finger shot out, like a torpedo pointed at Stahmer's heart. 'Why?' he hissed.

'Gruppenführer,' Stahmer began. 'I have clear orders to ensure that there are fatalities ... which will include innocent employees of the radio station and German police officials. No one can order me to do that.'

Gestapo Müller gazed at Stahmer for several moments, and his eyes were almost sad.

'No one?' he said softly. 'Not even Heydrich?'

'Even Heydrich cannot demand that I kill fellow-Germans. That is murder,' Stahmer said, with iron determination.

For a second, Müller seemed astonished, even frightened.

'And why don't you tell him that yourself?' he asked hoarsely.

'Because he is not here.'

'Well, perhaps he might come especially, seeing as it's you,' Müller said sourly, peering at his fingernails.

'I don't know what's got into you,' he continued, in a dangerously soft voice. 'You don't usually make such a fuss about nothing. I have to do for a hundred or more. Not for my own pleasure. I can tell you that, Herr Stahmer, but for the Führer and Greater Germany. Got that?' Now he was screaming at the top of his lungs. 'And you get on your bloody hobby-horse over two or three clapped-out characters ... Herr Stahmer, what do you want, government-issue corpses?'

Müller launched himself at the tall man and began to scream into his face. Stahmer's face tightened, but he said nothing and expressed nothing. He was still overwhelmed by his recent discovery – of the fact that he had a conscience.

Then the Gruppenführer stood stock still.

'Government-issue corpses?' he said to himself, with an almost childish wonder. A weaselly smile was spreading over his face. 'Good God!' Beside himself with delight over his idea, Müller punched Stahmer in the chest. 'Man, that's an idea. Of course. Sit down, Stahmer,' he said expansively.

Stahmer had no idea what was on the Gruppenführer's mind.

'You're all right after all,' Müller continued, with an oily benevolence that was almost worse than his anger. 'You're quite right, in fact. Why sacrifice good German racial stock, when we have plenty of those other pigs.'

Stahmer still had not understood. A minute before, he had thought he was finished with all this, and now his rebellion seemed to be ending with yet another shabby compromise. A postponement, which would keep him alive until he finally got his – at the R.S.H.A.'s convenience.

'You will return and wait for the code word. Don't concern yourself with anything else.'

'Very well, Gruppenführer,' Stahmer answered bleakly.

The heat was turning the day into an endurance test. The tarmac was bubbling. The water tenders of the fire brigade had already given up trying to control the rush of fires. The capital of the Reich sprawled helpless under the pitiless sun. It was not until early evening that some vague rain-clouds started to gather on the horizon, signalling the hoped-for break in the weather. Tens of thousands of Berliners, seeking relief from the burning streets, crowded together on the shores of the Wannsee lake. But the rain didn't come.

In the Prinz-Albrecht-Strasse, the windows were firmly shut. The upper storeys were cooler than elsewhere, and blackout curtains were already in position. The sentries in front of the building sweated under their heavy steel helmets. The chief of the R.S.H.A. had scarcely left his headquarters for days. Cars had come and gone. Messengers had been dashing all over the place. The phone had never stopped ringing. After all, this was the eve of the Second World War …

Hitler had kept the final decision for himself. In the late afternoon, Heydrich had received the first indication – full alert at Wehrmacht headquarters in the Bendlerstrasse. Then high excitement at the Foreign Office in the Wilhelmstrasse. Comings and goings at the Reich Chancellery. Rumours started to spread like wildfire, fanned by conversations between government officials. Orders were rescinded, then issued again. Soldiers were already crouched at battle stations. Adolf Hitler was making history, in his own peculiar way.

War was certain; only the precise day and hour was in doubt. Even Heydrich didn't know exactly. He was the only leading Nazi who had dared to argue against Hitler. The Obergruppenführer wanted war, but he maintained that the probable date was too premature. Not that such reservations would stop him from pressing the button when the time came.

Around seven that evening, the R.S.H.A. boss received the telephone call he had been waiting for.

'Thank God,' he said.

A gesture to his adjutant was enough. High-priority call to Gestapo-Müller. And then one word: 'Operation Himmler'.

The radio on Heydrich's desk was spewing out the usual stream of accusations and distortions. Hitler's desire for peace. Final talks with Daladier, the French prime minister. Chamberlain making threats against Germany.

Heydrich's lips curled up in a superior smile.

'Well,' he said almost jovially, 'Goebbels seems to be doing his usual stuff.'

He switched off the radio, stood up, and paced backwards and forwards. His watery-pale eyes were surrounded by red circles. Tomorrow he would change his uniform. Satan was flexible: he would alter his colours from midnight-black to field-grey.

An adjutant stormed in and snapped to attention.

'Gruppenführer Müller has confirmed the order,' the man said crisply.

Heydrich looked at his watch. Two hours to go.

'Make sure that we can receive the Gleiwitz transmitter. Loud and clear,' he commanded.

The code word, Werner Stahmer thought as he picked up the receiver. 'Understood,' he answered calmly. He nodded to himself, like a criminal acknowledging the hangman. It was time. His cold-bloodedness took over from here; the professional drive that rode rough-shod over thoughts, conscience, nerves.

From now on, the stopwatch ruled everything. Stahmer alerted his accomplices by means of the 'snowball' system: he rang up one man, who passed on the word; and the sixth rang back to Stahmer to confirm completion. The initial phase of the plan lasted eight minutes. One of the men was to stay behind in Stahmer's hotel room to keep up contact with headquarters.

Stahmer went out into the street. He was on foot, because there was plenty of time. They had synchronised their watches. The briefcase he was carrying dragged with the weight of a machine pistol and two hand grenades. The girl Sybille was on night duty. For a moment, Stahmer felt almost bitter that everything kept on going so right.

Nine forty-eight. The deadly visitor reported to the doorman, an elderly man, with a round, red face and thick glasses.

'Where are you for?'

'To see Fräulein Knapp.'

'Your business?'

'Private,' Stahmer said with a suitably sly leer.

Hesitantly, obviously disapproving, the doorman reached for a check-in form and gave it to him. Stahmer filled it out. The man made a phone call upstairs. Then the way was free. For now ...

Stahmer knew every inch, every room and corridor of the building by heart, though it was his first time there. He passed through the network of corridors and knocked on the door of room seventeen.

Sybille Knapp was pursing her lips into her makeup mirror, still checking her rouge. She smiled at the man as he came in, then reached for her handbag.

'I'm ready,' she said.

'What's the hurry?' he murmured, staring around the room with feigned interest.

'Well, the office isn't really the right place for ... '

'For what?' Stahmer asked. He had to gain time. He looked around some more. 'Nice,' he said.

Sybille giggled. 'I'd like to know what's nice about this place,' she said, shaking her head.

He went over to her and put his arm on her shoulders, pressing her gently down into her seat.

'Not here,' the girl hissed quickly. 'My boss ... '

'Let's smoke a cigarette,' Stahmer said. He looked at his watch. Still sixty minutes to go. Why couldn't those bloody hands move faster.

'I've had trouble with Horst,' the girl said.

Stahmer nodded absently.

'Because of you.'

He shook his head, failing to summon up any interest.

'You're not very attentive today,' the girl pouted.

'I'm sorry,' Stahmer said through clenched teeth.

Four minutes left. What the hell was he supposed to do with her? Knock her down? Leave her standing? She might run into the business end of a machine pistol. Christ, he should have chosen some other way into this place.

He stubbed out his cigarette. The two of them hadn't

193

spoken for a couple of minutes.

'What's wrong with you today?' Sybille asked, genuinely angry now.

'Nothing,' he said, snatching a quick glance at the hands of his watch.

The Second World War was due to start in one hundred and twenty seconds ...

Suddenly there were footsteps in the corridor outside. Slow, regular, shuffling – the weary feet of a man who was longing for going-home time. Stahmer tensed. This was all they needed, he thought. In a minute or two, Operation Himmler was due to start. The stopwatch was the director, the one who staged the Gleiwitz spine-chiller. Produced by Satan, whose name was Reinhard Heydrich and who was watching from Berlin.

There was someone else in Berlin, too: a girl named Margot. Heydrich gave orders. Margot waited. Anyone who served the Devil was not supposed to have feelings. And he was Satan's right hand, thought Stahmer bitterly.

The footsteps carried on past their room. A door opened and shut. Silence again. Stahmer relaxed slightly, though his mouth stayed dry, his face strained. He stared at the desk, looking at the briefcase he had brought with him; it was the kind of briefcase people used to take sandwiches to work, but there were no sandwiches in this one – only grenades. Stahmer hardly dared look up and meet the eyes of the girl who was sitting behind the desk.

'Look, are you going to tell me what's wrong, or not?' the girl said, her pretty face flushed with anger.

'I can't,' he said dully.

It was no use, he thought; he would have to use violence. For her own good. A harmless little girl. God, he was a bastard. He could have got in here some other way ...

'Have you been drinking?' she persisted.

'No,' Stahmer answered, checking the time again.

His brain was working as precisely as that stopwatch. No, he shouldn't have got Sybille mixed up in this, he mused. Now he would have to make sure she stayed in here, so that she wouldn't get involved in the shootout. He looked quickly at the door. No key in the lock. Christ almighty.

'I'm going now,' the girl said defiantly. 'And I don't want to see you again ... never.'

Stahmer nodded.

The girl mustn't be allowed to scream. He would have to go for the windpipe. A few seconds' pressure ... The palms of his hands were already burning with anticipation – but in shame, not fear. He walked quickly over to the door and leaned against it, facing her, blocking her way out.

'No,' he said, his suave Berlin film-maker's purr long forgotten. His voice was harsh, commanding. 'You will stay here. I cannot explain everything to you. What will happen now is for your own protection, even if you don't understand.'

He looked at her searchingly, almost with a brutal suggestiveness.

Sybille stood still, trapped by those steel-hard eyes. She hesitated, and her lip began to quiver. Then she laughed, humourlessly, with an undertone of hysteria. It had to be now, Stahmer thought, and prepared to launch himself towards her.

At that moment, seconds before the attack on the Reich radio station at Gleiwitz, the telephone rang.

Sybille picked up the receiver mechanically. That was good, he calculated; he wouldn't have to attack her from the front. He moved round, ready to take her from behind.

Sybille turned round, her face a caricature of astonishment.

'It's for you,' she said tonelessly.

For a second, Stahmer felt as if his whole world was

collapsing. Then he pulled himself together and took the phone out of the girl's hand, as gently as he could. Something must have gone terribly wrong ...

'Yes?' he said crisply into the receiver.

He recognised the caller's voice immediately. It was the contact-man they had left behind in the hotel.

'They've rung through from Oppeln,' the man was saying quickly. 'The operation's been called off. Not to go ahead under any circumstances.'

'Understood,' Stahmer rasped.

He hung up, grabbed the black briefcase, and headed for the door. Sybille stepped into his path; he hurled her to one side, sending her hard against the wall. As he left, he saw her crumpled on the floor, moaning and rubbing the back of her head.

Stahmer dashed along the corridor. God almighty, he thought. How long was the bloody thing? How many steps were there? He took the steps several at a time, careering down towards the exit. He reached the door and stumbled out. For a second he was blinded by the bright lights in the yard ...

The doorman's lodge. Stahmer forced himself to move. He could hear steps behind him; the people in the building had found out about the incident with Sybille.

A car was coming to a halt.

Two shapes leapt out. By the outer wall stood a man with his raincoat-collar pulled up. He nodded to the new arrivals. Two more were coming from the other side of the street, heading for the doorman's office. One of them had a big pistol at the ready, carelessly hidden in his sleeve. Ten paces to go, maybe fifteen ...

'Stop!' Stahmer roared at the top of his voice.

The man with the weapon spun round and pointed the barrel at him.

'Stop!' Stahmer bellowed a second time. 'Mission aborted! Get out of here!'

They wavered. Were they going to realise who he was, he thought? Or would they cut him to pieces with that bloody piece of ironware first? That would be beautiful – he would be the corpse he was supposed to be providing.

But Stahmer was in luck. The gorillas may have been moronic, but they got the message, though they took their time about it. He had to come full out of the darkness. A few vicious, well-chosen words sent them on their ways as if the whole company of hell was after them.

The doorman came out of his little lodge.

'What do you think you're doing?' he called roughly.

Then there was Sybille, standing behind Stahmer, her hair in a mess, sobbing convulsively. He put one arm round her shoulders and dragged her back towards the building. The briefcase in his other hand was threatening to take his shoulder out of its socket. Grenades are heavy.

'Come on,' said Stahmer, tender and comforting now.

'Let me go!' Sybille squealed, fighting against his grip.

'No,' he said. 'I have to explain to you, I ... lost my head ... '

My kingdom for an excuse, he thought frantically, for a lie, no matter how clumsy, for some ounce of conviction ...

'You were right,' he said, hardly aware of the words that were coming out of his mouth. 'I had been drinking ... '

'I don't want to hear it,' she sobbed. 'You behaved like a ... an animal.'

'I know,' he broke in. 'But you don't understand ... '

He was surprised how assured his voice sounded. 'I have a sister ... my only living relative ... and today she was run over ... dead.' He stood still and let go of the girl. 'Don't you understand? I just didn't know what I was doing, I was so fond of her ... '

'And the men just now?'

'Friends,' he improvised wildly. 'They brought me the news ... I'd gone off to see you, and then they found me. They were supposed to be looking after me, you see ... '

Anyone who believed that had to be totally wooden-headed, he thought despairingly. She couldn't be that stupid ...

But suddenly he had an ally: pity. A wave of emotion swamped the girl's reason. She forgot the details of the last few minutes. All she could think was: here was a lonely man who needed help, who had just undergone a terrible experience.

She put her arm nervously in his. And so they walked on, in silence, through the warm summer night. At five past ten. Three minutes after the attack that never took place. Why not? Stahmer had got out of the habit of asking questions. The only man who had that right was the one who gave the orders: Reinhard Heydrich. He wore uniform, and he was blond. And his eyes were as small as cut diamonds and as cold as ice.

They heard the murmur of voices from a bar. At the regulars' table, they were drowning their fears about war and peace. Sybille followed Stahmer into the place, as if she had no will of her own, and they sat down in a quiet corner. Stahmer ordered cognac. A whole bottle. He poured the schnapps out quickly.

'Please don't drink,' the girl implored.

'I have to,' Stahmer said curtly.

He hardly noticed the first glass at all. The second burned at his tongue. The third tasted good. The fourth brought some kind of relief to his shattered nerves.

'Please be nice,' Sybille said.

Stahmer nodded. He had to get back to the hotel, where the rest of them were bound to be waiting for him.

He paid and left half the bottle where it stood. Then he took the girl home. Sybille hesitated when they got to her front door. He took her in his arms and kissed her, hastily, almost indifferently. She seemed as lifeless as a rag doll. Her face was hot, but her lips were cold. And they stayed shut.

198

'You won't do any more stupid things, will you?' the girl asked.

'No,' Stahmer promised.

Then he turned and went on his way. Out of her sight, and out of her life.

The night air was close, oppressive. Clouds of summer mist drifted along the horizon, like moving shrouds. Thousands of soldiers were crouched in damp dugouts, in fields of stubble, by the side of streams, in barns. They were waiting for the order to attack. It was still peacetime, but these men were already at war. The fuel-tanks of their vehicles were brim full. Their weapons were fed with live ammunition, stacked in neat pyramids, waiting. Their provisions bags were filled with iron rations. They smoked and whispered, staring into the night, into the dark melancholy of late summer.

The soldiers' positions lay in Upper Silesia, but their thoughts were far away, at home. But in one small grid square on the military map, just outside the village of Dreilinden, near Oppeln, the whole plan for attack had gone out of the window. Suddenly, without any reason being given, a battalion of sappers had been ordered to leave the area that afternoon.

The regular unit was replaced by a very strange outfit indeed: a hundred men in striped fatigues. As they stumbled rather than marched along the little country road, a truck drove slowly behind them, with a car bringing up the rear. Beside the driver sat an S.S. Sturmbannführer, the equivalent of a first lieutenant in the Wehrmacht. There was the sound of a whistle, and the column halted.

'Form a circle!' the officer yelled.

The hundred men grouped round him. In the first row, on the left, stood the concentration camp prisoner

199

Rosenstein and his friend Mersmann. The carriage had taken a long time to get from Dachau to Oppeln. And every inch of the way, every man on that train had been asking himself: What are they going to do with us?

'Men!' the Sturmbannführer shouted. 'I have to inform you that the Reichsführer S.S. has seen fit to pardon you. From this moment, you are no longer prisoners. You are to be given the opportunity to make up for your past misdeeds ... immediately ... '

The men were silent. Their eyes sparkled with a feverish energy that was part hope, part fear. Herbert Rosenstein stood expectantly, as if preparing to defend himself, slightly bent forward, strangely unattentive. He was thinking about the way he had been fattened up. He was thinking of the fact that they had trimmed his hair so that there was no trace of the usual concentration camp inmate's shaven skull. He was remembering that for the past four weeks he had not been beaten, scarcely shouted at. And he knew from experience that these torturers were at their most diabolical when they put on a veneer of human decency ...

'The Poles have thrown down a challenge to the German people,' the Sturmbannführer droned on. 'The Führer has finally lost patience. We are going to strike back! You have been chosen to play a part in the German advance into Poland, and to do your duties. You are no longer prisoners, but soldiers, and you will be kitted out ready for marching. Strike at the enemy wherever you find him. Show yourselves worthy of the generosity that the Reichsführer S.S. has displayed to you!'

The Sturmbannführer sneaked a look at his watch. Another hour to go. He would have to be careful to get out of here in time.

Three kilometres away, men in uniform were clambering

out of carefully camouflaged trucks. They were men of the S.S., disguised as Poles, proud of being given the chance to show their mettle, of being allowed to commit murder for Führer, Folk and Fatherland ... and to be killed themselves. The last detail was, of course, the one they hadn't been told about ...

It all went very smoothly. The hundred men at Dreilinden tore off their hated striped fatigues and got into the Wehrmacht uniforms. There was a rich choice. Their supervisors were careful to ensure that everything fitted, that everything was perfect down to the insignia of rank. Then they were issued with rifles.

'Ready loaded,' growled an Unterscharführer.

'But I don't know how,' Mersmann muttered to his friend. 'If they're thinking of sending us to the front without any training, they can stuff their bloody war ... '

'Hold your tongue!' the Sturmbannführer bellowed. Then he switched back to his jovial tone. 'You'll soon get the hang of firing those things. In any case, the Poles are a useless bunch, can't fight for peanuts. You'll sort 'em out, big strong lads like you ... '

He looked at his watch again. He didn't intend to end up as a target.

Rosenstein managed to get hold of an Unteroffizier's uniform, but Mersmann had to be content with private first class. As they buttoned up the tunics with the eagle insignia on them, more than one of them began to have a strange longing to be back in stripes. Then a few of them were put on guard detail. The Sturmbannführer and his aides gathered slightly to one side, out of hearing of the men.

'I hope to Christ none of the buggers tries to make a break for it. That'd really drop us in the shit,' muttered the S.S. officer. 'Still half an hour to go ... just keep an eye on the goods.' Then he cupped his hands round his mouth: 'Get down in the grass!' he bawled to the 'recruits'.

They obeyed automatically. They couldn't explain any of this, but then they were used to reacting to whistles and shouts – and the hell they had lived through at Dachau had never been explained, either. At least it was a night with no barbed wire! They breathed in the pure country air. They stared at the starry, cloudless sky. Here, a man could dream again. In any case, what could be worse than Dachau? A little hope was better than none.

And it wasn't just themselves the men were thinking of. Every one of them had a wife, a mother, or a child at home. Every one of them wanted to survive, somehow. Every one of them believed in a better future, in some final remnant of humanity in the world, or in God.

Rosenstein lay on the ground, his chin propped up on one arm. The long grass was prickling his body. He could hear grasshoppers chirping, dogs barking in the distance. Somewhere close by he caught the rustle of a hedgehog or a field mouse. He was on the earth, not on a prison yard. And the man who had suffered and borne everything they could throw at him suddenly forgot where he was.

He was thinking of Maria. He could see her, young and sad, fearful and trusting. In his mind, he was running his fingers through her hair, kissing her lips, feeling her breath on him, the beat of her heart, the touch of her skin.

'What's wrong?' he was asking in his waking dream.

'Nothing,' she was saying. 'It's just that I can't believe we're together again.'

'Yes,' Rosenstein whispered. 'It's a miracle. A real miracle.'

His friend Mersmann poked him in the ribs. Rosenstein turned to face him, reluctantly.

'I'd just like to know what their bloody game is,' Mersmann said.

Rosenstein nodded.

'Maybe it's better we don't know,' he answered wearily. Slowly, reluctantly, he drove Maria from his mind. His eyes became clear again, and he was alert to the world around him once more. Rosenstein was about to speak again, then he noticed that his own voice was praying softly, as if under its own power, The prayer came from deep within him, sincere, with a kind of simple faith he had never known before.

He was calm and peaceful now. They could do what they liked with him now, he thought; there was a part of him they could never hurt. Never. His hands were stroking the earth that would soon open to receive him – for ever. They stopped and rested on a little shrub, just as they had rested on Maria's shoulder in his thoughts a few minutes before.

At that moment, the Sturmbannführer looked at his watch for the last time. He nodded to his men. Time to disappear. Operation Himmler was under way; they were getting ready with the entrenching tools, the grenades and the rifle-butts.

The weekly newsreel was going to show the whole world what swine those Poles could be ...

11

Everyone was asking questions during that night's confusion, and one above all: What was going on? No one seemed to know, everyone was trying desperately to find out. Wehrmacht units were being shoved around the countryside. The Reichstag had been called together, then the sitting had been cancelled, suddenly, by telegram. The Propaganda Ministry's hacks had been put back on the leash at the last moment, and the army commanders had been told to hold their fire.

It wasn't until the late evening that the men in the Prinz-Albrecht-Strasse learned that the Second World War had been postponed until further notice – for reasons of foreign policy. Ribbentrop, the Nazi Foreign Minister, had flown to Moscow and was negotiating a non-aggression pact with the Soviets. The talks seemed to be reaching a breakthrough-point, and Hitler was beginning to calculate now that the British and the French would stay out of any war. And so he decided to re-open direct 'negotiations' with the Poles, who were now in a weaker position.

Hitler and Stalin arm in arm: the free world shuddered at the thought of an alliance between Red and Brown barbarians. It was the biggest political sensation of the decade. Poland had already been divided up between Germany and Russia in a secret agreement, a cynical deal that made nonsense of history.

Shortly after nine-thirty that evening, Heydrich was told for certain that the pre-arranged 'border incidents' at Gleiwitz and Dreilinden were to be called off.

High-priority call to Oppeln.

'Yes, Obergruppenführer,' Gestapo-Müller bawled down the line. He looked at the time, and his forehead filmed over with sweat.

Another call. This time to Gleiwitz. Werner Stahmer, it turned out, was already on his way to the radio station. The consequences were incalculable. But the contact-man in the hotel room managed to reach Stahmer at the last moment. The programmes were not interrupted. Stahmer raced to Oppeln, cursing, fighting his way through the columns of Wehrmacht vehicles that were clogging the roads. The villages were full of chaotic, frantic activity. Engines growling in low gear, orders, curses. Somewhere a Panzer had run over a private car. Stahmer himself only just managed to brake in time to stop himself from killing half a dozen confused civilians on the road. Eventually he reached Oppeln and was shown into Müller's requisitioned office.

He had never seen the Gruppenführer as he was now.

Müller's whole pudgy body radiated fear, like an animal scent. He was running about his quarters like a rat in a trap, casting terrified glances at the telephone, then from the telephone to the clock. He didn't dare tell the Prinz-Albrecht-Strasse the disastrous news, but he knew he had to.

'Christ, Stahmer,' the chief torturer quavered. His eyes glinted like a madman's, his voice was a strangled croak, and his hands twitched like a man in a fever.

'I have to do it,' he mumbled, as if to himself. He picked up the receiver, hesitantly. Stahmer watched him, repelled and strangely gratified. So that's what these bastards were like when they crawled out of their cosy holes and had to take part in a real-life operation – the kind they usually ordered so casually.

'Müller here,' the Gestapo boss squeaked into the phone in a voice that was more like a whimper than a military

205

report. 'Yes ... get me Obergruppenführer Heydrich ... immediately, immediately!' He looked as if he was hanging on to the receiver like a lifebelt. Stahmer saw his body start to shake convulsively when he was connected with the R.S.H.A. commander.

'What's wrong, Müller?' asked Heydrich.

'Contact's been broken off,' the little man panted. 'I can't reach our men from Bernau. They ... they're already on their way.'

'What are you saying?' The voice in Berlin was icy now.

'I can't stop Operation Himmler!' Müller was moaning, almost incomprehensibly.

There was silence for a second from the other man. Then the voice came again. Almost casual, drawling out the words slowly. Stahmer couldn't help himself; he moved closer to the telephone so that he could hear.

'Listen to me, Müller,' Heydrich said. 'If you don't stop this business, I shall have your head. I'll have you put up against the wall, the whole lot of you.'

End of conversation. Müller hung up, bathed in sweat, his eyes hollow pits – eerily similar to those of the victims he so loved to torment in the cellars of the Prinz-Albrecht-Strasse.

'It's incredible,' he stuttered. 'The Führer has switched to a peace policy, and the business in Dreilinden is going ahead.'

Werner Stahmer nodded indifferently.

'Well, don't just stand there like a spare piece of furniture!' Müller gibbered. 'Do something!'

'I await your orders, Gruppenführer,' the agent said mockingly.

'You ... you!' Müller exploded. 'That's all you bastards can do!'

He wrenched open the door to the outside office. The messengers leapt up from their chairs.

'Still no answer, Gruppenführer,' said one of them stiffly.

Müller almost staggered back to his desk.

His face was as grey and featureless as the wall in the execution yard at the Prinz-Albrecht-Strasse – where Reinhard Heydrich would make him pay the price for failure.

Midnight. A hundred men in uniform had realised that they had been left alone. A few of them were asleep, some of them were eating, and many of them dreamed of escape. But to where? How far would they get? They were in a total police state, without money or papers, with their descriptions and photographs on file all over the country.

'Senseless,' said Rosenstein to his friend Mersmann.

They stared out into the night.

Then they saw the shadows. Out there on the edge of the forest, near the path from the road. Nonsense. It couldn't be. Just their nerves playing tricks. But the shadows were becoming more numerous all the time, more distinct. Then, suddenly, they melted into the grass.

'Deep cover,' the company commander had whispered.

Eight minutes past twelve. Heydrich was staring at the telephone with as much attention as Gruppenführer Müller. In the other offices, his adjutants were moving about on tiptoe, talking in whispers. The chief was pacing uneasily around his room, like a savage animal in its cage.

Müller had not phoned again. Heydrich knew what that meant. It was inconceivable, a foul-up of epic proportions. The whole propaganda machine had been switched over to peace, and any minute now all hell would be breaking loose in Dreilinden. Try hiding that ...

Should he inform Himmler? The Reichsführer S.S. would find out soon enough. How the hell could that idiot Müller have let them break off contact! These bloody amateurs! Heydrich wore his usual sour smile, but this time it hid a real anxiety and uncertainty.

During those few minutes, even the Devil knew fear.

A Wehrmacht motorcycle rattled along through the darkness. The man hanging grimly onto the handlebars wore S.S. uniform and protective goggles. The machine was careering across country, threatening to go out of control at any moment: the rider was driving like a drunk, or a madman – or a man afraid for his life.

The extreme secrecy with which 'Operation Himmler' had been prepared was rebounding on the plotters now. No one knew exactly what was going on; because it had all been carefully arranged so that the left hand didn't know what the right was doing. The killers in Polish uniforms had been away from their quarters for an hour now, while their victims were stuck out in the countryside somewhere. And there was no doubt that the 'incident' would start punctually, to the minute.

In four minutes' time.

That was how long the despatch-rider had to stop it. He gunned the motorcycle past the customs post at Dreilinden. All he knew was that some sort of raid was being staged in the area between Ratibor, Gross-Rauden and Rybnik, in a meadow near a wood. And however hard the man looked, however desperately he tried to penetrate the darkness, all he could see were meadows and woods. He had been travelling for an hour now, and he had come off the motorcycle twice. It was a miracle that the heap of junk was still moving. As for the despatch-rider, he was bleeding from his forehead, but the Gruppenführer had sent him out, and he had very little desire to displease Gestapo-Müller.

Three minutes to go now. Christ, where were they? He pushed the machine even faster, and it shot forwards, bouncing through the air like a stunt bike. For God's sake don't crash, the rider thought, for sweet God's sake don't crash! If he didn't find the S.D. group from Bernau ... If he didn't stop the massacre ... Idiots, not keeping a line open to Oppeln. In three minutes, there would be machine gun fire, grenades, screams, and the whole operation would drown in its own blood.

And so, thought the despatch-rider, would he.

They had their targets in their sights. The men lay close together, sprawled flat against the ground, as they had practised so many times in the sandy soil around Bernau. No talking. They lay in tense silence, staring at their victims four hundred metres away. Even at that range, they could pick out their targets easily; the prisoners-turned-soldiers were bunched together, like a herd of sheep.

The company commander looked at his watch and nodded. A German command was on the tip of his tongue, but he choked it back. It had to be Polish ...

'*Nasadzig bagnet*,' he called hoarsely. 'Fix bayonets.' It was done. With a perfect parade-ground unity.

'*Nabij-Gotow*,' came the next command. 'Load.'

The company commander crawled ahead of his men and into the meadow. He waited for a few seconds, then raised one arm. His men followed him, almost soundlessly, with an uncanny obedience, coming closer all the time, as if nothing could stop them. They had been ordered to kill their victims in hand-to-hand struggle, not at distance. No chances were to be taken. Not a single sacrifice was to escape the knife. Orders were orders, and schnapps was schnapps. The 'Poles' had had enough schnapps during the last few days in their billet, a disused dance hall. The bloody dance was about to begin.

The officer heard a rustling noise behind him, and he looked round reluctantly. A man was crawling towards him. Clumsily. Completely against instructions. Those men down there on the meadow would be sure to see him. Now the idiot was launching himself headlong, and had landed by the officer's side. He was speaking German. German!

'Order from Gruppenführer Müller,' the man panted. For a second he couldn't speak; he had to catch his breath. Wheezing as though his lungs were about to burst, he grabbed the company commander firmly by the arm. 'Don't,' he croaked. 'Abort assignment. I ... I've come straight from Oppeln ... been looking for you for the past hour.'

'Who are you, anyway?' the S.D. officer hissed.

'Doesn't matter.'

'Show me the order.'

'No written order. No time,' the rider said desperately.

'You must be off your head,' growled the S.S.man.

For a moment, he had completely forgotten his own ban on using German. Then he glowered at the new arrival, waved to the men in the Polish uniforms. They squirmed forward until they were level with him.

'It'll cost you your head!' the despatch-rider called out angrily.

'Idiot,' the man from the S.D. answered, unperturbed. He had about as much intelligence as he had conscience. In the next few seconds, he would decide whether a hundred men would die – or be saved for another day.

Europe hovered between life and death, peace and war, for

another full week. Those statesmen who genuinely wanted to avoid conflict were condemned to watch and wait, like helpless doctors who know that operations or transfusions can do a patient no more good. Hitler needed those seven days to 'prove' to the world, with typical mealy-mouthed hypocrisy, that he did not want war. Goebbels supplied headlines in the muzzled German press, hammered out the message on millions of radio sets. Never, on the eve of a war, had there been more talk of peace. The German soldiers in their dugouts and assembly-points were waiting for the signal to attack. Rumours piled on rumours.

The terror of the night when the Second World War had been almost unleashed by mistake was over by the first light of dawn. At the last moment, Gestapo-Müller's messenger had managed to persuade the commander of the 'Polish' S.S. unit to call off his attack. The S.D. trainees from Bernau had marched off back to their dance hall, for another week of schnapps, double rations, and waiting.

By two o'clock that night, Müller had been able to inform the Prinz-Albrecht-Strasse that the panic was over. Then, just when Heydrich should have been relieved, he had raged: 'If the slightest foul-up happens next time,' he bellowed down the phone, 'then you're finished, Müller! Make sure those incompetent fools are replaced ... immediately!'

Werner Stahmer, the Devil's agent, was back in Gleiwitz the same night. The hundred 'canned goods', the concentration camp prisoners in Wehrmacht uniform, settled themselves into a barn.

The next morning, the Sturmbannführer who had been in charge of them – and who had made himself scarce too soon, breaking off the link with Müller in Oppeln – turned up back at the scene of the crime that never was, complete with his henchmen. He looked in a bad way. His face was puffy, his breath stank of alcohol, and he stared at the world through half-closed, bloodshot eyes. More or less the usual picture of a member of the 'master race' before mid-day. What he didn't know, as he took charge of his 'flock' again, was that the events of the previous night meant a lot more than just a bad hangover.

Müller arrived at one o'clock that afternoon. Even in front of a hundred concentration camp inmates, he didn't mince his words.

'You cretin!' he roared at the Sturmbannführer. 'You are dismissed ... for gross incompetence!' The Gestapo boss made a gesture that made his plans for the squad leader clear. The man was to disappear. Permanently.

Müller had brought the commander's replacement with him: a taciturn Hauptsturmbannführer. The Gruppen-führer giveth, the Gruppenführer taketh away.

Back in his headquarters in Oppeln, Gestapo-Müller pondered over the details of 'Operation Himmler' once more. Where were the weak links? Was there any way another mistake could happen? The plan stayed unaltered. The massacre was postponed, but not cancelled. Müller worried at the scheme, his machine-like policeman's mind ferreting out the last technical problems. Of course, they had forgotten to tattoo the 'canned goods' with their blood-group symbols. The error was corrected. From now on, the victims carried the same mark of Cain as their guards. And a hundred dead, Müller thought, wasn't right either, it was too neat. He smiled with malevolent satisfaction. Because now he knew how he could change that.

Then he gave instructions that the men guarding the concentration camp prisoners were only to withdraw after the shooting had begun. And they were to be issued with a field telephone.

Müller carried on examining the Devil's plan: Gleiwitz. Admittedly, Stahmer had done all right. He had got into the radio station building and had even been able to withdraw without attracting too much attention. In any case, the next attack on the transmitter was put forward by two hours: it was to begin at two minutes past eight.

But Werner Stahmer had lost credit in Müller's eyes. The Gestapo chief didn't trust him any more. His refusal to open fire on his fellow-countryman was disturbing. But Müller knew him. Heydrich's favourite pupil was no windbag, and the Gruppenführer needed him, so he couldn't be disposed of now. Even afterwards, that would be difficult in Stahmer's case. He was too well known; he stood under Heydrich's protection; Himmler had talked to him, and the Führer had shaken his hand.

Müller phoned the agent.

'Everything all right?' he asked.

'Yes,' Stahmer said, without mentioning Müller's rank.

'Listen,' the Gestapo boss continued. 'I am sending you an extra man.'

'I don't need one,' Stahmer answered. 'That would only complicate our operational plans.'

'Nonsense,' Müller cut in, brushing off his objections. 'You don't need to worry about this man ... he'll be working on his own.' Then he hung up.

Stahmer paced up and down his hotel room. So that was it: the first sign of distrust. Müller was putting in someone he didn't know, to keep an eye on him. Let him do it, Stahmer thought, sick to his stomach. He knew the men he served.

Werner Stahmer settled into a hermit-like existence at the hotel. The waiting was a strain on his nerves. He had no desire to see Sybille Knapp again; he would have to find some other method of getting into the transmitter building. He bought a blue overall, and decided to disguise himself as an electrician. He only went out onto the streets at night, so as to avoid meeting the girl by chance. Time went slowly, painfully slowly. Every time the telephone rang, his whole body tensed.

Now, he thought as he picked up the receiver for the

tenth time. But it was just a routine call from his men, who had to report to him at regular intervals.

The Prinz-Albrecht-Strasse had set Werner Stahmer down in the grey industrial town of Gleiwitz. But his mind and his feelings had stayed in Berlin. With Margot. He could see her every moment of his solitary day, smiling, turning away so that he could not see how sad she really was. He couldn't be with her. His name wasn't even Stahmer any more. His passport contained another, strange name. He wasn't even allowed to wear his own suits; they came from a men's shop in Warsaw. He didn't even keep his own personality – that came off a peg at the Prinz-Albrecht-Strasse, too.

A wild idea was beginning to enter his head, burrowing and fixing itself in his brain. Margot didn't know where he was. He was forbidden to write to her. It was an assignment like all the rest: he was supposed to kiss her goodbye and disappear. Then, one day, he would come back ... or maybe not. Until the next time, or the last time. Until he too died on one of the dirty roads of the invisible war. And his pact with the Devil was written in blood.

For a few crazy moments, Stahmer forgot the Prinz-Albrecht-Strasse and his orders. He went to the post office and booked a trunk call to Berlin. He was lucky. Margot was at home.

'You,' she said in blunt amazement.

'Yes,' he answered quickly. 'Please forget where this call comes from.'

'Fine,' she said calmly.

Then there was silence on the line, like a vacuum.

'It's bad,' Stahmer said then. 'Very bad. I ... I would like to be with you.'

'I know.'

Christ, Stahmer thought, he shouldn't have rung her. It only made things worse: he couldn't say what he thought, and what he said was nowhere near what he was thinking.

It was the usual problem on the phone: the eternal misunderstanding between two people who loved each other. A blessing of technology, and a curse.

'Come back to me,' Margot said.

'Yes,' he said. 'Soon.'

'In one piece ... ' the girl added.

'Sure,' he said. And hung up. How was he to know that he had just made the most serious mistake of his life?

The Hauptsturmführer checked the time and got to his feet.

'Listen, all you men,' he shouted to the 'canned goods'. The hum of conversation subsided immediately. And a hundred dumb faces asked the old question: What are they going to do with us?

'I have just heard,' the S.S. officer began smoothly, 'that the Polacks may attempt to cross the border and attack the territory of the German Reich. Tonight, under cover of darkness. You are soldiers! You must return fire immediately! Is that clear?'

'Yes, Herr Hauptsturmbannführer,' they murmured mechanically, but there was fear in their eyes.

They had been sitting here for six days now, still with no training of any kind. They had been given more good food to keep their spirits up. But the stuff was beginning to stick in their gullets these days.

Rosenstein was lost in thoughts of his Maria. Mersmann stood next to him, as always. Both friends knew that they were sure to die; they just didn't know how and when. And despite everything, they accepted these last few days thankfully, as a gift – like a few real late summer days in a grey autumn without end, like a glimpse of light in the gloom of their lives. They lived and suffered shoulder to shoulder, as always.

They had told each other everything that needed saying,

215

a hundred times. They both knew each other's home addresses by heart; if one of them survived, he would bring a last greeting from the dead friend to his family. If ...

'One more thing,' the Hauptsturmführer added. 'I need a volunteer. Who's willing?'

No one moved a muscle. The S.S. officer smiled wanly. Then he walked over to them. At random, like a robot's metal feeler, his arm whipped out. A cook, reaching into a water tank and snatching a good, fat fish.

'You,' he said, and tapped Mersmann on the chest with his forefinger.

The prisoner looked around at his friend, and his face was sad and fearful. Rosenstein nodded, without looking at him. Then their eyes met for a fraction of a second in a last, desperate, deeply-felt farewell. Neither of them said a word; their eyes held everything they wanted to say.

A hefty poke in Mersmann's ribs broke the scene. An armoured car was waiting outside. An S.S. man spat on the ground and pointed to the seat next to the driver. Hans Mersmann got in, and the car moved off quickly, taking him to his future – or what was left of it.

The prisoner didn't bother to look at the countryside. The car stopped so abruptly that Mersmann cracked his head against the windscreen. Now he realised that he was in Oppeln, in front of a building that looked like a barracks.

'Come,' the driver said.

The prisoner in uniform followed him, half a pace behind, through a maze of corridors. Then the guard shoved open a door, and Mersmann felt the smell of disinfectant. As they entered the room, two medical orderlies stood up and looked at him listlessly. One jerked a thumb in the direction of the treatment-room.

Seconds later, Mersmann was standing in front of a beefy S.S. doctor.

'There you are,' the man said, looking past the prisoner.

'You have been selected for a special assignment. I have to examine you. Strip to the waist.'

It all happened very quickly. Fate had smiled on Hans Mersmann. All he had to do was to die. Nothing else. Almost without realising it.

'I don't like the sound of your heart rate,' the man said. 'I'm going to give you something for it.'

The needle was already primed. An orderly held his arm. Seconds later, Mersmann slumped to the floor. Like a dying man. They had given him a heavy dose of morphine. But it was only enough to make him unconscious. Not enough for death.

The code word came. Werner Stahmer tensed; the operation was under way at last. He pulled on his blue overall and the last of his men rang in to receive orders. It was seven o'clock. In one hour and two minutes, a German radio station would transmit a speech that had not been personally edited by Goebbels – for the first time in six years.

The main problem was the doorman at the radio building. Would he recognise him?

'I'm from … ' he named some firm or another. 'I've come to fix the wiring.'

The doorman nodded absently.

The way upstairs was free. Pray he didn't bump into Sybille; she was nowhere in sight, as it turned out. The stopwatch was driving Stahmer on. Three minutes to go.

In the privacy of a toilet cubicle, Stahmer took two grenades out of his briefcase and clicked off the safety catch of his pistol. He shoved the weapon in his right-hand overall pocket, where he could keep his finger on the trigger. Only twenty metres from the studio area. There couldn't be more than three people there, he thought; even if he was faced with a couple more, he should be able to

217

keep control through sheer surprise. He swallowed hard, then listened. Almost no one in the building. Christ, he hoped they would be reasonable, he thought, and not play the hero. It wouldn't do them – or him – any good. They and he were all in the same bloody boat.

The second hand ticked over to the full minute. Stahmer kicked open the door with the red light that meant 'no entry', and pushed his way into the room.

'What the hell do you think you're doing?' a man's voice roared.

At the back of the studio, a girl was sitting in a room that was separated from the main studio by a glass partition. Stahmer left the door open behind him, then reached into his pocket, as if he was getting out a cigarette. A second later, he was levelling the barrel of his pistol at the man.

'Move,' he said harshly. 'Stand in the corner. Any noise and I'll shoot ... you too,' he added, gesturing at the girl.

The two of them sat there, totally astonished.

'What's going on?' the man yelled again.

His secretary laughed hysterically. Stahmer whipped his pistol into the studio director's forehead, and the man crumpled to the ground like a jack-knife, with a faint, still-astonished moan. The girl's eyes were like great moons of terror.

Just then, the Devil's bloodhounds were let loose. There was a flurry of pistol shots outside, the sound of station employees rushing panic-stricken through the corridors. Two came to the door of the studio and were about to come in; then they saw Stahmer's gun and lurched off.

Then Stahmer's men came. First the squad's technician. Two of them came into the room, while the others stood guard in the corridor, their guns trained on the terrorised station staff.

'The bastards turned the bloody thing off at the last moment,' the technician said.

'Use the emergency equipment,' Stahmer rasped.

The prepared text was in Polish and German:

'The hour of liberation has arrived ... Rise up against your German oppressors ... Upper Silesia will be Polish ... Act now! ... The free world will support your struggle!'

Stahmer knew the speech by heart. As the squad's 'announcer' rattled off the final sentence, he reached into his pocket and took out a whistle. The shrill scream of the whistle echoed through the building. Retreat. The 'Poles' moved back along the corridor, their backs to the wall.

They got down as far as the first floor. Still no serious incidents. Then Stahmer heard the sirens. Police. This was where the going got rough.

'Everyone here?'

'Yes,' his men chorused.

The howl of the sirens was getting closer. The doorman was slumped unconscious at his desk. The staff members had got up enough courage for pursuit now, and were sneaking along the corridor behind Stahmer's squad as they reached the entrance hall. Stahmer fired off a few rounds between the figures in the corridor. Too high, deliberately. One of his men threw the first hand grenade of the Second World War. Just as it exploded, policemen came tumbling out of a squad car.

They swarmed into the open, found themselves being shot at, and hurled themselves to the ground. The cops had only pistols. Stahmer's men shot around wildly, as had been planned; the worthy town cops of Gleiwitz hadn't the faintest clue what was going on. They squirmed forward, bellies on the ground. A grenade went off right in their midst, and one of them screamed horribly. His arm was a bloody mess of torn and scorched flesh. The first German victim.

'Take cover!' one of the police commanders bawled, obviously deciding to wait for reinforcements before trying to handle these maniacs.

'Back!' Stahmer yelled across the yard.

They had to resist for a time, on orders. The uneven duel had to last ninety seconds exactly. The police were choosing their targets now, trying to wear the raiders down. The man next to Stahmer gasped and slumped to the floor with a bullet in his throat, pumping blood. Stahmer cursed, then watched as his men prepared for the getaway. Now. Stahmer was the last to retreat, firing aimlessly behind him as he backed through the building and down the stairs. No trouble: they had already picked a side exit for the getaway. Then, in the growing darkness, Stahmer stumbled across something soft just in front of the door.

A man. He looked as if he was asleep – or dead. Stahmer bent quickly over the motionless shape and peered at the man's face. He didn't recognise Hans Mersmann; after all, he had never met him.

'Get out!' hissed a voice behind him.

'What's this?' Stahmer asked.

'Orders of Gruppenführer Müller.'

Stahmer peeled back one of the man on the ground's eyelids with one finger. The man was still alive, he thought, just unconscious. Then he stood up – and the Gestapo boss's man grinned quickly before loosing a whole magazine of ammunition into the body, sending it into strange puppet-like convulsions.

Whistles. Shouts. Bawled commands. No time to wonder why. Stahmer dashed towards the wall, hauled himself up, leapt over, landed like a cat and looked around. They hadn't yet managed to surround the radio station properly. Amateurs, he thought with a relieved sigh. Too much confusion for their sleepy provincial heads to cope with.

Part one of 'Operation Himmler' had succeeded. Five dead, though Werner Stahmer didn't know it. He only knew about the man in the doorway, the man whose face haunted him ever after. And the gorilla who had been shot next to him during the gun battle.

Heydrich could be satisfied, he thought savagely. Blood had flowed.

It was sweltering hot in the Prinz-Albrecht-Strasse, as throughout all that summer. Heydrich had had special high-power radio equipment installed in his office. Along with a few hand-picked cronies, he followed the live broadcast from Gleiwitz: the choked-off shouts for help, the steps, the shots, the screams. It all sounded even better than the real thing. Even though normal radio sets would only have been able to pick it up in Upper Silesia, that still meant that there would be thousands of German witnesses – people who would only realise years later that they had been subjected to a monstrous confidence-trick. The 'Pole' who took over the microphone spoke quickly and clearly. At the end came a few sentences in broken German, then more shots, and then, for two or three minutes, the airwaves were deadly quiet. Finally, an obviously unpractised, mildly hysterical voice came on the air: 'The Reich radio station Gleiwitz is closing temporarily because of technical problems.'

Heydrich smiled. Werner Stahmer had delivered the goods, as usual. The first part of his bloody project had gone off according to plan, and now it was the propaganda boys' turn. The first announcement came on the late-evening news: 'While the Führer is still making desperate attempts to preserve peace in the world, Polish insurgents have entered the territory of the German Reich illegally in the neighbourhood of Gleiwitz and committed their most outrageous attack yet. They occupied the radio station at Gleiwitz for some minutes. The Polish terrorists were involved in an exchange of fire with the German police.

There have been deaths on both sides. Here is the German network radio; we shall now be continuing our programmes.'

Only a very few men outside the room in which that meeting took place knew who the real attackers had been.

'Get me police headquarters in Gleiwitz,' Heydrich said.

A major in the auxiliary police answered the Obergruppenführer's call.

'This is an outrage!' Heydrich bellowed. He was determined to play the whole deadly farce with absolute seriousness. 'Have you caught these swine?'

'No,' the major said. 'I mean, we have one of them, but he's dead.'

'Identified?'

'Identity not known, Obergruppenführer, but the man is Polish, that's for certain.'

'Good,' the R.S.H.A. boss rasped. 'And what further measures have you taken?'

'The whole city has been sealed off. No one can get out. We'll get those animals.'

'Listen to me,' Heydrich growled back. 'I must have them alive. We have to show them to the world. Understood?'

'Yes, Obergruppenführer.' You could practically hear the man's heels click together over the line.

Heydrich hung up. His cronies grinned. They all knew that Stahmer was long gone from Gleiwitz, along with the survivors of his squad. They had got out of the city before the police chief there had managed to organise his security cordon. Nevertheless, the Gleiwitz police department would have to carry on inquiries for months yet, on Heydrich's orders – pursuing investigations that would never get any results, and were not meant to.

'So,' Heydrich said with a tight smile. 'Now Oppeln.'

A high-priority call to Gestapo-Müller.

'The men are already on their way,' Müller said dutifully, trying to keep the nervousness out of his voice.

'Good,' said Heydrich. 'I wait your report when the operation has been carried out.'

The Obergruppenführer paced his office, rubbing his hands. The Führer would be pleased with him. He had given him his justification for war. Tomorrow Hitler would be able to address his tame Reichstag, spitting with outrage and injured innocence the words that meant the beginning of the bloodiest war of all time: 'Poland has fired on regular soldiers on German territory for the first time. Since five forty-five this morning, German troops have been returning fire. From now on, we will answer bullets with bullets, bombs with bombs ... '

The air was almost too hot to breathe. The new-mown cornfields were strangely pale in the sparse moonlight. Thousands of men lay packed together, staring upwards. They might have been looking for the Great Bear, or the Pole Star, or the Milky Way, but tonight they wouldn't find them; the sky was starless, overcast. The heavens were millions of light years from the men in uniform, and far above even them, somewhere in the universe, was God. So far as the system was concerned. He was a legend who had outgrown His usefulness; someone they couldn't reach with a burst from a machine gun, and who therefore didn't exist. Heydrich trampled on His works every day, with impunity. For now ...

The men were moving along in Indian file, with occasional barked orders in Polish to keep them in the right direction. Side arms jingled, leather webbing chafed, rifle butts bounced against their backs. They had been told to march out of step, but unconsciously this ghost-unit had fallen back into the regular Wehrmacht stride, the old one-two.

None of them spoke. They all just stared ahead. They had reached their first target. Gestapo-Müller had thought up another refinement; before they turned their attention to the 'canned goods', they were to burn down the customs post at Dreilinden. Men at the rear carried canisters filled with phosphorous. The column came to a halt, and the company commander took one man and went forward. He looked through his binoculars. The place was only two hundred metres away. Easy.

'Fan out,' he said in Polish.

Moving in from three directions, rifles at the ready, the men in Polish uniforms advanced towards the house. A dog started barking. A man's head appeared out of a window.

'Who's that?' he shouted. 'Anything wrong?'

'Fire!' bellowed the company commander in Polish.

Hundreds of shots tore through the night. The men were still firing into the air, in accordance with their instructions. The customs official fled. A woman and a child ran frantically into the darkness. From the other side of the border, a searchlight flickered, groping towards the scene.

'Move. Quickly!' the commander yelled.

They emptied the canisters onto the ground, and a few seconds later the house and outbuildings were an inferno. There was the tinkle of breaking glass; jets of flame twenty metres high clawed holes in the night.

'Withdraw!' the company commander rasped. They withdrew to the wood at a trot, moving round and lining themselves up for the next target.

'Load!' the order came. This time they wouldn't fire their rifles into the air. Now their targets would be real flesh and blood.

At first the policeman thought his visitor was drunk. Friedrich Holzmann, farmer from Dreilinden, was still so shocked by the nightmare he had seen that he was unable

224

to frame words. Then the policeman understood. The man who had got him out of bed was claiming to have seen a whole company of Polish soldiers. On German soil. Unbelievable! But the village cop went to his telephone and contacted headquarters.

A minute later, he was getting his motorcycle out of the shed. The farmer plonked himself uneasily on the passenger seat, and soon they were at their goal: the police barracks in Oppeln. Careful questioning. No one seemed to know what to do. Some of them thought the farmer was crazy, others said they could believe anything of the Polacks. There was an official from Berlin around the building somewhere, one of the local policemen said; some big wheel in the Gestapo who was here on hush-hush business. To be on the safe side, the station chief decided to check with him.

'Bring him here,' Müller ordered.

The witness got a fright when he first walked into the room. Müller was standing with his back to the door, looking out of the window, and from behind the master of terror looked just like a shaven-headed concentration camp inmate.

Müller turned round slowly.

'So you've seen some Polacks, eh?' he asked.

'Yes,' the farmer said nervously, twisting his cap in his boney hands.

'Where?'

The witness thought, then hesitantly named the place.

'Incredible,' said Müller to the local police chief, 'but take a statement for the record, just in case.'

The two other men left. Alone again, Müller went back to the window. He was smiling. Fate had given him a genuine witness.

So far as 'Operation Himmler' was concerned, farmer Holzmann was worth his weight in gold.

*

Herbert Rosenstein had been put on guard duty. The bizarre unit had taken up position in the meadow once more. The concentration camp inmate in Wehrmacht uniform was standing about fifty metres from his comrades, peering out into the darkness. Distantly. His thoughts were with Maria; she would be getting ready for sleep now. Finally he felt a light breeze coming up, whispering through the wood, rustling leaves. But wait a minute ... was it the breeze that was whispering?

Nonsense, Rosenstein thought – constant fear could make a man imagine things. Like the shapes there on the edge of the wood. And they were starting to move.

No, Rosenstein thought. His instinct had been right. The shadows were spreading out, close to the ground but moving, bobbing and weaving. Twenty, thirty, forty of them; a whole platoon, black as night and threatening. At the front of them, in the middle, he saw an arm raised and then the others came hurrying forward.

His tongue felt like a piece of dried-up leather in his mouth. His throat was constricted, and the sweat was pouring over his forehead. He dared not hesitate.

'Alarm!' His voice croaked like a lost soul over the meadow. The comrades behind him lurched sleepily to their feet.

A second later, the massacre began ...

The inhuman scream cut through into the men's sinews; it seemed to float above the meadow, then come back as an eerie echo, tearing them out of their restless slumber, breaking into their dreams, eating away what nerves they had left.

'A-larm!' Herbert Rosenstein shrieked, over and over again, before hurling himself to the ground. His comrades stumbled over to the pyramids of stacked rifles, took cover, looking anxiously for the shadows that were coming closer, slowly and inexorably. Suddenly the stretch of meadow where the hundred victims were crouching was bathed in the dazzling glow from two searchlights. Floodlit slaughter. Mass-murder, *son et lumière.*

In those few, interminable seconds, the hundred men knew the answer to that question: What are they going to do with us? The hundred prisoners marked for death knew why for the last few weeks they had been given chocolate instead of the whip, generous rations instead of kicks and beatings. They stared into the gloom, at the shapes that meant their deaths, and they knew everything. Their guard, the S.S. Hauptsturmführer, roared before they could make out the details of the approaching figures: 'Those are Polacks. Kill them!'

Then he leapt to his feet, followed by his cronies; he was intending to get out of the searchlight's beam, so as not to be trapped in the field of fire from his own S.S. people. The beam followed him, shimmering, almost casually.

'Not me!' The S.S. officer moaned. 'I'm not one of them. Be careful, you idiots!'

Then the machine guns chattered. The first burst sliced through the top half of his body like an electric saw, sending him kicking and gurgling against a tree trunk. Legs splayed out weirdly, he clawed at his shattered, crimson chest, then he subsided slowly. He must have been dead before he finally made contact with the damp earth. The fire arced round, chewing into the men beside the officer, sending them the same way, hurling them into the hedges and ditches. For a second there was silence, and the searchlight stayed on the scene briefly, as if it was gloating over its first harvest, before switching round to concentrate on the main body of the prisoners once more. The killers on the other side of the meadow had very precise orders: no one – but no one – was to escape. Those who tried to run were to be mown down; the rest had to be killed in close combat, as bloodily as possible.

The first of the S.D. trainees in Polish uniforms were within fifty metres of their victims. Now came the second part of the assignment. The hard part. These men knew all the theory of killing. But they still had to learn how to massacre totally defenceless human beings. They didn't yet know how a bayonet grated when it hit bone; or how men's eyes begged in the face of death; how a man would cry before he broke and died. They were ordinary soldiers, even though they had been brain-washed, still boys many of them, full of faith and even a perverted idealism.

They came closer, hesitantly almost, clutching their rifles as if they were talismans against the evil eye. Then the first hand grenade exploded; the company commander had hurled it. The 'canned goods' started to return fire. With blanks.

They didn't realise it. Not in that first moment. The lucky ones never had time to see the truth. The others still had another few seconds, even minutes, to live.

A few of the victims got to their feet and began to make for a way out of the trap. The pitiless arc of the machine gun cut them down before they had managed more than a few feet, at point-blank range. Then the men in Polish uniforms moved forward, bayonets at the ready. The machine guns stopped. Grenades were no longer to be used now, their orders said. Firearms were for emergencies only. The company commander set an example by lashing out at a moaning, cringing figure on the ground with an entrenching tool whose blade had been honed until it was as sharp as a stiletto.

They moved forward, straight over the corpses, the wounded, the screams of mutilated human beings. Thrust, twist, pull, finish off with the rifle butt. No witnesses, no survivors – Operation Himmler was an exercise in state-supported massacre; the Reich had staged the perfect murder. Here, on the bloodsoaked edge of a wood in Upper Silesia, Adolf Hitler was making history ...

But the process was slow. Death had many faces that night, all of them cruel and ugly. There were some who lay still and waited for death. Others made a run for it, trying to draw fire onto themselves, hoping for a quick death. And one group, made brave by fear of certain death, launched themselves at their attackers, wielding rifle butts, and sold their lives as dearly as they could.

Herbert Rosenstein found himself writhing on the ground with his fingers pressing round the windpipe of an S.S. man who had tripped over him in the darkness. Everything the concentration camp prisoner had suffered in those last few years, all the fear, all the hate, the will to live, was concentrated in the relentless power of those fingers as they squeezed the life out of another human being. When the other finally jerked one last time and lay still, Rosenstein found himself staring into the dead, distorted features of a boy young enough to be his son.

Then he saw the machine pistol lying in the grass. He wrenched himself to his feet and emptied the whole magazine at the attackers, until he himself was sent flying by a grenade.

The last phase. Little bunches of men squirming and writhing on the ground. The searchlights moved in closer, probing. There was a babble of orders. The last resistance had been broken. The killers stopped speaking Polish. A shot. Another. A last, choking scream.

A jackboot thudded into Rosenstein's belly, then moved on. Two metres away from him lay a comrade from the same hut in Dachau, wounded. The man lifted one arm. His face was contorted in a last, desperate plea for life. And those eyes: huge, begging, suffering.

The eighteen-year-old S.D. trainee stood staring down at him, hesitating. Then the Hauptsturmführer came clumping up behind him.

'Come on!' he roared at the young S.S. soldier in the Polish uniform. 'Finish him off, you cowardly bastard!'

Herbert Rosenstein shut his eyes, waited, listened. For the shot. For the blow. Blood was running down his face;

he had stabs of pain in his arms and legs, he felt light-headed with fever. Any minute now, he thought. Reality was becoming more remote; his mind was preparing itself. Soon it would be over. And he found himself astonished how slowly even a tormented, shattered, martyred, miserable body like his own let go of life ...

12

Three minutes past midnight. The high tide of death on the edge of the wood was ebbing. The shots were becoming isolated; it was a mopping-up operation from now on, the cleaning out of the trap – plus a little cosmetic work on the meadow, making sure that the corpses were displayed in an effective, aesthetically satisfying way.

The Prinz-Albrecht-Strasse was waiting for news of the operation's success. Heydrich was phoning Himmler. Himmler was phoning Hitler. Hitler had already given the order for the invasion of Poland. The Panzers would start to move in four hours. The Wehrmacht High Command had worked out everything down to the last detail; the whole campaign was planned to last four weeks at the most. The amateur ex-private gave the orders, and his diligent generals obeyed. After the war they would tell how much they hated the man who had given them medals and promotions – and who allowed them to send so many to a 'glorious death'. They would give clever speeches at veterans' reunions, would even act as prosecution witnesses at war crimes trials. And they would draw very healthy pensions ...

The night was heavy and close. Millions slept fitfully, or lay awake in the oppressive heat. Ration cards had been given out. Even the most optimistic of them couldn't believe there would be peace now. The best that could be hoped for was that it would be a short war.

Margot Lehndorff stood at a window in her villa and stared out into the darkness. In spite of the warmth, she was shivering. The coldness came from within, not from outside; she had felt it ever since she heard the news of the

231

'Polish' attack on the Reich radio station at Gleiwitz.

Stahmer had telephoned her from the city in Upper Silesia a few days before. She could see the connections, but she tried not to think too hard about them, though something told her that Werner was mixed up in the business. He had sounded so tense, so exhausted. And Margot was used to reading behind the words when she spoke to him.

What did the future hold? It was a question she never stopped asking. And she never got an answer. She told herself to be strong, and when Werner Stahmer was with her she hid her doubts and her tears as best she could. But when she was alone, all the weaknesses came out and her nerves were stretched like taut wires. How long could she live on the past? Was there any sense in sticking with Werner when one day he would lie in the grave he had long dug for himself?

Yet again, Margot found herself mentally writing the goodbye letter she would never send. At that moment, as she stood at the window, she couldn't remember what life had been like before she had met him. She had been young, innocent in her way, 'a father's daughter', who wanted to become 'a man's wife'. She had played with Werner, answered his charm with mockery, dismissed him as a brutal careerist; until she had asked herself whether he could be gentle, and had been surprised at the answer; until she had understood that it was too late to be free of him.

In the middle of the night, the doorbell rang. At first she was more astonished than afraid. She saw two shapes from the window. Big men.

Two minutes later, she learned that they had come to take her away.

Slowly, gradually, he regained consciousness. A last,

ragged volley of shots brought the wounded man out of his feverish sleep. For a moment, Herbert Rosenstein's thoughts were on Maria, the woman he loved. Maria, he was saying, don't cry, believe me, it's better like this ... for both of us.

Heavy footsteps just by his head brought Rosenstein back to the present. The meadow. The massacre. He looked cautiously round. He was lying in a row along with his murdered comrades. They must have thought I was dead, he thought. He mustn't move. Or should he? What difference would it make?

Then Rosenstein heard a noise very close by. A young S.S. soldier in a Polish uniform was throwing up into the grass. A human being among all these murderers, he thought. Somebody with more of a conscience – or maybe just a weaker stomach – than the rest.

'You pathetic ninny!' his company commander was bawling at the boy.

The soldier straightened up and looked round.

'Give us a hand!' someone yelled at him.

'Three of our own men dead,' a third reported. 'Two seriously wounded. Shall we take them away?'

'No,' the company commander said quietly. 'Lay them out over there, to the right.'

His voice was thick, hoarse. Even a professional killer like him shrank before the last part of that order. There were to be no witnesses, no wounded. Even his own men had to be given the coup de grace if they couldn't be moved.

A wounded man in a Polish uniform was carried past Rosenstein.

'Bullet in the stomach,' one of the men said.

'Water ... ' the S.D. man whispered.

Don't give him any, Rosenstein thought feverishly. Liquids were fatal with stomach wounds. He knew that from his own service in the First World War.

233

'Move out!' the company commander ordered.

He picked out a few to stay behind, among them the boy who had been sick. Rosenstein could see him out of the corner of his half-closed eye, standing helplessly a short distance away, paralysed with fear and horror.

Orders. The sound of steps. At first they seemed to be almost tiptoeing away. Then, as they moved off, the pace picked up.

'It's no good,' the company commander said again. 'Maier, take a man with you ... do it so that they don't see what's coming.'

Steps again. A click. A shot. And another. A third. A long pause, then: 'Order carried out, Sturmbannführer.'

First the living had to dispose of the wounded, then the war would start on the living.

'Take a torch ... let's have another look at them. I have to be hundred-percent sure.'

Now, Herbert Rosenstein thought. He shut his eyes. But he could hear steps. Then they stopped. The glare of a light.

'Hmm ... that one looks ... '

Onto the next. Death parade. And the shattered men no longer needed to be told to look straight ahead. Their eyes were empty, glassy, lifeless.

Now, thought Rosenstein again.

Perhaps he moved slightly. Perhaps a twitch, a slight expulsion of breath. The boy stopped, looked at him, with panic in his eyes.

'He ... he's still moving,' the young soldier panted.

The Sturmbannführer came over.

'Good lesson for you!' he roared at the boy. 'Get on with it!'

No point in pretending any more. Rosenstein's eyes were open now, staring into the face of the murderer. The boy. He watched him as he unshouldered his rifle and levelled it, aiming straight between Rosenstein's calm, unwavering eyes.

'Not like that!' bellowed his commander. 'Save ammunition! Use the butt, man!'

The boy obeyed automatically, tensing his hands round the barrel. He swung it back and froze.

Rosenstein gazed back at him. Soon, he told himself; it will soon be over. Just a blow that he would hardly feel. It wasn't this boy's fault – whatever he did, he was better than the rest of them: Father, forgive them ... for they will be cursed for all eternity. Amen.

The rifle fell out of the boy's hand and clumped dully to the ground.

'You pansy,' the company commander screamed. 'Carry out the order!'

'Yes, Sturmbannführer,' the boy answered. He bent over, picked up the weapon again, then let it fall.

'I can't ... ' he sobbed.

Yes, thought Rosenstein. They could take a man's mind from him, but not his feelings.

Then he saw a face, the crazed features of the Sturmbannführer, as the man wrenched his pistol out of its holster and fired. The officer seemed beside himself. Perhaps it had something to do with the fact that Herbert Rosenstein was smiling.

'Shift yourselves!' the officer called out.

All five of them moved out. Somewhere there was the sound of car engines approaching.

'Out!' the leader of the killer-squad bawled. 'We'll just have to hope the others have made it back to quarters.'

Actually, they were less than two hundred metres from their refuge. No songs of victory. Just silently marching. Into the old village dance hall, home from the dance of death on the meadow. To drink and wait; wait and drink.

Until their turn came.

By the time the men had taken off their Polish uniforms and got back into their S.S. kit, the first police cars had reached the meadow by the wood. The gentle slope was covered with a heavy, grey cloud of mist, as if God had decided to draw a veil over the suffering and hate caused by his creations.

In the middle of the night, a rumour began to circulate, spreading like a forest fire through the city of Oppeln: the impossible had happened. The Poles had attacked, had dared to cross the border; they had set fire to a customs post and then wiped out an unsuspecting Wehrmacht unit. The good citizens stood at their doors, thin coats over their night clothes, excitedly discussing the outrage. So it hadn't been propaganda after all! The Führer had been right again.

The police and the Wehrmacht were mounting a joint hunt for the Poles. There were more and more reports from witnesses who had seen the soldiers in foreign uniforms, and every statement was carefully noted down. In his office at the police headquarters in Oppeln, Gestapo-Müller drew the threads together. Berlin was pleased with the Gruppenführer; 'Operation Himmler' had succeeded. The newsreel had been alerted, and that very same night they had hauled foreign journalists out of their beds in the capital, piled them into a bus, and taken them off to view the scene of the atrocity.

Gestapo-Müller in person acted as guide to the press. The reporters had no idea of the enormity of the incident. As they approached the spot, the German 'counter-strike' was under way. German planes were bombing and strafing targets inside Poland. Panzers were rolling eastwards, followed by infantry divisions. The reporters passed by the army units on the roads, and at first they were far more

236

interested by them than by what they were being taken to see.

Then the bus stopped. No one spoke. The corpses in the meadow had been covered with tarpaulins. Before Müller ordered the covers to be removed, he decided a few well-chosen words would add to the effect: 'Gentlemen,' he said to the assembled journalists. 'What you are about to see here is so appalling, so monstrous, that it needs no further comment.' He gestured to his minions. The newsreel cameras whirred, and their glass eyes took in every detail of the grisly scene, lingering on the grey, swollen faces and torn bodies of the dead men.

'This was a cowardly attack, from behind,' Müller continued after a few minutes. 'Nothing has been changed here. You can see how unsuspecting our soldiers were when they were ambushed by these murderers; they were not even able to defend themselves with live ammunition. We have found dozens of spent blanks.'

There were about twenty journalists present, seasoned reporters with strong stomachs. Most of them had to turn away. They couldn't look, and still less could they understand what they saw. Those who came from democratic countries would have believed Hitler capable of any atrocity. Confronted with such a barbaric scene of slaughter, however, all cynicism disappeared. They believed the Gestapo chief's every word.

'You will understand,' the Gruppenführer concluded, 'that the Reich cannot allow these sort of outrages. We cannot simply sit with our hands folded.' He lifted his hand and looked around at the pressmen gravely. 'Here, in the face of what you see, in the presence of these brave German soldiers,' he intoned, 'who have been shot down by a cowardly enemy, we must abandon the attempts at peace. Our nation and its Führer has shown willing. Now we must see who is the stronger.'

A column of Wehrmacht soldiers was passing the meadow. The young soldiers stared at the corpses on the grass, turned away, shocked and filled with hatred for the Poles. The Gruppenführer announced that the meadow would be opened to the general public.

All the time, the propaganda machine was in motion, using the nation's horror and anger to stoke up enthusiasm for the war. 'Operation Himmler' was over. The Second World War had begun.

And afterwards? The nameless concentration camp inmates, the deadly 'canned goods', were buried with full military honours, amidst a fanfare of publicity. The newsreel was there, too. As they lowered Rosenstein and the others into the earth, a Wehrmacht band slowly played the old soldier's song: 'I had a comrade ... '

Werner Stahmer arrived back in Berlin days later, during the late evening. The detours that the R.S.H.A. had forced him to make had been so absurd that for a while he had suspected that they were trying to get rid of him, too – as a dangerous witness. Had it come to that? Or would he be the one exception?

Stahmer had no idea. But now, he felt, he knew his own mind. He was finished with this business; neither his heart nor his head was with it any more. He had been an accessory to murder. What other men called courage was simply cowardice. He was afraid to leave. He should have realised it at the time of the Formis affair; and perhaps he had, but he had postponed the decision, again and again. He had been lured to the Prinz-Albrecht-Strasse by a lust for adventure, because he was terrified of spending his life in an office, of being 'ordinary'. Now he was in a position where he envied everyone else, who had worked and studied, who lived a normal existence, even the men who would be called into the army now. If they survived, at least they would have a home, something to cling to, security. His future, if he had any, lay among the damned, on the road of danger and despair. He had avoided recognising the fact, drawn Margot to him, though he knew that a man like him was poison for her. Now he was responsible for her, too, and the thought was almost unbearable.

Berlin seemed hostile and brutal. The moment he had arrived, he had been afflicted with a strange unease. He rang Margot from the station concourse to announce that he had come back from the dead again.

Her father answered the phone. The old man's voice sounded weary and flat.

'Please come here,' he said.

'Is something wrong?' Stahmer asked incredulously.

'Yes,' the old man said. His voice seemed infinitely far away. 'But we can't discuss it on the telephone.'

Stahmer took a taxi to the deserted-looking villa in Dahlem. No lights burned. No guests, friends dropping around, as it had always been before. Margot's father's face was ashen and drawn; his eyes held an unspoken accusation.

The moment Stahmer saw that look, he knew everything.

'What's wrong?' he asked. His voice was harsh and gravelly.

'Margot has gone.'

'What do you mean?'

'Arrested,' her father answered. 'Two weeks ago.'

'And where is she?'

The old man shrugged helplessly.

'Have you contacted the police?' Stahmer said. He felt as if the ground was about to give way under him. Soon he would be falling, just endlessly falling ...

'I did,' Herr Lehndorff said slowly. Then he paced up and down wearily for a few seconds.

'I ended up in the missing persons' section,' he continued. 'The people there took a statement. At first they were very keen and helpful. Then, suddenly, they didn't want to know. I'm sure they know where she is.'

Stahmer's head sank down between his shoulders. His fault. His fault. He hardly dared look at the old man.

'It must be something to do with you,' Lehndorff concluded with a bitter sigh.

'I know.' The telephone call from Gleiwitz, he thought feverishly. They must have been listening; he should have realised they would have put a tap on Margot's phone. And they had simply made her disappear. Perhaps they had only taken her into custody, or they might have gone the whole hog ... and now they would settle with him, with the agent who had broken his vow of silence, like a novice.

For a fleeting moment, Stahmer wondered what his worth would be for some foreign power at the present time. For a neutral country, perhaps. What would happen if Werner were to turn up at an international press conference somewhere and say: Yes, I was the man who lit the fuse for the Second World War. The order came from Hitler, and was passed on by Heydrich after Admiral Canaris of the Abwehr had refused to play along.

And Margot? Stahmer asked himself.

If she was still alive, it would be the end for her, that much was certain. And not just for her. They would revenge themselves on his mother, on his sister, perhaps Margot's father, too. The secret police had started to use that technique to hinder people from escaping these days, and they wouldn't hesitate to use their powers. If a man evaded their clutches, he could be sentencing his own mother to death.

Werner Stahmer trudged through the dark Berlin streets. He thought and thought, calculated and weighed things up, but he still kept on coming back to the same conclusion. He knew the way Heydrich operated.

240

Headquarters was taking out an insurance; the Ober-gruppenführer had decided the time was ripe.

He felt like a leper when he stood in Heydrich's anteroom the next day. No one spoke to him. They all knew he was in disfavour. How far would Heydrich's disfavour go? Could Stahmer retrieve the situation? And was there any point? The next assignment would just mean more killing. Suddenly he felt a deep hatred for Heydrich, because the Obergruppenführer had turned him into a weakling. But then it wasn't for his sake that he was here, but for Margot's, for the woman he loved. An agent wasn't supposed to have any feelings. He was supposed to move when headquarters told him to, in the deadly twilight, with his finger ready on the trigger. And his eyes on his next victim. Orders were orders, and murder was murder.

'Come,' the adjutant said curtly.

Heydrich was standing by the window, looking out onto the street. He turned slowly when Stahmer came in. His lips were curled slightly in a faint, mysterious smile.

'Oh, so it's you,' he began, as if surprised.

'Order carried out, Obergruppenführer.'

'Do you think so?' said Heydrich calmly. He went to his desk, rummaged among the papers on its surface, and lit himself a cigarette.

'Are you a beginner,' he asked, 'or are you getting old?'

Stahmer felt the fear creeping up his spine, but he stood ramrod-straight, determined not to crack.

'You ignored my explicit instructions,' Heydrich continued in a conversational tone. 'You endangered Secret Reich Business by a ridiculous telephone call. You are no longer completely reliable, Stahmer.' Heydrich swiped at the air with his ruler a few times. Then he continued. 'You managed the business in Gleiwitz well enough, I'll admit. But I don't like men who talk too much.' He stared hard at Stahmer, as if savouring his fear, apparently pondering on what to do with him. A pathetic

241

piece of theatre, Stahmer thought, a cheap trick. This comedian wasn't the Devil. He was just playing at Satan.

'We are working on a new project,' Heydrich went on, deliberately changing the subject. 'Perhaps I will remember your past services and give you a last chance to redeem yourself. Then again, perhaps I won't. Understood?'

'Yes, Obergruppenführer,' Stahmer answered mechanically.

'Good,' said Heydrich dismissively. He turned back to the window. 'Now make yourself scarce.'

Stahmer hesitated for an instant. And Margot? he thought wildly. He ignored Heydrich's irritated wave of the hand. The Obergruppenführer was looking at him out of the corner of one eye, and Stahmer could feel sweat running down his back and gathering in his palms. Usually he clicked his heels, made an about-face and marched out of the office. But today he just stood there, strangely bowed, motionless.

'Is there something else?' the R.S.H.A. boss asked coldly.

'Yes, Obergruppenführer,' Stahmer said. 'My wife-to-be, Margot Lehndorff, has disappeared.'

'Disappeared?' Heydrich raised one eyebrow and smiled. The word seemed to amuse him.

'Yes,' Stahmer answered.

'Then you had better go and look for her,' Heydrich said mockingly. Then he became direct. 'I have had her arrested,' he hissed. 'And now, please, tell me why.'

'The telephone call was stupid,' Stahmer murmured, 'and I am responsible. I ... not Margot.'

Heydrich put his hands in his trouser pockets and cocked his head to one side. His expression was almost schoolmasterly. He wandered slowly back to his desk, then swivelled on his heel.

'Don't be so romantic, my dear little knight in shining armour,' Heydrich said with a cynical grin. 'Whatever happens to the girl, you are responsible. You alone.' He looked at his manicured fingernails. 'You see, I still need you,' he said. 'You're going to get out there into the field and work like you've never worked before. You're going to be the most glittering jewel in my crown. You're going to be falling over yourself to take on the craziest assignments. Do you believe me?'

'No, Obergruppenführer,' Stahmer answered stiffly.

With a jovial wave of the hand, Heydrich passed over Stahmer's unheard-of insolence. 'You are life insurance,' he went on, 'the girl's life insurance. So long as you behave yourself, she stays alive.'

'You ... you can't do that,' Stahmer croaked.

'Oh, I can do anything,' drawled Heydrich. 'And from now on I want us to discuss what you can do.'

Stahmer forced himself to hold his tongue. He was shaking – not with fear, but with sheer, venomous hatred. Just a little more pushing, and he would have been prepared to go straight for his boss's throat. But his reason told him it would do no good. His thoughts must have been written on his face. He could see that Heydrich thought the whole affair extremely amusing.

'I believe in justice as well,' Heydrich continued, 'though doubtless you find that hard to accept. Naturally I would far rather put you behind bars than the girl, but you are necessary to the war effort. We're not playing games here any more. We're in the front line now. You have made a mistake, and I am almost grateful, because now I have a hostage, an assurance that you won't make another. The more you care about the girl – ' he pursed his lips ' – the more energetic the efforts you will make in future for Führer, Folk and Fatherland!'

Heydrich threw his cigarette end to one side, sending it

243

curving over to the other side of the room in a wide arc. He looked straight at Stahmer and nodded. Stahmer went. Like an automaton.

'You will keep yourself at my disposal,' the Obergruppenführer called after him.

13

War created a power for the R.S.H.A. that was beyond Heydrich's wildest dreams. For years he had been preparing, gathering his forces. Now he could throw caution to the winds; there was no limit to excess now, no rein on madness. Heydrich's strategy in the war situation was to use limitless powers for unrestrained accumulation of influence. The R.S.H.A. turned into a many-headed monster, a monster whose black shadow grew longer over the Reich by the day. Nothing was too trivial – or too important – to be kept out of the files of the Prinz-Albrecht-Strasse. Bitter remarks made in air-raid shelters were registered, along with jokes that did the rounds of the beer halls. Human life – and human death – became a matter of economics. They had already worked out on paper how many cubic metres of Zyklon B would be needed to kill a thousand human beings, and how the daily 'production' could be increased. They were already building crematoria, calculating in advance the profit they would harvest from the gold teeth they would wrench from the victims in the concentration camps.

The headquarters in the Prinz-Albrecht-Strasse became a Mecca for all kinds of strange and malevolent forms of life. Anyone who could leave his conscience at home was sure of a career with the R.S.H.A. Gauleiters began to fear it, industrialists began to finance it in the hope of currying favour. The power that was growing in Heydrich's hands was even putting him beyond the reach of Himmler, whom he dominated effortlessly.

Perhaps the pasty-faced Reichsführer S.S. was already fearing the monster that he himself had created; perhaps he felt the theoretician's sense of inferiority in the face of a cold-blooded man of action.

The strange thing was that the R.S.H.A., which had absolute power at its disposal, had no official function in its own right. Technically, it was simply an umbrella organisation, a sort of clearing house for various bureaux, an administrative convenience. But under Heydrich, who had carefully concentrated all posts in his own person, it became the most perfect secret police empire the world has ever seen.

Its powers were deliberately kept vague, so that Heydrich could play one department off against another, and use a combination of patronage and threat to hold the final say in all of them. He had cunningly gathered together a motley collection of completely opposite types at his macabre headquarters: bull-necked beer-hall pugilists from the Nazi Party's 'heroic' period along with sallow-faced academics, working-class characters side by side with aristocrats, adventurers with desk-bound specialists, fanatics alongside totally unpolitical careerists.

The whole network was, nevertheless, organised along strictly bureaucratic lines. The departments of the R.S.H.A. were divided into sections with strange names:

Section I   Personnel Department
Section II   Office for Organisation, Administration and Legal Matters (budget and finance)
Section III   S.D. Inland (reporting on the state of the Reich)
Section IV   Research and Combating of Opponents (Gestapo)
    IV-E   Counter-Espionage Inland
Section V   Office for the Combating of Criminality (police)
Section VI   Office for Overseas Information Gathering (espionage)
Section VII   Archive and Office for Research and Evaluation.

Whenever the Obergruppenführer was in Berlin, he would meet his department heads almost every day and discuss new plans and projects over lunch. New atrocities were dreamt up between the soup and the main course; numbers of those to be liquidated were confirmed over dessert. The R.S.H.A. 'dining club' was a typical example of the way in which the R.S.H.A. was a hotbed of intrigue, even at the top.

At that table sat Gestapo-Müller, the primitive cop, next to the highly-qualified lawyer and S.S. Gruppenführer Arthur Nebe, an extremely able official who rose to the head of the Reich Criminal Police and whose blind ambition was so overwhelming that he himself sat behind a machine-gun during a massacre in the East to show his men 'how Russians are liquidated'. Nebe was a man who inwardly rejected the régime he served with such fervour, who could ruthlessly persecute and then show a strange compassion. He was Müller's chief opponent, a technical expert who could have been just as successful anywhere in the world. Nebe was an art-lover and a mass-murderer, a typical 'fellow-traveller'. He was finally executed for his part in the Resistance against Hitler.

Then there was Walter Schellenberg, who had no qualifications beyond an intermediate legal examination pass and a history of denunciation as an 'honorary' spy for the S.D. He had a pleasant appearance and good manners, and that, coupled with total servility and great skill in office intrigues, seemed to suffice to raise him to the directorship of Heydrich's entire overseas espionage network. He became the Obergruppenführer's chief guide in a jungle he didn't understand, and which he stumbled through with a clumsy innocence. Schellenberg was a cowboy; it was typical of him that he had a machine pistol worked by a foot pedal built into his office in the Prinz-Albrecht-Strasse. Just in case. Schellenberg was, however, by no means the nastiest of the reptiles that crept around Heydrich's nest, and it may have been his colourless mediocrity that saved his neck after the collapse of the Reich in 1945.

Müller, with his peasant cunning, survived too. He simply disappeared, though he was known everywhere and sought for years all over Europe.

Occasional guests at Heydrich's 'high table' were the S.S. generals Pohl and Ohlendorff, completely opposite characters, but both due to end on the gallows: Ohlendorff in full recognition of his guilt – Oswald Pohl, the man who developed the whole machinery for financial and material exploitation of the concentration camps' harvest of death, protesting loudly to the last.

Slowly but inexorably, Heydrich drew closer to a position of untrammelled power. He used the legal system, which operated completely in his shadow. He was the one who set aside verdicts or confirmed them. Judges were his puppets, for all their impressive robes; he gave the orders, and heads rolled.

The R.S.H.A. had become a totally self-sufficient monopoly. The espionage services maintained by Ribbentrop's foreign ministry and the overseas department of the Party didn't need to be taken seriously. Only the traditional military espionage organisation stood in the way of Heydrich's limitless ambition. The Abwehr, entrenched in its stronghold on the Tirptiz-Ufer, was under the command of the crafty Admiral Canaris. And the S.S. parvenu Heydrich hated Canaris with all the venom of the outsider; the Admiral was one of the few men to whom he, deep inside, felt inferior. The Abwehr was without doubt technically more proficient and, above all, quieter and more discreet. There were no rules in the espionage struggle, of course, but at least the Admiral's agents put on gloves before they stooped to the unpleasant tactics demanded for success on the 'invisible front'. So the R.S.H.A. and the Abwehr ran parallel to each other, like two crocodiles of equal size, constantly sizing each other up, but afraid to try to eat each other up. Canaris was indispensable, though few Nazis trusted him. But Heydrich, who kept tabs on everything and everyone, was waiting, patiently and nervelessly, for his chance to cause the Admiral's downfall.

Meanwhile, Heydrich decided to substitute quantity for quality. It was a mistake. The Prinz-Albrecht-Strasse had its successes – like the freeing of Mussolini later in the war – but its achievements were by no means impressive when compared with those of foreign espionage networks. There were very bad foul-ups, and the basic cause was always amateurism. The R.S.H.A. never reached maturity, though, since it tried just about everything, it was bound to score isolated successes.

Heydrich himself had the instincts of a territorial animal and a highly imaginative brain. So far as the outside world was concerned, he seemed a cold servant of the system. In reality, however, he was obsessed by his own personal position. He expended most of his energy in personal vendettas. His suspicion of everyone was so extreme that he could only work with men who were totally at his mercy. And he persecuted even the most highly-placed ministers and officials if they refused to show the correct respect for his might. He measured his success by the degree of fear shown to his empire by other sections of the state.

The Prinz-Albrecht-Strasse became a sort of crossroads of fortune. In the mansion that housed the R.S.H.A., men of power bought information, industrialists asked for protection, concentration camp commanders received their authority, and spies grubbed for money. It all went on side by side – the con-man rubbed shoulders with the homosexual, the 'poached' Abwehr expert co-existed with S.S. men, the Austrian adventurer Otto Skorzeny met the German-American Dash, who talked them into sending him to the coast of the U.S.A. along with a submarine full of accomplices, all of whom he sent to the electric chair later in order to save his own skin. Then there was the Hindu crook who claimed to be able to produce fuel out of thin air, and who was wined and dined because the R.S.H.A. was desperate enough to consider alchemy as a serious proposition. They also had their own pet forger, who had been a criminal yesterday, and now produced English pound notes and American dollars for the war effort. The R.S.H.A. kept a stable of contact-men in neutral Spain, whose only function was to provide luxury goods for a privileged group of S.S. leaders, every item bought out of secret state funds. Deep within Heydrich's spider's web sat a pale-faced Obersturmbannführer with fanatical eyes and the weird title of 'Jewish Expert': Adolf Eichmann, embittered by the fact that for security reasons he was allowed only comparatively modest rank, although he had the power to slaughter millions of human beings like vermin. Later in the war came Erich Gimpel, perhaps the most bizarre spy of World War Two, who was sent to America by U-boat at the end of 1944 in order to gather information on the Manhattan Project, code name for the atom bomb. Incredibly, he managed to land at Frenchman Bay, along with an American traitor, because the entire coastal security system, including radar, had been switched off in anticipation of final victory.

Such were the types who were at home in the Prinz-Albrecht-Strasse, and between times there rose and fell endless waves of weird and wonderful characters who were perhaps most typical of the Third Reich's underworld. There was a saying: that National Socialism had been built on the sufferings of the workless for the benefit of the work-shy.

And swimming in this evil-smelling sea of exotic and savage fish was one man who had long given up thinking, or feeling, who had no schemes, no room for manoeuvre, but who had not yet completely given up hope: Werner Stahmer.

Heydrich's cruel reasoning had been amply justified: Stahmer functioned. He had to, because Heydrich held the only important card in the game: Margot Lehndorff. The Obergruppenführer knew it, and he enjoyed his knowledge.

Werner Stahmer had travelled all the mile-posts on the road of despair. More than once he had been abroad, with forged papers, in a country where he would have been greeted as an important witness against the Nazis. One telephone call, and he could have been a free man. But he had used all his professional skills and experience to ensure that he carried out his assignment and returned to a country whose rulers he hated and despised to the bottom of his being.

The Obergruppenführer liked to play games with him. He would postpone Stahmer's missions or send him for special training. He said he was going to send him on a routine assignment to North Africa, then suddenly ordered him to the border post at Venlo, with instructions to kidnap two Dutch and one British officer in broad daylight. Heydrich made ready to drop him into England, then recalled him at the last possible moment.

Stahmer became hard and uncommunicative. He learned patience, finally won his way through to a kind of calculating obedience that had nothing to do with resignation or hopelessness. At first he had tormented himself with thoughts of the girl, made life hell for himself. Margot in a concentration camp. He had pictured the female camp guards, the Führer's harpies, with their sagging breasts, lumpy faces, flat shoes. Margot would have to pay for not being like them. She would be whipped, insulted, stripped – and worse – for her beautiful hair, her pretty face, her full lips; above all, they would make her suffer because she could still love, believe, hope, laugh and cry.

Sometimes it seemed as if Heydrich, in a fit of generosity, was about to set his hostage free. But it always turned out to be part of the cruel game. Stahmer was known in the R.S.H.A. as their most daring and reliable agent, the man they could give any job to, trust with any secret, any cache of money, who never boasted, and who always left others to take the credit. Perhaps only Heydrich really knew the hatred that burned underneath Stahmer's dutiful façade.

Stahmer knew that one day he would free Margot from the women's concentration camp; all he hoped was that it would not be too late. Time had brought with it a distancing. After a while, he had no idea of what his true feelings about Margot were. He wasn't sure if he still loved her; his memories of her had become vague, fragmentary, like photographs in a dusty family album that only comes out on rainy days, then gets put back in the cupboard until the next time. It wasn't a matter of personal emotions any more. Stahmer knew only one thing: that he was responsible for what had happened to the girl, and that he had to make that up to her, whatever the price, without regard for his personal fate. It was a cross he had taken up, of his own free will, a method of penance for all the evils of the last years, the crimes he had committed at Heydrich's order.

Time seemed to slip through his hands. He measured it by assignments. Stahmer always came back; his luck, like his energy, was uncanny. He was mechanical and precise, the faultless technician of the invisible front, without a will of his own, without feelings, or nerves. A credit to any secret service, anywhere in the world.

And just as he was about to finally resign himself to his fate and put an end to everything, came a sudden, shattering change.

At the beginning of September 1941 the press carried a report that caused worldwide astonishment. Quite unexpectedly, the German News Agency announced in a short press release that Hitler had appointed Reinhard Heydrich, chief of the security police and the S.D., to the post of Deputy Reich Protector of Bohemia and Moravia – the German-occupied remnant of what had once been Czechoslovakia.

What had been going on behind the scenes? In all totalitarian states, rumour is the only true source of news. On that day, whispers and rumours were everywhere. In Berlin just as much as in London. Newspaper editors chewed their pencils down to stubs, and Germany's Nazi bureaucrats asked each other anxiously who they were supposed to obey now. Versions claiming to be 'the truth' surfaced in the morning and had been shot to pieces by mid-day. It seemed from Party sources that Hitler's governor in Prague, Baron von Neurath, an old nationalist politician from pre-Nazi days, was considered to be too weak. The land of the Czechs, ever restless, needed a firm hand. In the Prinz-Albrecht-Strasse, they knew that the Obergruppenführer, once Himmler's golden boy, was in disfavour with the S.S. chief, and that recently he had come into conflict with Reichsleiter Martin Bormann, who was building up his own power-base.

Were they trying to get Heydrich out of the way? Were they using his own weapon of 'divide and rule' against him, because they feared that the huge bureaucracy he controlled was becoming an end in itself, an irresistible personal machine that would sweep him into sole power?

Heydrich himself saw his new position as a promotion. He was in genial form as he strolled through the offices at his headquarters, clapping his underlings on the back, doling out praise, full of his plans for the move. It was already crystal-clear that he intended to carry on running the R.S.H.A. from Prague.

An air shuttle, operated by lightweight aluminium-framed Junker 52s, came into being, whisking men and reports between Berlin and Prague. But Werner Stahmer was not the only one to breathe a sigh of relief that the boss he hated and feared was going to be controlling things from a distance.

Heydrich's reputation as a hangman had gone before him to Prague. The Obergruppenführer was in fact far more notorious abroad than at home in the Reich. The general public in Germany only glimpsed him occasionally, kitted out for a fencing match (he had represented Germany in the 1936 Olympics) or at a riding competition, or snapped during one of the active service missions at the front that he had been in the habit of leading until Hitler forbade him. For the Allies, however, Heydrich was a symbol of the Nazi system.

When he appeared in Prague, supplied with absolute powers that turned the man who was technically Reich Protector into a mere figurehead, the Czechs got their heads down and feared the worst. They expected a series of show trials; reductions in rations; an escalation of terror; the sort of martial law they had in Poland; laws and rulings that only allowed release from custody or death; the extermination of the Jews; an increase in the influence of collaborators; and total enslavement. Then, to their total astonishment, none of those things happened. In Prague, with full powers to write his own rules, Heydrich seemed to change. He may have been a beast, but he was a highly intelligent one; the perfect policeman showed himself to be a clever politician.

After he took over, the political climate became relatively tolerant. The new master in the Hradschin Castle even went so far as to apologise for individual German outrages against the population. The Czechs could hardly believe it. Hitler's hated S.S. general was behaving more humanely than the elegant, 'refined' Baron von Neurath.

It all went according to plan. The psychological consequences that Heydrich had predicted became a reality. The whole country became more peaceful, though there was no increase in police activity. The number of attacks on German soldiers declined sharply. Hatred and resentment began to be less widespread. The Resistance started to lose support – and not just into prisons and Gestapo torture chambers.

The results that the R.S.H.A. boss and Deputy Reich Protector could point to on his visits to the Führer's headquarters were sensational – and genuine. If Himmler and Bormann had really arranged for their rival to be shunted off into a quiet siding in Prague, then their plot had rebounded on them. Now the Obergruppenführer, whom Hitler approvingly called, 'the man with the heart of iron', had been given a new opportunity to show his talents. And since the rest of the Nazi élite, with the exception of Goebbels, were intellectual mediocrities, it was proving a relatively easy matter.

But Bormann, the intriguer, and Himmler, the political hypochondriac, were not the only ones to see danger. The Czech Resistance realised, too, that it was finished if it didn't manage to do something about Heydrich.

It is one of the supreme ironies of history that Heydrich dug his own grave when, against his habit and his instinct, he decided, for purely political reasons, to play the peacemaker.

Obergruppenführer Reinhard Heydrich had been in Prague for eight months now. Margot Lehndorff had been rotting in a women's concentration camp for eight more months, while Werner Stahmer vainly tried to sound out his superiors for a chance to set his plan into operation. For eight months, he had been commuting between Prague and Berlin, constantly summoned to meetings in the Hradschin – meetings where skilled experts trembled, never knowing in advance whether they would be loaded with praise or thrown to the wolves.

But this journey to the capital of the so-called 'Protectorate' held no fears for Werner Stahmer. It was a social occasion. In the middle of the war, the Obergruppenführer had taken it into his head to stage a strange spectacle: He had invited all the top officials of the counter-espionage organisations and the Abwehr, the whole jungle of plotters and intriguers, to the ancient city for a sort of old-boys' reunion. Heydrich sat quietly at the side of his enemy, Canaris, and the rest sat side by side round the table. Men who couldn't bear each other, and who were longing for the opportunity to cut each other's throats, toasted their new-found 'friends'. And all eyes were on their host, Reinhard Heydrich, who was charming everyone with his wit and modesty, behaving like a venerable company chairman at the firm's jubilee dinner.

The hotel rooms were decked out with flowers. Specially-provided mementoes were laid out on the bedside tables. Not forgetting expensive bottles of old Czech brandy.

Objectively, the secret servicemen's jamboree had absolutely no purpose. It was true that in the middle of the two-day party, the Obergruppenführer gave a short talk on what he called the 'Ten Commandments' for German espionage organisations. For the rest, it was forty-eight hours of boozing, visits to the theatre, and morale-boosting over first-class food. Perhaps Heydrich, heir apparent to the S.S. empire, simply wanted to show that he was still master of the Prinz-Albrecht-Strasse, and that he would take up his police duties again with a total single-mindedness when he was freed of his pacifying mission in Bohemia-Moravia.

For two days the Obergruppenführer had been snubbing Werner Stahmer. When, during the farewells, he shook hands, his eyes were already on the next departing guest. It was the old game, and one of its rules was that Heydrich never acknowledged the game's existence. Stahmer was glad to get his boss back at arm's length.

After his return to Berlin, Werner Stahmer recognised an old face around headquarters once more: Standartenführer Löbel had just come back from Russia, where he had been in command of an S.D. murder-squad Heydrich had sent the man who had already killed millions of Jews and Russians on paper off to the front, and he had left him there for a long time. The gap between theory and practice had brought the S.S. officer into disfavour. Löbel still stood by the theory, even now, but he had learned that it was easier to kill human beings in their millions on paper than to actually go out himself and murder them in cold blood, particularly using the old-fashioned method of a bullet in the back of the neck. The 'success-rate' of Löbel's squad had been modest compared with that of other squads. The Standartenführer was still convinced that it was necessary to liquidate whole sections of the world's population, but when it came to the crunch he hadn't the icy nerves of a Gestapo-Müller or the savage ambition of Arthur Nebe. Heydrich had noticed the 'inadequate' statistics of Löbel's killers, and that was why he had let him languish in the depths of Russia, doing the Reich's dirty work, for months longer than other senior officers.

Now Löbel was back, trying hard to regain favour with Heydrich. He offered Stahmer his hand, with a jovial smile. But the hand was trembling, and it was clear that Löbel had aged in the last year. He walked with a slight stoop, his eyes were misty-yellow, with prominent red veins. His gaze was shifty and unsteady; he tried to fight back the scent of blood with schnapps, but morning always brought the hangover – and the memories.

Löbel had been detailed to the foreign espionage desk, for which Stahmer had been working over the past few years.

'Come in,' the Standartenführer said, going ahead of Stahmer into his office. He closed the curtains and checked, quite pointlessly, that no microphones were hidden around the room. The old spy-drama stuff. Stahmer had never liked him; now the man sickened him. The Standartenführer slapped a bottle of schnapps down onto the table, then began to hold forth at astonishing length. 'Sweden,' Stahmer heard him say, without understanding. His mind was elsewhere. With Margot. In some anonymous camp.

'We have "turned" this man,' Löbel was saying, 'and now is the time to start building up our own network. We're dealing with a well-organised German Resistance group that is said to have good connections with the Wehrmacht High Command. If it's true, that would be quite a blow.'

'Yes, Standartenführer,' Stahmer said listlessly.

'You would be the ideal man for the job,' Löbel continued, downing his drink and pouring himself another. 'Everything depends on the impression you can make on these bastards. You would have to convince them that you're a deserter.'

Stahmer smiled crookedly. A work of art, he thought. Just take these chains off my legs and I'll play the most convincing deserter you ever saw ...

'That's the most important thing,' Löbel said. 'Maybe the way would be take some sort of emigré or something with you, someone who can vouch for you.'

Suddenly Stahmer was totally alert, his instincts

operating at full power. He had let Löbel's ramblings wash him over, without consciously paying attention. Now he was listening hard, to make absolutely sure he had it right.

'May I?' he asked, picking up the bottle. He had to gain time. Carefully he poured out two full glasses.

'It doesn't seem quite right,' he muttered, looking dubious. 'They'll realise the whole thing is fake, even suspect blackmail.'

'Yes, but ... '

'Better to take someone who offers a cast-iron alibi. Do you understand, Standartenführer?'

'Not quite,' said Löbel dully.

'We need a Jew or whatever ... someone we can let go, and who knows he owes me his life.'

'Hm,' the Standartenführer sighed. He went back over to the window, opened a chink in the curtains, and looked down onto the courtyard.

'I've had too much experience,' Stahmer said, still stirring for all he was worth. 'I don't like getting involved in things that go wrong.'

'It mustn't go wrong, whatever happens,' Löbel said, turning round to face him. 'Listen,' he said. 'You're the only other person who knows about this business. No one else. I'll take full responsibility. I know,' he lowered his voice, 'that I'm exceeding my powers, but I want to have something clearcut to present to the Obergruppenführer. I want an unmistakable success; one that you and I have scored all on our own.' He came up to within inches of Stahmer's face. 'Just the two of us,' he whispered.

'Let me find myself a Jew, then,' Stahmer changed the subject.

'It's hard with Jews,' Löbel answered, just as Stahmer had expected him to. 'The Reichsführer S.S. has a thing about them.'

'Or any other concentration camp inmate. Someone like that will be glad to be given a chance.' Stahmer smiled.

'And I'll make sure he doesn't get up to anything silly ...
you can rely on that, Standartenführer.'

'It's worth some thought,' Löbel agreed. 'Work out a
plan, in writing, but it'll have to be quick.'

'I've already had experience of something similar,'
Stahmer added, almost as an afterthought. But he was
springing his trap. 'With a woman. You know, the Formis
case. Years ago.'

'Christ, yes.'

'And a woman is easier to control than a man,' Stahmer
murmured with a man-to-man leer.

'You're absolutely right,' the Standartenführer boomed,
obviously delighted with the idea now. 'I knew you were
the right man for something like this. Bugger the written
plan. We'll go straight into action, eh?'

Stahmer nodded. His face was expressionless, though he
could feel an almost unbearable pressure in his temples.

'Absolute powers,' Löbel burbled. 'Search all the
concentration camps. Look in our files for a suitable
prisoner. But quick, get your skates on. How long will you
need?'

'Three days, at the most,' Stahmer said.

'Anything else?' the Standartenführer asked.

'A written authorisation to show to the concentration
camp commander ... a family passport for Sweden ...
foreign currency and ...'

'Agreed,' Löbel cut him off. 'Just one condition: keep
your mouth shut.'

'Very well, Standartenführer,' Stahmer responded,
springing to attention with a crisp firmness he hadn't
shown in years. He knew he was on his way to his goal.
And without any risk – so long as he moved quickly.

They had been standing lined up in squares for hours, and
they had waited: maybe for nothing, maybe for a beating,

an inspection, or some new, more refined insult. Life was precarious and unpredictable; only the guards' cruelty had system. These women had no names, only numbers. Ready for torture en bloc and mass-murder.

A fine, almost invisible rain was falling. It was May, but the neutered beings on the exercise yard didn't experience it as spring; for them it was always autumn, late autumn. Their faces were grey, grey like everything in this department of hell; grey like the uniforms, grey like the food, grey as the walls, as the concrete of the yard. Even the little patch of green near the kitchen hut was sparse and pale, as if it was frightened of drawing attention to itself.

A number was called. A four-figure one. This one must have been here a long time, the women thought – those whose brains still bothered to function.

An emaciated figure emerged from the front rank. No one was moved at the sight of her. Here they were all emaciated, and all feeling had died, good and bad, hope or fear. So no one looked when number 3402 stepped out of the ranks; curiosity was a luxury that could prove fatal, and so it had gone the way of all luxuries in this women's concentration camp.

Number 3402 was still young, but it would have been difficult to have told it from her appearance. Even to realise that she had once been pretty would have taken more power of imagination than anyone in that place possessed. Years as a hostage of the Devil had marked her terribly. Margot Lehndorff had even forgotten why she was here. Numbers don't ask ...

Number 3402 had taken the route to the orderly room countless times. As a new arrival, she had gone in hope and fear – hope for help, fear of a beating. Margot had hoped and starved, cried and cursed, just like the rest of them. She had tried to resist, then had collapsed before the brutal power of the system. She had gone through every stage from resignation to despair, until she had learned how to use the only weapon of the concentration camp inmate: the emotionless apathy which enabled them to exist from day to day without finding madness or death.

Number 3402 had reached the orderly room and was standing to attention in front of the woman guard, just as she had a hundred times before. A flicker of the eyelid, a deep breath, a word too many or a laugh in the wrong place, and it could mean torture, or deportation into a field-brothel, or transfer to the vivisection unit. The stunted being who was examining Margot now, a sort of female sergeant-major, had the power to dispense every humiliation and atrocity that could be inflicted on a woman, and she enjoyed that power.

Margot had feared all the terrible alternatives. But they had not come. She had carried on fearing them – until that blessed apathy came, and with it the death fear. Her heart still pumped. Her arms and legs functioned. Even her mind still operated after a fashion. Only one thing was missing, and it had been destroyed when they finally broken her resistance: her soul.

'Here,' the guard said. 'Sign this.' She shoved a piece of paper over her desk top towards number 3402. It was a form, already filled out except for the signature.

Margot Lehndorff looked at the form without curiosity, as if its contents were a matter of total indifference, as if she was interested only in the place where she was supposed to put her name. There was a declaration under the heading: 'Oath of Silence'. Without realising it, Margot had promised not to mention anything about the conditions in the women's camps. It was a formality that preceded release. And because there were so few people released from the camps, it was more or less irrelevant.

Number 3402 stood swaying slightly, waiting for the next order, careful not to meet the woman guard's eye. There was an almost obscene intensity about the way the wardress was looking at her, a human being who was about to escape her absolute authority. Perhaps she was thinking about making recompense for the atrocities she had inflicted; then again, she may simply have been regretting that she hadn't taken her chance earlier and sent 3402 to the S.S. doctors' block – from where the lucky ones came back mad, or cripples.

'Go in there,' the guard said, pointing to an adjoining room.

Margot went, looking neither right or left, ignoring the pangs of hunger in her stomach and the swimming feeling in her head. She noted without interest that there were four people in the room, but that was all.

One of them looked so horrified that it made an impression. Margot looked up fully. Suddenly her wasted body felt as if it were made of lead. She held onto the wall for support and closed her eyes, breathing heavily, trying desperately not to scream. She had just seen a ghost.

'I thank you for your help, in the name of the R.S.H.A.,' a voice rasped. She knew it, and that was unbearable. 'I shall not fail to mention in my report how you have given us every support.'

No, number 3402 wanted to scream, this wasn't possible. She felt naked, pathetic. Once she had waited for this man, not only to free her but also because she had longed for his presence, his touch. Now it seemed the final humiliation, the camp's last cruel trick.

Margot felt an irresistible urge to run. But she couldn't. He already had a firm grip on her arm and was pushing her out of the door. She obeyed, like a shabby puppet. Someone threw a coat over her shoulders. Another clicked his heels. There was a car parked in front of the door; Stahmer wrenched open the door, shoved her in, turned to wave, then drove off.

Now she felt fear, a burning, choking terror ... that voice. She tried to hide herself, burrowing into the upholstery of the seat. Even when she closed her eyes, there was still a blinding, painful light. She was frightened to look, frightened to hear, and she couldn't know that Stahmer felt exactly as she did.

It had been easier for him; at first he had been able to play his part as one of Heydrich's agents. He had prepared himself for the meeting with Margot, and he had told himself a hundred times that the biggest danger would be when she recognised him – and perhaps revealed that she was not some anonymous tool of the R.S.H.A. Stahmer had concentrated everything into ensuring that the handover went without incident. He had known a bit about conditions in concentration camps. God knows, he had spent enough sleepless nights imagining what it must do to a woman. Yes, he had thought he was prepared for the worst. He had been wrong ...

So he sat at the wheel, desperately searching for a bridge to her, but he felt helpless. What was he supposed to say? Was it bad, darling? Or: I'm sorry, I'm a little late, but it won't happen again? Or: Things will be all right now that we're together again? Or: What would you like for dinner? Or: How many of you did they hang today?

Werner Stahmer said nothing. He had got what he wanted. But he had come too late. Perhaps it would have been better if they had killed Margot straight away. He felt ashamed of his thoughts, but he knew he was right. Then he realised that it was precisely his 'rightness' that made him feel ashamed.

Margot had aged, she was almost ugly, and there was a lifelessness about her. The hollows at the corners of her mouth, which had been so charming once, had become deep furrows, hard lines that proclaimed the face of a camp inmate to the world.

They had been driving for an hour or more. Neither of them had said a word; both sat with only the drone of the engine for company. They reached a village and found themselves stuck behind a horse and cart. Stahmer was thankful for it; he could concentrate on his driving, occupy his mind. He drove slowly behind the farmer and found himself hoping wildly that the cart was going all the way to Berlin. He dare not look to his right. He knew that every glance from him would seem like a distorting mirror to the wreck of a human being next to him. And Stahmer had promised himself that he would stay with Margot, whatever happened, to love her, however ugly she was, to never betray her, whatever temptations came his way. He had told her that all those years ago, and it had been easy, because the way to heaven seemed open; a heaven on earth that would never exist again. As he drove, he was praying that he would be able to keep his word.

Werner Stahmer had overtaken the horse and cart and had the open road in front of him again. He was horrified at the cruelty of his own thoughts. If Margot guessed, it would finally destroy her, and this time it would be his fault too.

He stopped for a rest. In the glove compartment was a packet of cigarettes. He held the packet out to Margot. She shook her head. Stahmer gave himself a deadline: three drags and then he had to talk.

'I tried everything ... ' he murmured.

Margot made no reaction. He put his hand on her arm; it felt like a piece of dry wood.

'I can't explain much now ... We're travelling to Berlin...' he was speaking quickly, urgently. 'We'll get you some clothes there. I have passports ... for Sweden. In two days we'll be over the border, and we'll never come back to Germany ... never, do you hear?'

Margot was staring out of the window. The skin of her face was like leather.

'At least until the war's over,' Stahmer conceded, as if his words had been responsible for her attitude. He paused. 'Your hair's the only really bad thing,' he lied.

'They mustn't realise that you ... the camp ... ' He stopped himself, but he knew it was too late. 'We'll soon find a good hairdresser for you,' he continued, with a false heartiness.

She was in shock, he thought. Christ, if only they had longer. What could he do? Her father, maybe? Impossible. He had already involved one person and got her into a concentration camp. Ira, her friend. No, Ira had been conscripted and was working for the Luftwaffe in France. A doctor? There was no quick cure for what Margot had. But he would get her over the border, even if he had to drag her bodily.

The rain had stopped, and the sun was breaking through. It was going to be a bright, sunny day. The people outside were talking loudly, walking cheerfully through the streets. The houses were decked with swastikas for some reason. To Margot they looked like hawks' talons. Why don't they tear the flags down? she thought. And why were those people laughing? Didn't they know what was going on?

Suddenly Margot began to shiver. Of course. She understood now. Those people were from the other side, they belonged with the women who wore boots and used whips, even if they looked different. Perhaps the guards were just more honest, because they realised their true natures.

The loudspeakers in the street were booming into life again. Special war bulletins. The people were standing, waving for all they were worth. There were only fifteen or twenty of them, but for her they seemed a whole world.

Then the procession came, from the left. The boy with the banner at its head was hardly into his teens, an angelic-looking blond lad just like the one Margot always wanted to have. Before ... He had grown up quickly, she thought. Her face was lit by a faint smile, like the first shaft of sun on a rainy day.

Then she saw the boy with the banner launch himself at an old man who had failed to salute the flags. He was bawling at him like a sergeant-major. The old man turned a deep shade of red and dropped his walking-stick; then he bent down, picked it up, and went on his way, shaking his head sadly.

Werner Stahmer drove on. He cursed. More and more processions, more and more flags and banners, more and more special bulletins. A world in uniforms, with laughing faces, with the will to victory and total contempt for the outsiders, the ones fit only for liquidation. The pathetic figure of number 3402 beside him seemed to have shrunk into itself, a piece of flotsam in a country, a way of life, that she wasn't part of any more.

Werner Stahmer managed to summon up more tact and tenderness than ever before in his life. He didn't expect too much of Margot. He got used to smiling at her in a way that didn't mirror her suffering. He thought out every movement, every word in advance. He was constantly re-arranging her pillows. He turned off the radio. He put gentle pressure on her to eat, though she could never remember afterwards what she had had. He told her about Sweden. He gave descriptions of the northern landscapes that were straight out of a child's fairytale book. He tried to explain to her how he had changed, learned the lesson she had been trying to teach him all that time ago. He took her by the hand and carried her back in memory to the Riviera. He painted pastel pictures of the sea, the sand, red wine and spaghetti. Stahmer was a superb psychologist, but he was up against a brick wall. Perhaps he would have made his breakthrough, if there had been time. If it hadn't been for their encounter with Dr. Pfeiffer.

They had been in Berlin for two days now, and tomorrow they were due to leave. Stahmer already had the foreign currency. The visas still had to be collected, but there would be no problems. From now on, it couldn't –

and mustn't – go wrong. But Margot was weak and exhausted; her eyes were red-rimmed. She couldn't sleep. Stahmer had given her pills, but they had done no good, though he knew she had to get some rest before the journey.

Stahmer took her to the doctor a few doors along the street. He turned out to be the worst one they could have chosen. He wore a golden Party badge on his lapel, and he clapped Margot on the shoulder as if she were a piece of meat for inspection.

'You look pretty bad,' he rasped. 'Carry on like this and you'll never be a good German wife and mother.'

The radio was switched on in the corner. Another special bulletin, telling everyone how many net-register-tons the fleet had sunk.

'But then our enemies make war on women and children,' the man prattled on. 'You only need to see their faces to see what a pathetic, inferior tribe they are … ' He laughed shrilly.

Stahmer tried to get the man to change the subject, for Margot's sake. He glanced at a photograph on the wall, a framed portrait of a young Luftwaffe officer.

'My son,' the doctor commented, his eyes shining. 'Fell in action three weeks ago. I can't tell you how proud I am of him … '

'The prescription, please,' Stahmer pressed. What he wouldn't have given to have been able to smash this stupid quack's face in.

'I'm sorry,' he said to Margot. She didn't react.

At a chemist's shop on the corner he bought the sleeping tablets.

'Have a lie down for a few hours,' he said. 'I'll fetch our passports now, and then … '

He took Margot back to the apartment, then went off to round off the unfinished business. They had to leave for Sweden the next day, because timing was all-important.

He was certain now that everything would be all right. A few hours still, then the journey, and finally over the border. Child's play for an experienced expert.

Werner Stahmer said his farewell to Löbel, and it lasted longer than he had expected. He wasn't too unhappy about the delay; it took his mind off things, and in any case it might be a good thing if Margot were left alone for a while to think.

He was wrong, though he couldn't be expected to realise it.

Margot's attack came quite suddenly. She felt a spinning, roaring sensation in her head, and collapsed in the middle of the room. The place seemed full of bats. Then they changed into vultures, with claws like swastikas. They were waiting for her, croaking, gloating.

'Stop it!' she shouted feebly, clambering to her feet. She went over to the couch and lay down. She could see the boy again, going for the old man, and she was ashamed for him. And the doctor. How proud ... His words hissed around the room, louder and louder, until they were deafening, but she could find no way of stopping them. Everyone was marching and singing. Then the fanfare came again. Bombs over England. A bulletin from Russia. In a few weeks the war would be over. And the Führer was making history. And there had never been a more heroic time than now. And I am proud that he is dead. Proud ... the voice droned on.

And Margot felt as if she was sitting at the doctor's desk, filling out a prescription, ordering sleeping pills.

Suddenly the noise stopped, and there was an unnerving quiet in the room. The whole witches' sabbath had disappeared. And a thought came into her head. It had nothing to do with the man who had brought her here, or her father; it didn't even occur to her that the decision she had come to was irrevocable.

Margot suddenly had a goal. It was only just more than

an arm's length away. She stood up and went into the bathroom. She took all three bottles and poured their contents into an empty glass, then filled it with water, mixing it into a repulsive mush. Then she lifted it to her lips, to finish with it all, to finish with sorrow ... to have rest, quiet, peace ... in an eternity without broken crosses on blood-red banners ...

14

The Deputy Reich Protector for Bohemia and Moravia had his seat at a requisitioned castle just outside Prague. The 27th May 1942 was a fine, sunny day, and a welcoming light was already flooding through the high windows of his residence while Reinhard Heydrich lay in bed. But the Obergruppenführer was not idle; he was reading the day's reports from the Prinz-Albrecht-Strasse. Even from Prague, he kept a tight rein on his secret empire. It was part of his system to put two or three experts onto a case, separately and without each other's knowledge, so that they would automatically keep an eye on each other. The whole apparatus he had built up was still completely under his control; despite the geographical distances involved, there was nothing that went on in the Prinz-Albrecht-Strasse that Heydrich didn't know about.

He had known for days that a German Resistance group in Sweden had forged links with the British secret service, and that his department had succeeded in 'turning' one of the refugees involved. It was common practice in their bizarre trade. Almost no one could know anything for certain in the maze of espionage and counter-espionage, cross and double-cross. When the R.S.H.A. in Ankara later succeeded in the enterprise known as 'Operation Cicero', their coup turned to dust. In Berlin they refused to accept the documents, because it was assumed that they had been falsified by the British and deliberately 'fed' to the Nazi spies.

In this case, things were different. Here they were dealing with opponents inside Germany itself, generals and politicians who were working in secret for Hitler's overthrow. It would do no harm to arrest them, even if the odd piece of information was strictly inaccurate.

Suddenly Heydrich saw Stahmer's name. He pondered it for a moment. Not a bad choice; the man was skilled, and he would do his best – whether he liked it or not. The Obergruppenführer carried on reading, then froze when he learned that Stahmer was supposed to be heading for Sweden along with a political detainee. Even before he came across the name of Margot Lehndorff, he had seen through Stahmer's plan and had realised that the agent intended to escape along with his boss's 'insurance'.

He buzzed for his adjutant, then jabbed a finger at the report.

'Put a stop to this business, immediately,' he said. 'Have Stahmer arrested and brought here.' Heydrich smiled thinly. 'I intend to interrogate him personally.'

He had seen through the agent's little ruse, and this renewed proof of his own cleverness put the Obergruppenführer in good spirits. At about eight thirty, he got out of bed, dressed, and ordered his car to be made ready. Today his regular chauffeur was sick, and a replacement driver would be taking him into the city. In view of the fine weather and his expansive mood, Heydrich ordered the man to take the hood off from his armour-plated Mercedes. And so the May sunshine made history, because it made possible the long-planned attack. The S.S. Obergruppenführer sat next to his chauffeur during the drive in through the suburbs. Scarcely any passers-by turned to watch, although the pennant on the car's bonnet clearly showed the identity of its passenger. Heydrich ordered the driver to keep at moderate speed; he liked to think on his journeys into the city. The capital was very pleasant today, tranquil, almost like a peacetime city.

Just by the municipal hospital, the Bulovka, there is a sharp bend in the road. It was there that two men stood, dressed as workers, apparently enjoying the fine morning.

From their vantage-point they could observe the entire street. The assassins had bicycles ready for their escape.

It all happened very quickly. As Heydrich's car approached, doing no more than thirty kilometres per hour, one of the 'workers' took a package out of his briefcase and tossed it into the open car. Heydrich stood bolt upright. A second later, the bomb went off. A few passers-by stopped, astonished by the noise, and no one moved as the two men on the corner swung themselves onto their bicycles. Heydrich had been gravely injured, but he was still on his feet; fuelled by some barbaric, superhuman source of strength, he managed to unholster his pistol and fire off a few harmless bullets in the direction of the fleeing partisans. None of the witnesses was aware, as yet, of what had happened. Then Heydrich collapsed. His driver had also been wounded. A crowd gathered. Then they transported Prague's master into the hospital and fetched the famous surgeon, Professor Hohlbaum, who announced that Heydrich had suffered serious internal injuries.

The Obergruppenführer was still unconscious when they took him into the operating theatre. Despite transfusions, he was losing blood at a tremendous rate. When they managed to get a look at the wound, the surgeons realised for the first time the task they were faced with: the wound was centred on the diaphragm, and the lungs had been barely touched, but the spleen was beyond salvation. It was a life-or-death operation. And during the hours while the surgeons were fighting for Heydrich's life, the news of the assassination attempt had unleashed panic in Berlin. The city was alive with rumours. Hitler, it was said, was terrified that the incident would act as a signal for a general uprising in the occupied territories. He sent Professors Sauerbruch and Gebhard to Heydrich's sick bed as medical representatives of the Reich government.

The first bulletin came on the radio that same afternoon: 'An attempt on the life of the Deputy Reich Protector, S.S.

Obergruppenführer Heydrich, was made in Prague this morning by as yet unknown assailants. S.S. Obergruppenführer was wounded during the attack, but is now out of danger. A reward of ten million crowns is offered for the capture of the assassins.'

The difficult operation had succeeded. Less than twenty-four hours later it was clear that the complications the doctors had feared were no longer a problem. Their patient seemed to be recovering with incredible swiftness, aided by a will of steel and a robust physique. Tanks rolled through the streets of Prague, and houses were ransacked for the attackers.

After a few days, the Obergruppenführer had recovered to such a degree that he was able to take up his work again, to issue orders and directives from his bed. There seemed no doubt now that the operation had succeeded. Satan had survived, to laugh in the face of fate.

Four days previously, Werner Stahmer had come back in the late evening to find Margot unconscious, just as the Prinz-Albrecht-Strasse had given the final go-ahead for the Swedish mission. There was something peaceful, almost beautiful, about her face that said more to Stahmer than all the professional optimism of the doctor who got to work on her with the stomach-pump. Seven hours later, they issued the official death certificate.

Number 3402 had finally given up the struggle.

Stahmer was a free man, but during those hours his freedom meant nothing to him. He realised suddenly that he had freed a dead woman from the concentration camp, and the thought paralysed him. He should have fled, but he stood by and watched while the Nazi bureaucracy took up the case; the system that killed the living didn't even leave the dead in peace. The death notice went from the police to the Party. The newspapers were forbidden to publish any reports or announcements, and restrictions were placed on the funeral. Only Margot's closest relatives turned up – along with an outsider who stood at a distance, not daring to look any of them in the eye.

It was only a few hundred metres to the freshly-dug grave, but to Werner Stahmer it seemed like an endless route-march. He listened to the monotonous, hypnotic rhythm of the prayers, but they were meaningless. The sun shone down on the wreaths, the ropes on the coffin as they lowered it, the black of men's suits and women's veils. There was a faint sound of bells. Any minute now, the parson, a dignified-looking old man, would stand up and deliver his fine phrases.

Stahmer saw it all, but it passed him by. In that coffin lay the girl he had loved, and whom he had drawn into his world, and whose death he was responsible for. And hers was not the only coffin. There were many, from the 'canned goods' to the little engraver Puch. There should have been thousands of coffins here – one for every innocent human being whom the Prinz-Albrecht-Strasse had sent to the grave. But this one was here. And in this coffin Stahmer concentrated his madness and his guilt, his hope and his despair.

He stood at the graveside for a long time, as if he hadn't noticed that the ceremony was over. There was no more to be said to the dead woman; he was settling accounts with himself, and he was sparing himself nothing.

When he finally moved away from the grave, his eyes were strangely blank and unseeing. Two men were waiting at the cemetery gate. He knew their faces.

'You're under arrest, Stahmer,' one of them said.

He nodded with something close to satisfaction. The same day, he learned that they were sending him to Prague. Heydrich's recovery, he realised without fear or regret, would mean his own death.

*

The Obergruppenführer's swift recovery from such a serious and complicated operation was almost a medical miracle. Heydrich's animal vitality seemed to have been the deciding factor.

After two days, Reinhard Heydrich was already seeing his department heads for short meetings in his room at the hospital. After three, he was reading newspapers, going through telegrams from well-wishers and working on R.S.H.A. documents. He was unquestionably past the worst when Professor Hohlbaum, a respected expert, decided to give him an anti-tetanus injection. In 1942 they had little knowledge of the problems of the spleen. Today it is a medical fact that to administer tetanus serum or oedemic preparations to someone who has lost his spleen can prove fatal. And so came the final, savage irony ...

On June 4th, seven days after the operation, they had taken his temperature and measured his pulse rate just after breakfast. Heydrich's condition was still improving. The doctors were wholly satisfied with their patient, and the Obergruppenführer himself showed good spirits and a hearty appetite. He had read the daily reports from the Prinz-Albrecht-Strasse, and had learned that Stahmer, his fallen favourite, was now under detention in Prague.

He ordered the man to be brought to him. Shortly before Stahmer's arrival, his nurse had brought him his lunch on a tray, complete with a bottle of fine red wine, on Heydrich's explicit instructions.

The R.S.H.A. thugs flanked Stahmer as he entered the room. Heydrich nodded and motioned for the pair to withdraw.

'As you can see, Stahmer,' he began. 'I'm still alive.'

The man in front of him made no reaction.

The Obergruppenführer ignored his dumb insolence. Heydrich smiled one of his palest smiles. His face was grey, his lips were bloodless, but his eyes held the cold, contemptuous gleam Stahmer knew so well.

'So you got the girl out of the camp,' he murmured. Heydrich poured himself out some red wine, then held the glass up to the light, as if his only concern at that moment was to check if the wine had the right tint.

'You know you are responsible for her death?' he added.

Stahmer continued to keep silent. He was filled with a strange sense of relief. For the first time in his life, he stood opposite this man and felt no fear. He was absolved, free. He would never again have to stand to attention. No more: 'Very good, Obergruppenführer.' He could see under the façade. He saw a cold, crippled Devil, and he knew that he had the strength to smash that smiling face if he wished.

'You're finished, Stahmer,' Heydrich drawled, savouring the words. 'Totally. Absolutely. You will be taken to a camp. And there they will break you into little pieces. Very, very slowly.' He paused. 'Can you imagine it, Stahmer?'

'Yes,' said the agent.

'Pity. But perhaps we shall be able to think up a few refinements that will surprise even you.' His voice became harsh. 'No one leaves me ... no one abandons my ship. I'm going to use you for the sake of the others. Do you understand that? You're going to be a demonstration.' He nodded comfortably and raised the glass to his lips. 'Cheers, Stahmer,' he said. Then he drank, slowly and with deliberation. When he put the glass down, he was smiling again, but the smile was curiously fixed. Suddenly he sank back among the pillows, and the glass toppled from his hand. His lips were working spasmodically; in those cold eyes was astonishment and ... yes ... fear.

Stahmer took a pace forward and looked at Heydrich with a savage fascination. Then he understood: his tormentor had had a relapse. He smiled. For the first time since Margot's death, he broke through his apathy and actually felt something. Within a few moments, the faint resurgence had become a storm of joy. He was really free. He took a deep breath, feeling that happiness filling him, killing the last remnants of fear. Let them do what Heydrich had ordered; it couldn't disturb or shatter his inner freedom. Stahmer glanced at the Obergruppenführer once more, weighed up his chances, and acted spontaneously. He wrenched open the door to the anteroom and bellowed: 'For God's sake. The Obergruppenführer!'

They all rushed in at once. Even the thugs who had brought him here. Within seconds, terrified nurses and the R.S.H.A. men were clustered round the bed of the dying man. Someone yelled for a doctor. It was several minutes later by the time the frantic panic had subsided. Precious minutes for a man on the run, like Werner Stahmer.

Now he was in his element. For the first time he used his powers for his own sake, not for theirs, covering his tracks, laying false trails, bluffing, making fools of his pursuers. He got through, gradually, zig-zagging away from Prague until he had crossed the borders of the Protectorate. Then he travelled the Reich from one end to the other, until finally he stood on the heavily-guarded border of a neutral country. He knew that he would make it, that he had to make it. Not only for the sake of his own skin, but because he knew that one day the men of the Prinz-Albrecht-Strasse would have to answer for their crimes.

It was a foggy night. The newspapers had carried the report: 'As a result of the attempts on his life on the 27th May, S.S. Obergruppenführer Heydrich suffered severe injuries in the areas of his chest and stomach. At first there appeared to be no danger to his life. On the seventh day, however, after an apparently normal recovery, an infection brought about a worsening of his condition which led to his death on Thursday.'

Hitler staged a grandiose state funeral for the late Satan. Heydrich's allies and enemies stood around the coffin and hid their relief at the fact that even an inhuman creature like Heydrich was mortal. And with him died his unique empire of torture and hate.

Werner Stahmer could hear the tinny drone of a propaganda loudspeaker in the distance as he picked his way along the forest path. Just short of the border he came into contact with a patrol, heard a dog bark and come slavering towards him, saw bursts of machine gun fire scything through the trees. One more lunge and he had to be on the other side. A few seconds more and he was through, a shadow disappearing into no man's land.

Werner Stahmer was eventually struck off the records of the Prinz-Albrecht-Strasse. Even the enemy gave up trying to trace him. No one knew whether he was dead or in hiding. Until the day when the Nuremburg Tribunal came to deal with the atrocities committed by the Prinz-Albrecht-Strasse. Then a man appeared in the courtroom, a tall, broad-shouldered man with clear-cut features, a man whom the thugs in the dock stared at with horrified, disbelieving eyes.

He looked straight back at them, raised his right hand, and swore to tell the truth about everything he had seen and lived through, the deaths and the torments, his crime – and its punishment.

FINAL HARBOUR
A NOVEL BY
HARRY HOMEWOOD

U.S.S. **Mako** is one submarine among many. In telling her tale FINAL HARBOUR speaks not only for its heroes. It speaks also for the unsung thousands of submariners who waged a bitter, hidden war beneath the ocean's depths.

Mako's crew is a cross-section of civilian reservists and trained seamen thrown together by the harsh dictates of war. Captain Hinman has welded them into a fighting team as deadly and efficient as the steel predator in which they sail. At sea they are united against the enemy they would die to defeat. But on shore they are different men cherishing different dreams and loving many women. And before **Mako** can win her war each of her crew must fight many battles of their own.

FINAL HARBOUR tells the story of a ship, the men who fought in her, and the women they left behind.

WAR 0 7221 4795 3 £1.95

Tiger Hunt!
JADE TIGER
Craig Thomas

The bait: a defecting Chinese agent selling secrets.
The trail: every bolt-hole and hide-out from Hong
Kong to Berlin.
The quarry: JADE TIGER

JADE TIGER, the thrilling new masterpiece from
Craig Thomas, finds espionage veteran Kenneth
Aubrey facing his toughest assignment yet. In six
months he could crack the Chinese defector. But he
doesn't have months, he has weeks. Two weeks
before the Berlin Wall is bulldozed into history. Two
weeks to discover the truth behind the network of
misinformation coming his way . . .

JADE TIGER is the story of a race against time, a
chase across three continents. Ranging from the
heart of Communist China to the Australian
Outback. JADE TIGER is classic thriller writing of
the highest order.

ADVENTURE/THRILLER   0 7221 8451 4   £2.25

Don't miss Craig Thomas' other bestsellers:
FIREFOX
SNOW FALCON
RAT TRAP
WOLFSBANE
SEA LEOPARD
also available in Sphere books.

Heart of War

by John Masters

January 1 1916: Europe is bleeding to death as the corpses rot from Poland to Gallipoli in the cruel grip of the Great War . . .

HEART OF WAR
– follows the fate and fortunes of the Rowland family and those people bound up in their lives, the Cate squirearchy, the Strattons who manage the Rowland-owned factory, and the humble, multi-talented Gorse family.

HEART OF WAR
– during the years 1916 and 1917, the appalling slaughter of the Somme and Passchendaele cuts deep into the hearts of the British people as military conscription looms over Britain for the first time in a thousand years.

HEART OF WAR
– is the second self-contained volume in a trilogy entitled LOSS OF EDEN. It is probably the crowning achievement in the long and distinguished career of one of our leading contemporary novelists.

GENERAL FICTION   0 7221 0467 7   **£1.95**

And, also by John Masters in Sphere Books:
NOW, GOD BE THANKED
NIGHTRUNNERS OF BENGAL
THE FIELD-MARSHAL'S MEMOIRS
FANDANGO ROCK
THE HIMALAYAN CONCERTO

The Cambodia File

JACK ANDERSON AND BILL PRONZINI

A posting to Cambodia was like an invitation to a carnival in hell. Diplomat David Foxgrove thought that the Asian war would end when the last American Huey lifted off from the scarred and devastated war zone that had once been Phnom Penh. His Cambodian mistress, Kim, stayed in the ravaged city to face the murderous rage of the Khmer Rouge. For the generals the war was over, but there was no easy exit for the people who had lived a season in hell.

In THE CAMBODIA FILE Pulitzer Prize-winning war correspondent Jack Anderson and novelist Bill Pronzini have created an awesome tale of the cost of war and the price of love in the front line. Out of the battle-torn lives of a dedicated man and the woman whose nation he has betrayed, the authors have forged an epic tragedy of our time.

GENERAL FICTION   0 7221 7024 6   £2.25

A SELECTION OF BESTSELLERS FROM SPHERE

FICTION

THE MISTS OF AVALON	Marion Bradley	£2.95 ☐
THE INNOCENT DARK	J. S. Forrester	£1.95 ☐
THURSTON HOUSE	Danielle Steel	£1.95 ☐
MAIDEN VOYAGE	Graham Masterton	£2.50 ☐
THE FURTHER ADVENTURES OF HUCKLEBERRY FINN	Greg Matthews	£2.95 ☐

FILM AND TV TIE-INS

THE IRISH R.M.	E. E. Somerville and Martin Ross	£1.95 ☐
SCARFACE	Paul Monette	£1.75 ☐
THE KILLING OF KAREN SILKWOOD	Richard Rashke	£1.95 ☐
THE RADISH DAY JUBILEE	Sheilah B. Bruce	£1.50 ☐
THEY CALL ME BOOBER FRAGGLE	Michaela Muntean	£1.50 ☐
RED AND THE PUMPKINS	Jocelyn Stevenson	£1.50 ☐

NON-FICTION

GRENADA: INVASION, REVOLUTION AND AFTERMATH	Hugh O'Shaughnessy	£2.95 ☐
DIETING MAKES YOU FAT	Geoffrey Cannon & Hetty Einzig	£1.95 ☐
THE FRUIT AND NUT BOOK	Helena Radecka	£6.95 ☐
LEBANON, THE FRACTURED COUNTRY	David Gilmour	£2.95 ☐
THE OFFICIAL MARTIAL ARTS HANDBOOK	David Mitchell	£3.95 ☐

All Sphere books are available at your local bookshop or newsagent, or can be ordered direct from the publisher. Just tick the titles you want and fill in the form below.

Name _____

Address _____

_____

Write to Sphere Books, Cash Sales Department, P.O. Box 11, Falmouth, Cornwall TR10 9EN

Please enclose a cheque or postal order to the value of the cover price plus:

UK: 45p for the first book, 20p for the second book and 14p for each additional book ordered to a maximum charge of £1.63.

OVERSEAS: 75p for the first book and 21p per copy for each additional book.

BFPO & EIRE: 45p for the first book, 20p for the second book plus 14p per copy for the next 7 books, thereafter 8p per book.

Sphere Books reserve the right to show new retail prices on covers which may differ from those previously advertised in the text or elsewhere, and to increase postal rates in accordance with the PO.